**"Do you want a new Handler?"
Laurel held her breath, waiting for Devlin's
answer, praying he wouldn't say yes.**

Even though they had crossed the line, she didn't
want to lose him as one of her Paladins. Even if she
could convince one of the other Handlers to keep her
apprised of Devlin's progress, it wouldn't be the
same.

"No, I don't, but this can't happen again."

That much was true. She nodded, unable to
speak, her eyes stinging from the threat of tears.

"Not here, anyway." He leaned close enough so
that his warm breath tickled her skin. "On the other
hand, my dear Dr. Young, I can promise you this:
When you and I do go to bed together, it'll be someplace a hell of a lot more private than this. Because
nothing is going to stop us from finishing what we
started today."

And then he was gone.

Dark Protector

Alexis Morgan

POCKET BOOKS
New York London Toronto Sydney

An *Original* Publication of POCKET BOOKS

 POCKET BOOKS, a division of Simon & Schuster, Inc.
1230 Avenue of the Americas, New York, NY 10020

This book is a work of fiction. Names, characters, places and incidents are products of the author's imagination or are used fictitiously. Any resemblance to actual events or locales or persons, living or dead, is entirely coincidental.

ISBN-13: 978-1-4165-2036-8
ISBN-10:   1-4165-2036-8

This Pocket Books paperback edition July 2006

10 9 8 7 6 5 4 3 2 1

POCKET and colophon are registered trademarks of Simon & Schuster, Inc.

Cover illustration by Craig White

For information regarding special discounts for bulk purchases, please contact Simon & Schuster Special Sales at 1-800-456-6798 or business@simonandschuster.com

Manufactured in the United States of America

I would like to dedicate this book to the best and brightest that America has to offer—the men and women in uniform who serve our country, both at home and abroad. With prayers for your safety and my profound thanks, this book is for you.

Acknowledgments

I would like to acknowledge the following women for their roles in bringing my Paladins to life:

Michelle Grajkowski, my agent and friend, who listened to me nervously describing the initial idea and embraced the possibilities. I don't know if Mount St. Helens choosing that moment to blow her top helped or not, but you have to admit it made for an interesting discussion.

Micki Nuding, my editor, whose enthusiasm and encouragement have been a real joy. I know Devlin, Trahern, and the rest of the boys appreciate it.

And finally, Lorraine Pritchard, my wonderful mother-in-law, whose eagle eyes find all those nasty little typos for me.

Thanks, ladies.

Dark Protector

prologue

$\mathcal{M}$any opposites rule the ebb and flow of our lives: night and day, winter and summer, youth and age. Throughout history, men and women have drawn comfort from the natural way of things. But we also know that wherever the grasping fingers of darkness reach out to the bright beauty of the light, shadows lurk.

Deep within the Earth, our world shares a border with another: a world filled with darkness and evil. Its pale citizens covet the light that man takes for granted. A fragile barrier keeps the two worlds separate, but when the continents shift or a volcano erupts in fury, that barrier is breached. Then the Others pour through, bringing their darkness with them, tainting all that they touch.

As in days of old, Paladins stand ready to turn back the Others, driving the darkness back to where it belongs. These knights are the champions of light, fighting at the sharp edge of darkness for the sake of us all. This is their story.

chapter 1

*H*e fought free of the mists, drawing in painful gulps of precious air, vanquishing the last fetid vestiges of death. Slowly his heart began to beat again, taking its own sweet time to fall back into a remembered rhythm. Breathing in, breathing out, each sip of oxygen reluctantly sending life back into his limbs.

Damn, he hated this. He'd already died too many times—sometimes for a worthy cause, and sometimes for no good reason at all. Every time he came back from the edge was an agonizing process. And every time he brought back a little less of his humanity, until he barely remembered what it felt like to simply be a man. Over the decades, the shadows death had left on his soul made him stronger, but hard and edgy and angry.

"He's back." The familiar voice was not a welcome one.

"He needs to rest before you order him out again, Colonel," a female voice stated.

"He's needed now." The words had the clipped cadence of a man used to barking out orders and having them obeyed without question.

"Speaking as his Handler, I must protest your even being here. Sir." That last word was clearly a reluctant afterthought. "The transition is difficult enough for him without an audience. If you don't leave, I will have to register a complaint with my superiors."

Devlin smiled in his mind. *That's it, honey, give him hell.* Her protests would fall on deaf ears, but it would aggravate the man from Ordnance.

"Miss Young, I'm sorry," the colonel lied smoothly, "but as I said, he's needed as soon as he's up and about."

An unladylike snort followed. "It's *Doctor* Young. And according to Ordnance, he's always needed somewhere. If you keep putting him in these deadly situations without the proper care, you'll lose him altogether."

Despite her calm tone, there was a powerful undercurrent to her words, one Devlin couldn't quite decipher.

Colonel Kincade's voice took on an edge. "How I use him is none of your business, Dr. Young. He belongs to us."

The old bastard never could stand to be second-guessed, especially by a woman. The Handler had better tread softly.

"You may decide how best to use Devlin Bane's talents, Colonel, but *I* decide when—and if—he is ready for reassignment."

She stepped close enough to Dev's bed for him to feel the heat radiating off her. The normally calm Laurel Young's emotions were certainly running high today.

"You might as well take your papers and leave, Colonel. I'm not signing anything today, tomorrow, or maybe even the day after."

She'd grown some claws since he'd last been reborn, but the men from Ordnance had decades of experience in getting their way. When Devlin could speak, he would have to warn her to watch her back. He didn't need or even want her defending him.

He listened to the angry staccato steps of the colonel leaving the ward. Kincade would regroup and be back, but for the moment, he was gone. Already the air seemed fresher, more potent.

Cool fingers settled on his wrist, checking his pulse. He wondered why she didn't just accept the readings on the machines that beeped and whined and knew more about him than he did.

"You can come out of hiding now, Mr. Bane. He's gone."

Damn, he'd thought he'd done a better job of disguising his resurgence than that.

His eyelashes felt heavy as he struggled to open his eyes as ordered. It took several attempts and a considerable amount of effort before he could do more than squint up at his Handler. Her pixie face hovered over his, looking worried as she muttered under her breath. Laurel's face was more interesting than truly pretty, with wide-set, brown eyes the color of rich, dark chocolate. Looking up into that thickly lashed gaze had become his favorite part of reviving.

"I'm alive. Again." He wasn't sure he wanted to be. Not with the colonel and his friends already sniffing around.

"It took longer this time." Laurel frowned. "Almost too long."

Was that fear in her voice? He wished his hands weren't bound, so that he could offer her the comfort of his touch. The unexpected impulse shocked him. He'd jettisoned most of the softer emotions two Handlers ago, leaving him cold and detached.

Fighting against the Others made him that way. His nightmares were bad enough already, especially the one where he became one of them. That particular horror would become reality soon enough.

"Take off the straps," he demanded.

Regret shadowed her expression. "You know I can't. Not yet." She glanced past him to the clock on the wall. "We have to wait another hour at least. You ought to know the routine by now, Mr. Bane."

Yeah, but that didn't mean he had to like it. There were tests to be run, reflexes to test, various bodily specimens to collect and evaluate—all of it a waste of time, something he had precious little of. Besides, if he *had* turned Other, she would have known it the second he opened his eyes. Since she hadn't called for help, there must be enough humanity left in him to pass all the tests they threw at him.

He clenched his fists and tested the strength of the bonds. There was some give in the straps, but not enough for him to break free without risking further injury to himself. His body was still utilizing all of its resources to repair the damage from the other night. It would only delay his recovery further if he insisted on tearing himself loose from the bonds, even if he could muster enough strength to pull it off. He drew a breath deep enough to hurt and forced himself to relax, concentrating on easing the tension that left him irritated and angry.

"Good choice, Mr. Bane. Fighting it won't help either of us get our job done." Laurel stood a short distance away, her ever-present clipboard clutched to her chest. Her dark eyes flickered down the length of his body. "Would you like another blanket?"

"No."

He wasn't cold, especially not with that delectable female body so close by. One of the side effects of revival for him had always been the immediate and intense hunger to satisfy all of his body's basic needs—food and sex being at the top of the list. When he was younger, he'd usually given in to that impulse with the first obliging woman he encountered. Lately, though, he'd been less willing to be some nameless stranger's good time.

His senses, always sensitive but especially so after the journey back from death, were screaming with awareness of Laurel's feminine scent, despite the strong medicinal smells that permeated the laboratory.

He deliberately turned away from her to stare at the ceiling overhead, noticing that she'd changed the posters she kept up there for her clients' entertainment.

The buxom blondes frolicking on a beach wearing not much more than their smiles were a vast improvement over the kittens and puppies from last time.

"Nice artwork."

A smile tugged at Laurel's mouth as she glanced up. "One of your friends sent those to me after he got out. I didn't have the heart to throw them away without giving them a fair showing."

"Looks like something D.J. would have done."

She scrunched up her nose. "Right on the first guess. Personally, I preferred the kittens."

"You're not the one strapped to this damned table like some lab animal waiting to be dissected."

The brutal honesty of his words made her flinch, but it was the truth. If, in those first seconds after he came back, she had seen an Other instead of a Paladin looking up at her through his eyes, she wouldn't have hesitated to reach for the drugs that would end it all for him. For now, neither of them had had to face that little problem.

But eventually they would. Those were the roles they'd been assigned in this tragedy. Rather than talk anymore, he closed his eyes and pretended to sleep. She was too smart to be fooled, but she allowed him the small deception. A few seconds later, the lights dimmed and he slept for real.

Laurel wondered if Devlin knew he snored. She drew pleasure from listening to the rough, rumbling noise as she worked at the computer. It was such a homey sound, making Devlin Bane a little less frightening, a little more human. He wasn't—not completely, anyway—but she wanted him to hold on to whatever bit of humanity he had left as long as possible.

A small electronic *ping* announced that his waiting time was up, but she decided not to wake Devlin immediately. Since he'd actually fallen asleep on that steel slab, he probably needed the rest. She glanced back toward the dimly lit lab. No one had ever been able to explain to her why the table had to be so uncomfortable. Surely a little padding wouldn't compromise the strength of the steel. In her opinion, the Paladins deserved any possible comforts in their lives.

Not that any of them would admit it; they prided themselves on being the toughest sons of bitches around. And it was true. They all started off big and strong and added mean to the mix as time went on. Even the heavily armed guards posted outside her door moved carefully when a Paladin was in-house.

Especially Devlin Bane.

She sighed. Hardly a week went by that she didn't have one of the Paladins back in her care for at least a day or two. They fought, they died, and they came back to her to be repaired and replenished. Some were easier to deal with than others, but none of them was exactly easy to be around.

Even so, Devlin Bane was different.

His mere presence made her spacious laboratory feel cluttered and cramped, as if he took up too much of the air and most of the space. She turned again to study him.

His profile was strong and rather handsome, although his nose had been broken a time or two. His brows were two dark slashes across his face, one of them marred by a scar from some long ago battle. Her gaze lingered on his mouth. It was surprisingly sensual looking, almost out of place among his other features. Could he kiss as well as he did everything else he set his mind to?

Before she could mentally catalog anything else, she realized that his green eyes were open and staring right back at her with an intensity she could feel from all the way across the room.

"I'm sorry, I didn't realize that you were awake." She stood up, almost knocking her stool to the ground.

"That's all right. I guess you were too busy staring to notice." There was no humor at all in his words. "I want up."

She hid her embarrassment in a spate of medical talk. "I'll draw your blood first, then let you up. Once we've evaluated your current status—"

He cut her off. "I know the drill, Doc. Just get it done."

His words shouldn't have hurt, since she'd heard far worse over the years. After all, being dead tended to make the calmest of men a bit testy. Most of the time she could ignore their grumbling, but it was harder to do with Devlin.

He'd hate knowing that. In fact, if he even suspected how much time she spent poring over his records, trying to learn one more bit of information about what made him tick, he'd be beating on her boss's door, demanding a new Handler.

And it was imperative that she continue to oversee his care. Devlin Bane was one of the oldest known Paladins; he'd already outlived the average lifespan of his kind by two decades. If she could determine why he was showing resistance to the usual pattern of a Paladin's life, perhaps she could help the others live longer.

She released his right arm from its restraints, then tied a tourniquet just above his elbow. Never a fan of having his blood drawn, he winced and looked away as she inserted the needle in his vein. The blood pumped into the tube, rich and dark and red. She changed tubes, filling two more before loosening the tourniquet. After covering the needle with a cotton ball, she tugged it out of his arm.

"Bend your arm." Gently shaking the tubes, she walked away to set them in a rack, then returned to his side.

"Let me see the wound."

He sighed and straightened his arm. She checked under the cotton for bruising before covering the small puncture. It took all she had to keep from giggling when he saw that the bandage was covered with bright yellow happy faces. He clearly didn't appreciate the small bit of cheer.

"Very funny."

"They were on sale." Of course, so were the plain ones.

She unlocked the first of the straps that kept Devlin's legs chained to the table. Starting with his ankles, she worked her way up his body, studiously ignoring the fact that he was naked under the thin blanket. When a Paladin was first brought in, it was easy to remain clinical about such things. She tried to remember that as she undid the last of the restraints and Devlin sat up, the blanket pooling around his waist.

"How do you feel? Any dizziness or nausea?"

"No." He rubbed his wrists, working the stiffness out of them. "I feel just like I did the last dozen times I've been through this." He got to his feet, towering over her by nearly a foot.

She rolled her eyes in exasperation, not allowing him to intimidate her by his sheer size. "They won't open the doors unless I tell them to. I need answers."

He recited a litany of responses to her unspoken questions, all memorized from previous visits. "No nausea, no dizziness, I'm not seeing double or breaking out in strange rashes. And before you ask, I don't remember whether it was the sword stuck in my gut or the ax that shattered my leg that killed me. It didn't seem important at the time."

The list of wounds shouldn't shock her since she'd

been the one to repair the damage, but to hear him recite the list with absolutely no emotion bothered her a great deal. "And how does your leg feel? Any weakness or pain?"

"Look, Dr. Young, everything is in working order." He deliberately dropped the blanket to give proof to his claim.

She managed to stand her ground, but that didn't keep her from blushing furiously at the sight of all that masculine power. Devlin was a big man—all over. "I'll ring for your meal while you get dressed. Your clothes are in the locker."

He turned away. Rather than get caught staring at his backside, she retreated to her desk and picked up the phone.

"Please notify Dr. Neal that our patient is up and about. Also have Mr. Bane's favorite meal delivered asap. You know how testy he gets when he isn't fed right away." She deliberately pitched her voice so that Devlin would hear her.

"I can eat at home."

She jumped about a foot. How did a man his size move so darned quietly? He loomed over her, still buttoning his shirt and rolling up his sleeves. The combination of well-worn jeans and a faded chambray shirt did nothing to make him look less dangerous. His shoulder-length hair only added to his uncivilized air.

"Yes, you can. In fact, I'd recommend it. However, that doesn't mean you're leaving here until I know you can keep food down."

Before he could argue the point, the doors to the hallway slid open. Dr. Neal, Laurel's immediate supervisor and the head of Research, came through carrying a heavily laden tray.

"Devlin, you look a damn sight better than you did when you arrived five days ago." He set the tray down. "But I suppose none of us are at our best when we're dead. Go ahead and eat. I can wait."

Devlin gave Laurel's boss a thoroughly disgusted look before digging into his food.

"Dr. Young, may I see his data?"

She held out the clipboard. "I'll have the blood tests and other reports later this afternoon. So far, nothing surprising." Except he continued to hold off the changes normally associated with so many deaths with amazing success. She'd never mentioned her findings on that subject to anyone other than Dr. Neal, not even Devlin himself. Until she could account for the unexpected results, she didn't want to make a big deal out of them. Maybe they only meant that Devlin was lucky.

Dr. Neal flipped through the chart, his eyes quickly scanning her notes. When he'd read the last page, he handed her the clipboard. "I'd like him to return here every other day to repeat these tests until he reports back to the field." He made a couple of notes and then signed off on the chart.

Devlin looked up from his dinner glaring at both of them. "Like hell I will. Use someone else for a lab rat; not me."

Laurel's boss was a short, balding cherub of a

man, but that didn't mean he was a pushover. "I'll remind you, Mr. Bane, that your orders are to cooperate with my staff at all times. Now, we can do this one of two ways. You can promise to return when you're told to or we can just keep you here. Which would you prefer?"

The doctor got a string of obscenities in reply. He calmly nodded. "I thought you'd see it my way. Now if the two of you will excuse me, I believe I have kept Colonel Kincade waiting long enough." He peered over the top of his glasses at Laurel. "He seemed upset when he called. Is there anything I should know about beforehand?"

Laurel sensed Devlin's interest in her answer even though he didn't look in her direction. "He was here just before Mr. Bane woke up. He expressed his desire to see my patient released for immediate return to duty."

"And you said?"

"I simply reminded him that it wasn't his decision to declare Mr. Bane fit for duty; it was mine. I told Colonel Kincade that I will not sign any releases until I am satisfied that Mr. Bane has no lingering effects from his latest battle."

"And when do you expect to make that decision?"

The stress of the past few days, when her patient had hovered between this world and the next, had taken a toll on her temper. She glared at both men. "I'd like to know why everyone is suddenly in such a hurry!"

Dr. Neal frowned slightly. "I'm sorry, Laurel, but

Ordnance will be demanding to know when they can expect Mr. Bane to report back."

"I won't know for certain until I complete the follow-up examination in two days." Three, if she could stretch it that far.

"Thank you, that's better. I will pass that information along." He gave her a smile that was meant to be reassuring. "Mr. Bane, I hope I don't have to see you again for quite some time."

"Me, too, Doc." Devlin turned his attention back to his food.

When the doors swished shut behind Dr. Neal, Laurel sat down and stared at her computer screen. Her eyes burned with near exhaustion.

"How much sleep have you gotten since they brought me in?" he asked.

She rolled her shoulders, trying to ease the stiffness, then shrugged without looking in his direction. "I'd tell you that it was none of your business, but that has never stopped you before. Dr. Neal relieved me for about four hours each day." She leaned forward to rest her forehead on her arms and closed her eyes.

As he absorbed the meaning behind her answer, Devlin attacked the last of his meal. Judging from the dark smudges under her eyes, Lauren was close to collapsing.

"Dr. Young?"

No answer.

"Laurel?" He rarely allowed himself the privilege of using her first name.

No answer.

Finally, he picked her up in his arms and carried her to the cot she kept handy for when she had a critical patient. She stirred only long enough to find a comfortable spot on the pillow. He picked up the blanket that he'd dropped earlier and draped it over her, resisting the urge to press a kiss to her forehead. When he tucked a lock of her dark hair behind her ear, she smiled in her sleep. He felt it just as if she'd reached out to touch him.

He backed away. Damn, he needed to get the hell away from her. Even if she'd die before admitting it, her interest in him obviously went beyond that of a doctor for her patient. As long as he only saw her when he was chained down to her table, he could deal with it. He had to. She was the only thing that kept him anchored in this world, a lifeline who fought long and hard to drag him back from the abyss that he lived and fought in. He had a horrible suspicion that anyone else would have set him adrift years ago.

It was time to get out of there. He pressed the button that would summon the guards.

"Yes, Dr. Young?" The disembodied voice was a familiar one.

"No, it's Devlin Bane. Sergeant Purefoy, is that you?"

"Yes, sir, Mr. Bane. What do you need?"

"Dr. Young is resting right now, but she's signed my release." At least, he hoped she had. He wasn't about to wait around for her to wake up.

"I'll be right in."

No doubt armed to the teeth, with two or three others as backup. Devlin positioned himself in the middle of the room, doing his best to look harmless. It never worked; his reputation as one of the Paladins was too firmly entrenched for that.

The doors slid open and Sergeant Purefoy entered, his men right behind him. They fanned out, their weapons powered up and ready, until the sergeant checked to make sure Laurel was indeed sleeping and safe.

"Welcome back, sir." The man's smile seemed genuine. "I'll just verify the signature and then we'll see you safely out of the building."

"I'm in no hurry." Like hell. In here, he felt trapped and exposed.

The sergeant rifled through the clipboard, pausing every so often to read something. "Everything seems to be in order, sir."

"Good. Let's go."

Devlin walked between the men and out the door, relieved to leave the lab and the delectable Laurel behind. The last thing he needed right now was to break in a new Handler. There was too much at stake for that: the hands on the sword that had brought him down hadn't been those of an Other.

He closed his eyes to remember every detail he could of those last few minutes. The smell of blood and fear-tainted sweat. Grunts and groans as weapons were swung and made contact. The flash of a sword as it slid all too easily into his side. The shock had driven him to his knees as the blood splashed out of his body and onto the ground.

He never saw his attacker's face, but he had seen the hands gripping the sword as it was shoved through him and then twisted. Those hands had definitely been human. His last thought as he'd bled out onto the ground was the knowledge that one of his own people had tried to kill him.

chapter 2

*H*e's out."

The whispered message made his skin crawl.

"I warned you that they were difficult to kill. That should come as no surprise." Everyone with half a brain knew that Paladins died all the time. Getting them to stay that way was the hard part.

"When will you try again?"

The voice, dust dry and scratchy, grated on his nerves. He wished he had the balls to tell the bastard to go straight to hell, but that would be signing his own death warrant. Whoever wanted Devlin Bane permanently dead and buried was willing to pay big money to get the job done. It wouldn't cost a fraction of that amount to have someone come after him.

"I'm waiting." And none too patiently.

"Soon. Reports are coming in from all over the area that the pressure is building again. I'm guessing that

Ordnance will be sending out the Paladins within the next few days. Bane will lead the charge. He always does."

"We can't risk him near the barrier for much longer. He's bound to notice something."

Like the botched attempt on his life wouldn't already have put him on alert? He'd known this hit was stupid from the start, but all that money had drowned out the warnings his common sense had been shouting. "I know."

"The Paladins look to him for leadership. His death will distract the others, weakening their cause. We need them in chaos if we are to succeed." The voice stopped to draw a raspy breath. "There will be a bonus in it for you if he doesn't live to see the next shift in the plates." There was an audible *click* as the mysterious caller disconnected the call.

He slammed the phone down. "Fuck you, you bastard. If you wanted Bane dead so badly, you should have gone after him yourself."

He cursed himself as a fool for letting himself get caught between two of the scariest people in this world or any other one. It was one thing to be promised a bonus for killing Bane; living long enough to collect it was quite another.

Even if he succeeded, he'd spend the rest of his days looking over his shoulder. Paladins didn't take kindly to losing one of their number at the best of times. If they found out they'd been betrayed, they would be relentless in their pursuit of revenge. But he had no choice now. If he destroyed Bane, the Paladins might kill him. If he failed, the voice would for sure.

"Look who's back."

Another voice chimed in. "I've always figured him to be teacher's pet. None of *us* get to take five days off when the mountain is letting off steam."

"Both of you go to hell." Devlin said it because it was expected. If he'd failed to respond to his men's taunts, they would've been worried about him. He disappeared into his office and sat down. Despite his earlier assurances to Laurel, his leg ached and his head was pounding. But he'd had worse and survived—a bit of grim humor that made him smile.

D.J. followed him into his office and made himself comfortable on the corner of Dev's desk. "So how is the lovely Dr. Young? Does she miss me?"

"Not so you'd notice. She did hang up your posters, though, if that means anything to you." Devlin turned his attention to his computer and began working his way through the e-mails that had piled up since his death earlier in the week. Even after eliminating all the tongue-in-cheek condolences from his Paladin friends, there was a depressing amount of information left to deal with.

"Really? She actually put them up? I thought she'd come after me with a dull syringe." D.J. looked disappointed.

"I doubt she'll leave them up long. She still prefers puppies and kittens." Devlin scanned the first few entries, absorbing the most recent reports of increased pressure along the fault lines. "Any word from Ordnance when they want to send us out?"

D.J. shook his head. "No, but Colonel Kincade has been in several times throwing his weight around."

"He was at the lab checking on me, too."

D.J. frowned. "Why would he show up there? He knows that it's up to Dr. Neal and the others to notify him when we're ready to return to duty."

"I wish I knew." His mouth quirked up in a reluctant smile. "Dr. Young ran him off."

"Wish I could have been there to see that. Imagine, the big, bad colonel being chased by our favorite Handler." D.J. laughed, then dropped his voice to a tense whisper. "Think he'll retaliate for her standing up to him?"

"If he can without getting caught. He's a vindictive son of a bitch."

They all despised the colonel for his arrogance and casual disregard for the lives of those who served under his orders. He couldn't hurt the Paladins as easily as he could others, but over time, even they paid a high price for his carelessness.

"Did you warn her?"

Devlin shook his head. "Not yet, but I have to go back the day after tomorrow. We'll talk then."

And he'd give her an earful about a lot of things. He didn't want her interfering again in Paladin business. Her responsibility began when a Paladin was carried into her lab dead, and ended when he walked out alive again. It had always been that way and with good reason. Eventually she would have to make a decision to permanently end a Paladin's life. She had much too soft a heart already. If she made friends with her charges, it would destroy her when she had to put one of them down.

The door opened and Lonzo Jones poked his head in. "D.J., we need you to come look at something."

D.J. pushed himself back up to his feet with a long-suffering sigh. "What did you idiots do to the system this time? I swear, I walk away and you start pushing buttons and twisting dials just to watch the pretty lights flash."

Devlin was just as glad to have his office to himself for a while. D.J. was one of his closest friends, which meant he could see past the badass personality Devlin had spent decades perfecting. If someone was willing to kill him, anyone close to him might be in danger, as well. D.J. and the others could take care of themselves, but there was the little problem of Dr. Laurel Young.

He leaned back in his chair and closed his eyes, trying to relax for a few minutes. Under normal circumstances, he would have gone to his quarters and slept for a shift or two, but he couldn't allow himself that luxury until he caught up on everything that had happened while he'd been gone.

Five damn days lost, gone forever. No wonder Laurel had been muttering about how long it had taken him to come back. Normally it took two to three days to reclaim their lives. Four days wasn't unheard of, depending on the severity and number of injuries that their bodies had to repair. But five? Either his body was losing its inborn ability to recover or he'd been in worse shape than usual.

That thought brought a bitter smile to his lips. No one but a Paladin would understand the irony of knowing there were degrees of dead. He doubted his Handler would find the idea amusing, but then, she was the one who had to put them all back together again.

The scientists and physicians who made up the Research Department of the Regents had spent decades studying the physiology of the Paladins, seeking to understand how it was possible for them to be revived over and over again, their lives lasting decades beyond normal life expectancy.

Was one of the scientists behind the attack on him? He rolled the idea around in his mind, finally deciding that it didn't make sense. There was no real gain for anyone in Research if he died for good.

He rubbed his leg to ease the bone-deep ache. Eventually the pain and the scars would fade, but the memory of the ax shattering the bone and the blood that he'd lost would remain sharp and clear—until something worse took its place.

No, there was little reason to covet a life that consisted of waiting to fight, fighting until you could bleed no more, then being revived to start the cycle all over again. Not that he felt sorry for himself. The Paladins had a clear purpose in life, which was more than most folks could claim. The traits that they carried hardwired into their genes made them the perfect warriors: strength, skill with weapons, and a total commitment to a worthy cause. Their loyalty, once given, was unshakable.

Devlin stared at the array of swords and axes that hung on the wall opposite his desk. Razor sharp and maintained in perfect condition, they were the tools of his trade, used to drive back the darkness that seeped into his world every time fault lines slipped or a volcano belched fire and smoke and ash into the sky.

Devlin crossed to the wall and, using both hands, lifted his favorite sword down off the wall. He should have known one of the others would have retrieved it from the battle. The edge of the blade was nicked in several places, which didn't surprise him. The blackened scorch mark across the blade near the hilt did. Tomorrow he would carry it down to the armory to restore it to prime fighting condition. He had other swords, but none that fit his hand like this one did.

The carpet didn't quite muffle the sound of someone crossing his threshold. Before acknowledging his colleague's presence, he returned the sword to its place on the wall. Cullen Finley leaned against the doorframe and waited with his usual quiet patience before speaking.

"We almost didn't find it." He came the rest of the way into the room without waiting for a formal invitation. He knew that if Devlin didn't want company, the door would have been closed and locked.

Devlin returned to his seat behind his desk and motioned for his friend to sit down, as well. "I'm glad you did, Cullen. I would have missed it. Where was it?" He vaguely remembered dropping it on the ground, but he'd been too busy dying to care at that point.

His friend looked toward the sword and frowned. "It was stuck in the barrier. We had the devil's own time getting it out without causing further damage to it, or the barrier itself."

Alarm bells sounded again in Devlin's mind. "I was nowhere near the barrier when I went down. I'd gone down a side passage after a couple of strays." He should have realized then that something was wrong. It was rare for the Others to travel in pairs, but those two had stayed together even when the path had split. It was as if they'd known exactly where they were going, leading him straight into a trap.

Another piece of the puzzle that didn't fit.

"Is there anything else I should know about?"

Cullen took his time in answering; the others had nicknamed him "the Professor" for his tendency to deliberate carefully before giving an answer. And other than Devlin himself, the man had accumulated the most knowledge about the Paladins and their lot in life.

Cullen shook his head. "I can't figure out how the sword came to be where it was, but I'd give anything to know. It almost looked as if someone was trying to do serious damage to the barrier with it." He grinned, his smile wide and feral. "I bet whoever it was is nursing some serious burns on his hands. If the barrier was at full strength, he would have gotten quite a jolt running up the blade."

That thought cheered Devlin. "If you figure out any more about what happened, let me know." He raised his arms over his head and stretched. The little burst of energy he'd gotten from returning to his office was wearing off. If he didn't get home to his bed, he might just end up spending the night on his office floor.

"Did D.J. get the system straightened out again?"

None of them liked to call for assistance from the IT Department. They always acted as if the Paladins were a bunch of ignorant thugs who didn't know the first thing about running a computer, even though the organization ran on software designed and maintained by D.J. and Cullen.

Cullen smiled again. "It's fine. Sometimes I think Lonzo and the others like to mess with the system just enough to drive D.J. crazy. It always works."

A little horseplay helped alleviate the tension they lived with day in and day out. As long as they did no harm, Devlin wasn't about to complain.

"I'm still officially off the roster until Dr. Young and Dr. Neal finish poking holes in me and bleeding me dry. I'm going to turn in early, in hopes that a full day's rest will convince them to let me out of their clutches."

His friend cocked his eyebrow. "Dr. Neal's not my type, either. However, I wouldn't be in such a hurry to get away from Dr. Young, if I were you." He closed his eyes as if to savor an image in his mind. "All those brains, and a beauty to boot."

A surprisingly powerful urge to punch his friend almost sent Devlin diving across his desk. With no little effort, he forced himself to unclench his fists and to maintain a pleasant expression on his face. He placed his hands on his desk and pushed himself to his feet. Until he got himself under better control, he would be better off alone.

Cullen walked him out to the corridor. "Don't rush coming back. If we need you, we'll call."

"See that you do."

Once Cullen was out of sight, Devlin slammed his fist against the wall. Damn Laurel Young and those big eyes of hers. Did she have every single one of the Paladins drooling over her? Paladins weren't known for their sexual restraint, and if one of them managed to hook up with her, there'd be hell to pay.

Especially if that someone was anyone other than Devlin himself.

Laurel had wasted far too much of the morning watching the clock. If she'd been smart enough to give Devlin Bane a specific appointment, perhaps she would have accomplished far more than she had. She was thoroughly disgusted with herself and this foolish fixation. There were good solid reasons why generations of Handlers and Paladins had kept their interactions on a coldly clinical basis. But every time she let her concentration slip, her eyes went right back to staring at the minute hand and wishing it would move.

Paladins were the warriors who stood between their world and the dark one that threatened to seep in and destroy it. The Others were their enemies, not quite human but close enough to pass. They hovered on the other side of the barrier that separated the worlds. When the barrier was damaged, Others poured through the breach until the Paladins turned back the tide in bloody hand-to-hand combat, using weapons straight out of the Dark Ages. While they battled, others mended the barrier. When the damage was too great to be easily repaired, the Paladins stood shoulder-to-shoulder and held the line.

The cost to their souls was horrific. Laurel shuddered. No one knew why, but the more a Paladin fought and died, the more he became like the Others, uncontrollable and murderous. She hated the thought of destroying one of the valiant men she knew and respected, but she would do it when it became necessary.

She owed it to him and his companions.

Even if it was Devlin Bane. Especially if it was him. The man had fought longer than any man in the history of Paladins; he deserved to end his life with some dignity and not as a ravening monster. What the cost to her own soul would be, she didn't begin to guess.

The intercom buzzed. Not wanting to seem anxious, she waited a full five heartbeats before responding.

"Yes, Sergeant Purefoy?"

"Devlin Bane is here to see you."

"Give me a minute before bringing him in."

She'd be lucky if the guards could hold Devlin back half that time, but even those precious few seconds would allow her to make sure everything was in order. Her cot was safely stowed back in its closet, the blanket that Devlin had used to cover her was neatly folded and tucked away in a nearby cabinet.

Why she hadn't dropped it in the laundry hamper didn't bear thinking about. And how embarrassing was it to have fallen asleep while on duty, no matter how tired she had been? She'd spent way too much time wondering what it had been like to be held in Devlin's strong arms. She wished she remembered that as clearly as she did waking up surrounded by his scent from the blanket he'd used to cover her.

Damn, she had to stop doing this. That blanket was definitely going into the laundry. Before she could go three steps, though, the door to the lab swung open and Devlin Bane was escorted in by Sergeant Purefoy and his men.

Devlin was clearly not happy at having the guards tripping along at his heels.

"Thank you, Sergeant. I'll buzz you when he's ready to leave." She didn't like the rule that stated that a Paladin was never left to wander on his own, but she had to follow it. There were other, more important battles to fight than that one.

"Let's get this over with."

Devlin was already rolling up his sleeve, obviously

thinking that Dr. Neal had merely ordered a repeat on the blood work. Instead, he wanted a whole battery of tests run, starting with strength and endurance.

"Let's start off on the treadmill." She reached for her clipboard to avoid Devlin's gaze.

"Why the hell would I want to do that?"

Bracing herself for the explosion she was sure was imminent, she handed him the list. "This is what Dr. Neal ordered."

Devlin all but jerked the piece of paper from her fingers. "No way in hell, Dr. Young. I don't have time for this nonsense."

She didn't blame him, but she couldn't countermand her superior's orders. Dr. Neal was normally easy to work for, but if she pushed him too far he might relieve her of Devlin's care. Something she would not risk.

Maybe she could offer Devlin a compromise. "We could do half of the list today and the rest tomorrow."

Devlin stood glowering down at her. "Why is he doing this? What does he expect to find?"

"You'll have to ask Dr. Neal." Personally, she thought Devlin deserved the truth, but he wasn't going to get it any time soon.

"I'll get things set up." She opened a drawer and pulled out a pair of running shorts. "These will be more comfortable than your jeans."

Devlin watched her leave the room, the white lab coat doing little to disguise her long legs and feminine sway. He was still battling the side effects of being revived, and being around Laurel only made his sexual frustration worse.

He stripped off his shirt and reached for the snap on his jeans. Maybe a long workout on the treadmill would help. He'd refrained from his normal morning run: until he knew who'd tried to kill him, it wasn't smart to make a target of himself.

"Step up on the machine." Laurel held a bouquet of wires in her hand. One by one, she peeled the protective paper off the electrodes and began sticking them on his chest and arms. Each time her fingertips brushed his skin, a ripple of awareness burned along his nerve endings. He was glad that she didn't have the monitor turned on yet, or every wicked thought he was having would have been recorded. Like how he wanted to haul her off to somewhere private and kiss her senseless, for starters.

And what would Dr. Neal and his associates have made of those readings? When he smiled at the thought, Laurel instinctively backed up a step. Smart girl. If she was a little afraid of him, they'd both be better off.

"Start out at a slow pace, then gradually speed up. I know how fast you guys heal, but that was a bad break in your leg. I don't want to risk further injury to it."

"It's fine."

Not quite, but in another day it would be as good as new. He started off slowly, letting his muscles warm up and stretch out. After the first few minutes, he fell into the familiar rhythm of his early morning runs. It felt good to be moving again, to feel his blood circulating, his lungs drawing in air.

His leg was holding up so far, with no appreciable difference from the uninjured one. Even if it had acted up, he would have continued on as long as it would hold him. He needed to know if he could depend on it when he went back out into the field.

The likelihood of a major shift in the fault line that ran along the western edge of Washington was becoming more and more apparent. If the barrier went down, it could be a bloodbath and every sword would be needed.

Which reminded him that he still needed to go to the armory before the day was out.

"You can start slowing down." Laurel moved away from the monitor to add the final printouts to his chart.

Devlin kept up the pace for another few minutes, partly because it felt good, and partly because it allowed him that much control. Laurel ignored his little rebellion, maintaining her focus on the various readings the machine was spewing forth. He hated having everything about him being reduced to a series of endless numbers and charts, as if they were more real than he was himself.

He gradually slowed to a stop and stepped off the machine. Swiping a towel off a handy pile, he wiped the sweat off his face and neck and waited to see what she wanted to do next. He had a few ideas of his own on that subject, but doubted if she would be interested. Besides, this wasn't the place for such thoughts.

Cameras and microphones allowed the guards

outside to monitor everything that went on. If he gave in to the temptation of taking Laurel Young to bed, it wouldn't be with anyone looking on.

"What's next?"

One look at her face and he knew. He wadded up the towel and threw it in the direction of the hamper in the corner. Another damn brain scan, looking for proof that his grasp on his humanity was slipping away. "And if I refuse?"

Her chin came up a notch, her eyes flickering to the camera on the ceiling before returning to meet his gaze. "Is there a reason you would?"

"No, other than being tired of being poked and prodded." He gestured toward the thick chart on the counter. "Do you have any idea how many trees died just so you can quantify me?"

Some of the tension left her shoulders as she realized he wasn't going to refuse. This time, anyway. "Let's get it over with."

He followed her into a small room that held a narrow bed and yet another electronic console filled with gauges and switches and blinking lights. None of the Paladins liked this particular piece of machinery. It was their judge and their jury, a court where the accused was presumed guilty and had no chance to speak in his own defense.

And the price for being convicted was swift and immediate execution.

No matter how many times he'd been through the procedure, it never got easier. Very little frightened him anymore, but those tiny electrodes sticking into his scalp like tiny claws never failed to make his stomach roil and his head ache. He knew in his mind that he was still human enough to pass the test, but in his gut, where it counted, he feared what they would find when the machine chirped and buzzed as it recorded his brain waves.

He stretched out on the bed, only dimly aware of the cool cotton sheets beneath his back. Closing his eyes, he concentrated on his Handler to keep his thoughts from wandering down the ugly path of self-doubt. He'd always had a thing for brunettes with long legs, the kind made for riding high around a man's waist. Then there were those melted chocolate eyes. He could just eat her up.

Laurel's scent teased his senses, a mixture of shampoo and soap and something that was uniquely her. He dug his fingers into the bedding. The more he was around her, the stronger the temptation just to touch her became. When she leaned over him to apply the last of the electrodes, he bit his lip to keep from moaning.

Didn't the woman have the good sense to keep her breasts out of his face? He badly wanted to lift his head and nuzzle them. He settled for sneaking a quick peek, up close and personal. Her shirt was pulled tight across her chest, leaving him little doubt that her breasts were perfectly shaped to fit a man's hand, as well as his mouth. He bet they tasted sweet, like ripe berries and warm sunshine.

He shifted, glad that his shorts were baggy enough to partially disguise his immediate erection.

When Laurel stepped away, he let out a breath he'd hardly been aware of holding.

"I'll dim the lights. Just try to relax and think good thoughts."

As soon as the lights came down, she sat in the chair next to the bed and flipped the switch that would start the program running. He tried to relax, but it wasn't working.

"I know this isn't any fun, Devlin." Her voice was cool and soothing, her use of his first name a bit of a surprise.

Her hand came to rest on his shoulder before slowly making its way down his arm to rest on top of his hand. He turned his palm up, threading his fingers through hers. They were both playing with fire, but right now he needed all the warmth he could get. Maybe she would have done as much for any of the Paladins, but he didn't think so.

None of them had ever mentioned her conducting herself other than strictly professionally, and if she had, most of them were shallow enough to want bragging rights and would be unlikely to keep their mouths shut. Even D.J. and Cullen would have found some way to mention it to him. That little worry slid away for the time being.

Whenever he was hooked up to this machine, his sense of time was distorted. It rarely took longer than thirty minutes, but it always seemed far longer. Even if the results still proved him human enough to continue living, it marked his steady progression toward becoming Other.

He'd never bothered to ask how close he was coming to the end. It was unlikely that Laurel would even answer the question. Besides, knowing wouldn't change a thing. He would continue to fight and die alongside his comrades until his Handler revoked that privilege. That was something he was damn proud of.

Gradually, he relaxed as his world narrowed down to the dim pool of light reflected from the amber and green lights on the console. Turning his head slightly, he could see Laurel's profile and wondered where her thoughts were taking her as they waited in the silence.

Even with his better-than-average eyesight, it was difficult to judge her mood from her still face. Maybe she was making a mental list of what she needed to pick up at the store on the way home from work. Or maybe she was as painfully aware of him as he was of her. Did she ever lie awake at night and wonder how it would be between them?

He shouldn't even think such thoughts. What kind of future did he have to offer any woman? Even if a woman could find it in her heart to love him, how could she love the monster he would inevitably become?

The whir and beep of the machine signaled the end of the test, but when Laurel went to withdraw her hand from his, he clamped his fingers down and held it captive.

"Mr. Bane, please." So they were back to last names again.

His temper slipped free. Jerking the electrodes off his scalp, he ignored the sting of the tiny wounds and freed himself from the tangle of wires. He surged to his feet, trapping his Handler between the console and his body.

"I may be only a bunch of numbers to you, Dr. Young," he snarled, "just another interesting specimen for you to study . . ."

She looked up to protest his assessment of her, and he liked the way her pupils dilated and her nostrils flared in awareness of his extreme proximity. He stroked her wrist with the pad of his thumb, taking note of her quickened pulse.

He gentled his voice to a seductive whisper. "But I'm still a man with a man's needs, especially when it comes to a beautiful woman. Keep tempting me, and you're likely to find out the hard way exactly what those needs are and what it takes to satisfy them."

Then he dragged her up against his chest. Her dark eyes settled on his mouth as her lips parted, as if in invitation. And just that quickly, the battle was lost as he surrendered to the temptation and heady taste of Laurel Young.

chapter 3

Keeping her hand trapped within his, Devlin cradled her against the powerful muscles of his chest as his mouth plundered hers. Laurel was grateful for his strength, because at that moment not a single bone in her body would have supported her.

His tongue teased and tasted her, making her hunger for more. All rational thought had been banished the second she'd given in to the impulse to comfort him while they waited for the machine to weigh and judge Devlin's sanity. Judging by the outcome, maybe *she* should have been wearing the electrodes.

She wanted nothing more than to absorb his taste and touch and sheer power. Her fantasies hadn't even come close to the reality of having all that intensity focused solely on her.

He traced the line of her jaw with hot, damp kisses until he reached the shell of her ear and traced its delicate curves with the tip of his tongue. Then he breathed deeply, the current of warm air sending a surge of pure need burning through her. She yanked off her lab coat, letting it fall to the floor at their feet.

All of sudden she was tumbled back onto the bed with Devlin's delicious weight crushing her into the mattress. She spread her legs to welcome him, relishing the intimate connection between their bodies. Her mouth felt swollen and bruised from the onslaught of his kisses. And his powerful hands were everywhere, touching her first through the flimsy protection of her shirt and then sliding beneath it. His callused fingertips worked her buttons loose, giving him free access to her breasts.

He nuzzled his way down to them, his tongue setting her skin afire. When he unfastened her bra, he pushed himself up to stare down at her.

"I was right."

She wanted to ask him about what, but then he dove down to capture the swollen tip of her breast. He growled with satisfaction as he lavished attention on it, using his lips and teeth and tongue in such wondrous ways. The tugging sensations sent shards of need cutting through her to settle deep inside, and she yearned to absorb his entire body into hers.

The rasp of her zipper sliding down pleased her, his hand slipping inside her panties even more. His fingers tested her readiness, finding her already slick. Just that quickly, she was on the edge of shattering.

Suddenly Devlin froze, his head cocked to one side as if listening to something beyond the scope of her hearing.

"They're coming."

He rolled off the bed, pulling Laurel to her feet in the same swift motion. She could only stare up at him, her mind unable to understand what he was trying to tell her.

"Damn it, Doc, we've been in here too long. The guards are coming."

Finally she realized what he was talking about. Someone—no, several someones—were moving around in the lab outside the door. She fought down panic. If they caught her with her blouse unbuttoned and her pants unzipped, her reputation would be ruined and Devlin would have a new Handler by nightfall. That's when she noticed the flashing light on the console.

This was the one room in the lab that had no security cameras—thank goodness!—or microphones, because their electronic impulses interfered with the sensitive scanning equipment. To compensate, the Handler was expected to periodically send a coded message to the guards that all was well. The code was changed daily to prevent a rogue Paladin from discovering it and making use of it.

Missing her last check-in had triggered the alarm.

And unless she managed to defuse the situation, Sergeant Purefoy and his men were going to come charging through that door, ready to put down a rogue Paladin. She hit the button that was blinking to reset the alarm and quickly entered the code. It wouldn't call off the guards, because their assumption could very well be that Devlin now had the code and was using it, but at least they wouldn't be quite so quick to pull the trigger.

She managed to refasten her bra on the second attempt and swiftly rebuttoned her blouse. Patting her hair, she hoped she didn't look as rumpled as she felt. At least her lab coat would cover up some of the damage. Devlin had settled himself back on the bed after reattaching most of the electrodes. Just that quickly, his eyes were closed as if he'd drifted off to sleep counting the seconds until the test was over.

Laurel's hands were still shaking but her voice sounded calm when she spoke over the intercom. "Sergeant Purefoy, this is Dr. Young speaking. Code Alpha Zulu Beta. Repeat, Alpha Zulu Beta. This is not an emergency."

Dr. Neal answered, adding to her embarrassment. "Dr. Young, what is going on in there?" At least he sounded more exasperated than angry.

"Nothing, sir." At least not anymore. "If I may open the door, I can explain."

She hoped.

Devlin reached up to squeeze her hand before she reached for the doorknob. "Give 'em hell."

Just that small reassurance was enough to stiffen her spine. When the door swung open, she stepped through to face a room full of armed men and her boss without blinking.

A few minutes later, the room had been cleared of everyone but herself and Dr. Neal. Devlin still slept on, the muted sound of snoring giving wordless support to her shaky explanation.

"I am sorry, sir. I don't know how I managed to miss the check-in. I must have dozed off." She shook her head and shrugged, hoping her boss would attribute her reluctance to look him straight in the eye to embarrassment.

He looked past her toward where Devlin lay sprawled on the bed. "Then I would suggest you take off early today and get some rest. Falling asleep on the job, especially with a Paladin of Mr. Bane's advanced age, is foolish to say the least. Luckily for all concerned, no harm was done."

"Yes, sir. I'll leave as soon as Mr. Bane wakes up. That will give me time to finish my report."

"Are you sure you wouldn't like me to do that for you?"

She couldn't risk letting him discover the haphazard way that the electrodes were stuck to Devlin; there'd be no explaining that away.

"No, thank you. But if Mr. Bane hasn't awakened when I'm ready to leave, I'll call you."

Dr. Neal reluctantly left the room. Since there was every chance he might drop back in unexpectedly to check on her, she forced herself to wait a few minutes before approaching Devlin. The cluster of electrodes dangled down to the floor and her patient was propped up on the pillow, his expression unreadable and closed.

"You can leave whenever you want. Sergeant Purefoy will escort you out." She dropped his clothes on the bed and turned away to reset the machine.

Devlin's gaze weighed heavily on her back as he dressed. What was he thinking? If he had regrets, were they because they hadn't finished what they'd started, or because it happened at all?

The sheets rustled as Devlin got up and then she felt the warmth of his body close behind her.

"Do you want a new Handler?" She held her breath, praying he wouldn't say yes.

"No, I don't. But this can't happen again."

That was true. Still, her eyes stung from the threat of tears as she nodded in agreement.

"Not here, anyway." He leaned so close that his warm breath tickled her skin. "When you and I *do* go to bed, Laurel—and we will—it'll be someplace a hell of a lot more private than this. Because *nothing* is going to stop us from finishing what we started today."

Then he was gone.

Despite the near disaster at the lab, Devlin was in the best mood he'd been in for days. The delectable Dr. Young had proven quite a surprise. Behind that lab coat and clipboard lurked an amazingly passionate woman.

He couldn't wait to have her in his bed, naked and underneath him. They'd have to arrange it carefully, of course, but battle tactics were his specialty.

Arranging a secret tryst wasn't that much different from planning an ambush.

He turned down First Avenue toward Pioneer Square, a popular tourist spot. Below the streets lay a network of passageways known as the Seattle Underground. Tours offered limited access to out-of-towners and locals, and none of them realized that the tumbledown brick walls from the past masked the high-tech control center of the Paladins.

D.J. and the others got a kick out of watching the tourists as they were shepherded through the few parts of the Underground that were declared safe enough for the public. Devlin just considered them to be an inconvenience.

Habit had him checking to make sure he wasn't being tailed before ducking into the alley that offered the closest access to the Center. He nodded at the guard stationed near the entrance. Dressed as a down-on-his-luck drunk, complete with all the usual stains and smells, Penn's appearance was enough to ward off most intruders. If that didn't work, he had an impressive array of weapons hidden in his broken-down shopping cart.

Penn was even more disreputable looking than he had been the last time; the man obviously took perverse pride in his job.

"Cullen said for you to find him if you came in."

"Thanks, I'll track him down."

Devlin trotted down the staircase and keyed in the code to open the door. Once inside, his normal wariness eased. If he was safe anywhere, it was here.

Maybe Cullen had found out something about how Dev's sword came to be stuck in the barrier.

On the way to his office, Devlin stopped to chat with Lonzo and D.J. Neither of them had seen Cullen recently, but promised to let him know that Devlin was looking for him.

The stack of reports sitting on his desk was almost enough to make him turn around and march right back out again. He wasn't in the mood to read all those dry-as-dust statements about the current condition of the barrier. Hell, all he had to do was turn on the news to know that Mount St. Helens was spitting out steam and building a new lava dome.

If the unstable mountain decided to blow her top again, Devlin and the others would be on the front lines, fighting to keep the Others out of this world. He brought up a map of the area on his computer, one programmed to show the hot spots along the barrier. Sure enough, where it came close to the irritable mountain, the barrier was being tested from the other side.

He reached for the phone. "Lonzo, have we beefed up the coverage down near the mountain?"

"We doubled it last night when the first rumblings were reported. Ordnance okayed another squad to be on call if needed."

"Send them now, because I'm not sure even that will be enough. The activity on the other side is increasing steadily."

He wanted to get down there himself, but he hadn't been released back to active duty yet. If he'd stuck around the lab long enough to finish up the rest of the tests, he might have been free and clear. Still, he couldn't bring himself to regret anything that had happened—except for the alarm that brought the guards pouring into the lab.

Although maybe it had been a good thing they had. A quick tumble on that uncomfortable, narrow bed might have taken the edge off his needs, but not for long, not the way his body reacted whenever he was within sniffing distance of his Handler. Laurel deserved to be treated with more respect than that.

Normally he made sure a woman understood the transitory nature of their relationship, then they slipped off somewhere private and scratched a mutual itch. After he made sure his partner for the night was well satisfied, they parted company with no strings attached.

Laurel came loaded with complications. She might know intellectually that Paladins gradually lost their basic human emotions, becoming more unpredictable and violent right up until they crossed that final line and had to be destroyed. But what would become of her the first time she was forced to put down one of her assigned cases like a rabid dog?

What if it were him, especially when they became lovers? The man he was right now cared about that. The Other he was slowly becoming wouldn't. So how could he protect her from himself?

A light started flashing on his monitor, one that sent him running for the control room. Cullen and Lonzo, their faces grim, stared at the readings on their computers.

"What just happened? And where?"

"It looks like the mountain just sent up a plume of steam and ash. It's too early to know how bad it was."

He should have gone, with or without a clean bill of health from Research. "Has the backup squad gotten there?"

Lonzo tore his eyes away from the screen to check the time. "Not yet. Their ETA is in about fifteen minutes."

Devlin's gut knotted up solid. "And the barrier? How are the readings?"

Cullen answered, "It flickered on and off a couple of times. Right now it's up, but if the mountain decides to throw her weight around some more, there's no telling."

"Who's got the lead?"

"Trahern."

The knots loosened a bit. Blake Trahern was a coldblooded killing machine when it came to the enemy. If anyone could hold off a major onslaught with limited men and resources, he'd be the one. By all indications, the Others had been poised for invasion on the far side of the barrier, their numbers increasing daily as the pressure inside the mountain had grown. It would take more than a squad to hold them back. But if the barrier had indeed just flickered a bit, the Others would have come through in bursts instead of one overwhelming surge of hatred and weapons.

Devlin dragged a chair over by Lonzo and Cullen

and settled back to wait for the casualty reports to start rolling in.

"Send a copy of any incoming injury reports directly to Dr. Neal to give him a heads-up. Hopefully he won't need it, but it will make their job easier if they know who's coming in and what shape they're in."

He thought about calling Laurel directly, but decided against it. It wasn't part of the normal routine to call individual Handlers. If one of her Paladins were injured—or worse, dead—she'd be called in time to prepare. Once again, she'd face long hours and no sleep. She'd give as much as it took to save one of hers.

And she did it because she cared, not just because it was her job. That dedication made her much like the Paladins themselves.

"The second squad has landed and is moving in." Lonzo's was the voice of calm reason. No matter how bad things got, he never panicked. After it was all over he was likely to explode in a fit of violent rage, depending on the outcome of the battle. They'd learned to shuffle him away from the expensive equipment before that happened. There was a room down the hall outfitted with punching bags so he could let off steam in a burst of flying fists and vicious kicks, not unlike the fickle mountain to the south.

It would be awhile before any more reports came in. While they could still enjoy the lull, he returned to his office to send a second e-mail to Dr. Neal, asking for clearance to return to the trenches. The answer wasn't long in coming.

Devlin read it once and then again as he strung together the most vile curses he could think of. What could the man be thinking? The barrier was flickering, his friends were fighting and perhaps dying, and all that idiot doctor could think of was leeching a few more vials of blood out of his arm.

Well, he'd be parked on the good doctor's doorstep first thing in the morning, because come hell or high water, he was going to be on the next available transport down to the barrier.

Those who carried the makeup of a Paladin in their DNA were hardwired to fight when the barrier was damaged. Each and every one of them could feel it on some level when the safety of their world was threatened by a breach in the fragile barrier that separated their reality from the bleak one on the other side. The tension built until they had a target for their aggression, suitable or otherwise.

The Others were a constant threat to the stability of Earth's fragile ecosystems. Thanks to earthquakes and volcanic eruptions, enough Others had successfully made the crossing to jeopardize the balance between their dark world and the light of Earth. The damage to the ozone layer alone was enough to cause major trouble in the years to come.

Conditions on the other side must have worsened again for such sheer numbers to be trying to cross in one suicidal charge. Earth could absorb a certain number of the Others, and indeed had numerous times in the past. Based on recent strides in DNA mapping, it seemed that the addition of Others to mankind's already diverse gene pool had given rise over time to the Paladins themselves.

The scientists who worked for Research felt that explained the warriors' sensitivity to the barrier. That was the good news. The opposite side of the coin was a Paladin's tendency to become more and more like the Others as time went on. Now the organization was working on finding ways to prolong and strengthen a Paladin's hold on all that made him human.

Which brought him right back to Laurel Young, and her specific interest in him. Were her attempts to delve into his past more professional than personal? Or had the unmistakable attraction between them simply made her curious about her future lover?

He wished he could have seen her face when he had bluntly announced his intention to bed her. Had those dark eyes of hers been shocked or intrigued? Only time would tell. For now, he had a battle to monitor and friends to worry about.

He sat down at his desk and prepared to wait.

"Yes, Mom, I'm fine. My job is going great. And no, they aren't working me too hard." Except when she was on duty twenty-four hours a day to bring one of her patients back from death, but that was one of the many secrets she kept from her family.

Laurel closed her eyes and curled up in the corner of her sofa. She loved her mother dearly, but she wasn't in the mood for this particular conversation. Lately her mother had been on a mission to help her daughter find a nice man and settle down to the business of making her some more grandchildren, just as both of Laurel's siblings had done.

"Yes, Mom, I do know my birthday is coming up. If I can get away for a few days, I'll let you know."

She was still two years short of thirty and was proud of all that she'd accomplished. If only her parents could share that pride, as well. They meant well, of course, but they'd never understood quite what to do with a daughter whose test scores were off the charts and whose interests were science and medicine, not prom dates and homecoming games like the other girls in their small town.

High school had been a nightmare until the day a letter had mysteriously arrived from a group calling themselves the Regents, offering her a full scholarship to start college at the age of fifteen. There had been tears and arguments, but she'd packed her bags and caught the next plane to Seattle. Except for the occasional visit home, she hadn't looked back.

The Regents had saved her from the life her parents had planned for her, one for which she was particularly ill-suited. She loved her family and her hometown dearly; they were great. She was the one who didn't fit in.

Suddenly, Laurel realized that she'd missed something in the conversation. "What did you just say, Mom?"

"I was telling you that he'll be glad to show you around. It's been so long since you've lived here, I know you'd enjoy having someone point out all the changes."

A sick feeling settled in her stomach. "Who could show me around?"

"I swear, Laurel, you just don't listen unless the conversation is revolving around some disease." Her mother's long-suffering sigh came across the phone line, loud and clear. "I'm sorry, I didn't mean that. It's just that . . . I want you to be happy."

Her definition of happy, not Laurel's. "*Who* is going to show me around, Mom?"

"Why, your brother's new business partner, Carl. Who did you think I meant?"

Her parents sometimes forgot Laurel's excellent memory for details. "Is that the same Carl who has an ex-wife, a pot-belly, and no hair to speak of?"

"Well, yes, although you shouldn't judge a person on looks alone. I know he's had some problems in the past, but that's all over now. He's looking for a nice wife to settle down with."

"I wish Carl luck, Mother, but that nice little wife isn't going to be me. For one thing, he needs to be near his business, and my job is here."

Her mom's voice brightened right up. "But that's just it, Laurel. Like I've been telling you, the whole area is growing so fast. I was talking to Dr. Watson the other day, and he says he has more patients than he can handle alone. I know he'd be glad for your help, even if you wanted to just work part-time. You know, if you were to get married and all."

Laurel didn't want to hurt her mother, but neither could she let her go on thinking that Laurel's career was just something she did to earn a living, rather than an integral part of who she was.

"Mother, I'm sorry if this upsets you, but I'm not moving back home. My work here is too important." Lives depended on her particular expertise and training. "Besides, I'm not a general practitioner like Dr. Watson. My interest is in research, and I need specialized facilities for that."

She knew better than to hope that her mother would accept defeat. At best, she would withdraw to regroup.

"Well, we'll talk more when you get here. Let me know when you can come."

"I will. Tell Dad and the others that I love you all."

Her mother's voice softened. "We know you do, honey. We love you, too. Oh, look at the time! I'd better go get dinner started. Take care."

Laurel set the phone back down in its cradle. She wondered what her family would make of Devlin Bane. They certainly respected those who served in the military, which was the closest thing in their experience to the Paladins.

For a few seconds, she imagined what it would be like to take Devlin Bane home to meet her family. She couldn't quite see him sitting in her parents' small living room, spending a Saturday afternoon watching college football with her dad and brother.

Then her cellphone from work rang.

Laurel's heart sank, knowing it could only mean one thing: somewhere, Paladins were fighting and dying.

Everyone at Research was on high alert, waiting for the onslaught. Laurel had restocked her supplies, the stainless-steel table had been freshly disinfected, and the chains and straps checked for weaknesses.

Now all she could do was wait, trying not to think about what had almost happened the day before. She shivered, remembering the near disaster.

Going strictly by the rules, she should ask to be replaced as Devlin's Handler, but she wouldn't do so unless she was forced to. Her role was to decide what was best for her patient. How could another Handler, one who only saw him as another case file and not as an individual, make more informed decisions about Devlin's welfare? None of his previous Handlers had ever commented on the fact that his slowed progression toward the inevitable madness didn't fit the usual pattern. Since she couldn't believe that they hadn't noticed, she had to think that they had seen the numbers and either didn't care, or didn't bother to question them.

There was no time like the present to begin her campaign to take a more clinical attitude toward Devlin Bane. Her intense interest would only be because of the scientific value in knowing what made him different from the other Paladins. If it were a genetic anomaly, there might not be much she could do to extend his inborn resistance to the others. But if it were due to some chemical change in his bloodstream, that could lead to a world of possibilities. And maybe it would extend beyond the Paladins to normal human beings, as well.

The scientist in her took over as she began poring over his chart, comparing previous results against the most recent ones. The blood chemistries had remained constant for the three years she'd been his Handler. Measurements of his physical strength and endurance followed the same pattern, reflecting changes so minute as to be statistically insignificant.

But more interesting were his brain scans. She began to review the various markers on yesterday's scan, and with relief noted the beginning numbers were similar to his last scan.

About halfway through the test, though, the readings spiked and then dropped lower and stayed there. What would have caused that? By that point it was to be expected that he would have relaxed, but that didn't account for such dramatically lower scores.

She circled the ones that seemed most significant to puzzle over when she had time to compare those specific numbers against his readings over time. Once she had them all charted and lined up in neat little rows, she'd get Dr. Neal's opinion. Maybe they meant nothing at all, but a small voice in the back of her mind told her she was on the right track.

A shrill alarm screamed out a warning as lights began flashing. Laurel automatically closed the file and shoved it out of the way. She had only minutes before the first patient would come through her door. Her handpicked team of nurses and technicians streamed in to take their triage positions.

When the double doors burst open, a sense of calm settled over her. Pulling on a pair of surgical gloves, she took her place at the head of the examining table.

"All right, people, let's get him moved, and then we'll see what we're dealing with." Experience had shown her that if she reacted calmly to the horrific wounds they all saw on a frequent basis, her staff would do the same.

"On a count of three: One . . . two . . . three."

They grunted with the effort to slide the Paladin from the gurney to the table. Someone slapped the initial chart into her hand. She reviewed the preliminary findings as the others began hooking their patient up to monitors and cleaning away the blood-soaked bandages. She drew comfort from the fact that he was still bleeding; it took a heartbeat to make that happen.

For once, her patient wasn't dead, at least not yet.

"Get him on IVs and then let's get him stitched up."

"Which one is it?" Dr. Neal had just walked up behind her.

She glanced at the name and shuddered. Everyone thought Devlin Bane was scary, but in her opinion, he didn't hold a candle to Blake Trahern.

"It's Trahern. Get those restraints in place."

Judging from the speed with which her tech responded, she wasn't the only one who found Trahern and his cold gray eyes unnerving. His test scores weren't as far along as Devlin's, but they were getting worse faster. She secretly thought he was the most likely candidate to be the first she had to put down. As a result, she hated each and every time he came in.

"Does anyone know what happened?"

Dr. Neal had moved into position on the far side of the table. Working in tandem, they'd get the wounds closed and begin the healing process that much faster.

He looked up from the gash he was stitching shut. "I've heard it's bad, maybe really bad."

"The barrier?"

"According to the preliminary reports I saw, it was just flickering, so the Others were coming through in small bursts. The Paladins were doing cleanup, making sure no one got away. Then a large stretch of the barrier went down altogether."

"How many did we lose?"

"Enough that we're going to have trouble making room for them all." The worry in Neal's eyes sent a chill through her. "I had to release Devlin Bane to take charge at the breach until reinforcements arrive from other sectors. I warned Colonel Kincade that Bane wasn't at full strength yet. He's risking losing Bane for good if his leg gives out while he's under attack."

Paladins were hard to kill permanently, but it could be done if they went down under an onslaught of swords and axes.

"But it wasn't Colonel Kincade who asked for the

release; it was Bane himself. If I hadn't signed off on him, he would have gone underground into the breach anyway. I only made the inevitable easier for everybody involved until reinforcements arrive later tonight."

The doors slammed open again as a group of the guards came through carrying another pair of heavy examining tables, the straps and chains rattling with each shuffling step the guards took. The patients to fill them wouldn't be long in arriving, and Laurel braced herself for a marathon.

For Devlin Bane, all she could do was pray.

chapter 4

The jarring ring of the phone woke him out of a sound sleep; a harsh voice whispered, "Now is your chance. There are enough of the Others coming through to serve as a smokescreen for you." The line went dead.

He stared at the phone in his hand, wishing like hell that he had let the machine answer. It took two tries for his shaking hand to set it back in its cradle. There would be no going back to sleep now, not with his stomach churning as he tried to think of a reasonable course of action. By all reports, things were bad enough along the barrier that no one would think it too odd if he were to voluntarily show up in the underground passages, weapon in hand.

It wasn't all that unusual for the Paladins to request backup when the numbers of Others escaping across the barrier were higher than normal. He had some skill with a sword, although nowhere near the level achieved by the Paladins. Of course, they'd each had several lifetimes over which to hone their skills.

At least Trahern and a couple of the other scariest Paladins were already out of the game. That was something to be grateful for. Bane was bad enough, but he still registered some human emotions. Trahern's eyes were dead and all the more chilling because of it.

His own chances for success would greatly increase if he could score official orders to cover his reason for going underground. That way no one would question his presence. Having Bane die for good, though, could have one of two effects. Either it would leave the Paladins in temporary disarray with their leader gone, or else they would unite to hunt down Bane's killer.

It didn't take a genius to figure out that the Paladins would devise a particularly nasty death for anyone who had betrayed one of their own, especially if it were Bane. Son of a bitch, how was he going to handle this? He was poised at the edge of a slippery slope that led straight to hellfire and disaster. If he didn't want to sign his own death warrant, he'd have to tread carefully each step of the way.

Why had Bane been singled out for execution? His Handler would eventually have to pull the plug on his existence anyway. Not that it mattered now. The long-lived Paladin had obviously stepped on some pretty powerful toes somewhere along the line.

No matter how he looked at it, planning an execution was a hell of a way to start the day.

Devlin stood in the front of the elevator because he tolerated it better than some of the others. Lonzo, especially, needed his back against the wall until the fighting actually started. As the elevator hurtled downward, they all automatically checked their weapons, making sure that swords slid easily from their scabbards and that throwing knives were snug in their sheaths. A few of them used more specialized weapons. Lonzo carried a double-bladed ax he was particularly fond of, and a throwing hammer hung from D.J.'s belt.

"Any news on the numbers yet?" Lonzo asked from the back of the elevator.

Devlin shook his head. "Not since earlier this morning, but there will be plenty to go around."

"Hell yeah." D.J. loved a good fight, whether it was in cyberspace or up close and personal.

There was no group of men in this world that Devlin would rather have at his back. He glanced over his shoulder to see how the others were handling the tension. D.J. had a wad of gum stuck in his cheek as he hummed something off-key. Lonzo shifted from foot to foot, adrenaline making it impossible for him to stand still.

Cullen scanned his handheld computer, no doubt checking the most current data on the condition of the barrier so they'd know what they would be facing when they reached the bottom of the shaft.

Their mission was to shore up the defense of the barrier. He and Cullen would check it for weak spots and do what they could to strengthen it. From all reports, Trahern had been trying to stabilize it when he went down under almost overwhelming numbers of Others.

Luckily, reinforcements had arrived in time to drive back the attack. They'd managed to get the barrier stabilized again before evacuating their injured comrades. The last word Devlin had from Research was that Trahern had been badly injured, but they'd gotten him back in time to keep him from having to go through the strain of being revived again. Laurel and Dr. Neal would have him up and around within a day or two.

As thinly as the Paladins were deployed, Devlin was glad that the casualties were no worse. Unless the barrier flickered again, he and the others would begin mopping up the pockets of the enemy trapped in the passages. Until nightfall, the Others couldn't leave the safety of the relative darkness of the underground. It took them a fair amount of time to adjust to the intensity of Earth's sun, a weakness that the Paladins didn't share.

He could feel the hum of the high-energy barrier through the floor of the elevator. It danced along his nerves with a sweet taste that he and the other Paladins craved. From the restless sounds he heard coming from behind him, he wasn't the only one who was feeling its effect, making them all anxious to be about their business.

"Showtime, gentlemen." Devlin flexed his grip on the sword. "Let's send the bastards back across the barrier or straight to hell."

The elevator coasted to a stop with a soft thud. When the doors slid open, Devlin jumped forward ready to defend himself and the others, but the passageway appeared to be empty. The others fanned out behind him.

Something was wrong. The elevator was never supposed to be left undefended whenever the barrier had been breached. The last thing they wanted was for the Others to gain control of the main access point. Devlin held up his hand to signal his companions to freeze, then he closed his eyes and let his other senses take over. The ambient temperature felt right, hovering between fifty and sixty degrees. If the barrier had flickered or come down it would be a lot hotter, as the heat from the bordering world came pouring through. The air tasted stale and smelled heavily of damp rock. Again, nothing to be concerned about.

One by one, he identified the sounds that surrounded him. The elevator machinery, the pumps that kept the atmosphere breathable, the barely detectable rasp of air as his friends breathed in and out.

The sound of shuffling feet as their owners felt their way along the unfamiliar passageway . . . definitely Others. Devlin lifted his sword in one hand as he held up three fingers and motioned toward the left. Lonzo, Cullen, and D.J. headed off in that direction as the others moved right.

Devlin smiled. Gripping his weapon with two hands, he followed the curve of the passage, keeping the wall close to his back. Every few steps, he stopped and listened. Some of the footsteps had faded, telling him that the enemy was using their favorite tactic of splitting into smaller and smaller groups until each Other was on his own.

He'd always wondered what their world must be like, that they avoided one another's company so diligently. Or perhaps they operated under the theory that as long as they spread out, the Paladins would have a harder time tracking each of them down. The truth was, very few Others lived long enough to find their way into Devlin's world.

As the passages split off, so did the Paladins until Devlin was alone. The memory of the last time he'd tracked Others made him more cautious, taking his time to listen. When the tunnel ahead of him curved sharply to the left, blocking him from view of whoever was ahead of him, he sprinted forward to gain ground on his quarry. Just around the bend he knew the tunnel split in half, one side climbing upward toward the street overhead, the other winding back around toward the barrier.

He paused to listen.

Nothing.

He eased back a few steps and waited quietly. After a few seconds, his patience was rewarded. The low murmur of voices drifted down the passage. He cocked his head to listen. As the sound faded away, he crept forward, ready to charge as soon as he identified his target.

When he reached the split, he had to make a decision. If the enemy had gone to the right, they'd find themselves right back where they started. If they'd gone left, they could eventually find their way outside to the streets of Seattle. One or two escapees wouldn't have too much of an adverse effect on the environment, but over time the accumulated damage could be devastating.

He turned left and began the long, slow climb upward. About halfway up, he felt the air behind him stir as someone else moved into the passage. Whoever it was moved wrong to be one of the other Paladins, but he had no choice but to continue going forward until his mysterious companion revealed himself.

Rather than wait around, Devlin sped up in an attempt to gain ground on the Others. He was about to turn another corner when the battle cry of his enemy rang out in the narrowing passage. He'd managed to trap them between himself and the painful sunlight outside of the underground passages. Cornered and desperate, the Others turned to fight.

It was a pair of males, both heavily armed. Had they timed their escape better, there would likely have been a rash of murders before tomorrow morning in the city above. The two of them fought with the desperation of the about-to-be dead, intent on taking Devlin with them on the final journey into the afterlife. Devlin smiled grimly. Did they have any idea how many of their kind had fallen beneath his sword over the decades? Even if they managed to inflict a mortal wound, he would come back to fight their kind another day.

As they closed in on him, he did his best to avoid exposing his back to the open tunnel behind him. There was no way of knowing if their unknown companion was friend or foe.

"Why are you here?" one asked. The Others who crossed the barrier spoke a version of English, but the words sounded harsh and guttural to the ear.

Devlin's smile was wicked and his tone was nasty. "To send you back across or straight to hell. It's your choice." He brought up the tip of the sword to emphasize the idea.

"But we already paid."

Paid? Paid what? "I don't get paid for killing the likes of you. I do it for pleasure."

"I knew your kind couldn't be trusted!" Then he bellowed, "Die, human!"

The bigger of the two Others charged at him, swinging a long sword up and over his head, bringing it down at an angle meant to separate Devlin's head from his shoulders. It wasn't easy to kill a Paladin for good, but that would definitely work. Devlin danced backward and then lunged forward again, narrowly missing his chance to run the bastard through.

In a flurry of blows, the two of them fought with cold, calculated grace until both were breathing hard.

Devlin counted himself lucky that he wasn't having to fight both Others at the same time, but the passage was only wide enough for two to maneuver. If the second one joined the first, they would only hamper their own chances at success.

Despite the chill in the air, sweat poured off Devlin's face. His bad leg ached with the strain of the fight. His enemy quickly noticed that Devlin was favoring one side and kept attacking so that Devlin put the most weight and strain on his weaker leg. The steel of his blade rang with the repeated blows to his enemy's weapon as he tried to stay out of reach.

Finally, rather than letting his opponent lead in the deadly dance, Devlin spun to the side and then lunged forward, running his opponent through. The Other wasn't dead yet, but Devlin knew a fatal blow when he saw one.

He jerked his sword free and turned his attention to the second one. The youth moved with lithe grace; all it would take was one small mistake and Devlin would end up back on that stainless-steel slab in Dr. Young's lab.

As they circled each other, Devlin tried to come up with a compromise solution. Although he fought each battle with a fierce determination to protect his own world, he took no joy in killing.

"If you surrender, we'll send you back across to your world when the barrier flickers again."

A mad flurry of parries and thrusts were his answer, and he had to resort to brute strength to overcome his opponent. The crazed look in the youth's eyes told him that any further offer of mercy would be rejected. He did the only thing he could at that point and made the Other's passing mercifully swift.

As his lungs labored to catch his breath, Devlin wiped the sweat off his face and then the blood off his sword with a handkerchief. The bodies and weapons could be retrieved later, but for now he had a mystery to investigate. Slowly, he began moving back down the passage. Every few steps he paused to listen to the nature of the silence. It had an empty feel to it, as if whoever had been following him had abandoned the chase.

If it weren't for the previous attack, he would have passed it off as a product of his imagination. But his gut told him that someone had been there, someone who hoped that the two Others would damage Devlin enough to render him easy prey for an ambush. When that didn't happen, the coward had slunk off into the shadows to await the next opportunity. Devlin quickened his pace. It was time to rejoin his men.

The sound of footsteps whispered in the quiet, but this time he recognized the presence of another Paladin. Unless he missed his guess, it was D.J. coming toward him. Judging by his slow, deliberate pace, his friend wasn't in pursuit of any strays. Most likely he and the others had finished routing their opponents, and he was coming to offer Devlin any assistance he might need.

He sheathed his sword and leaned against the wall, glad for the chance to take some weight off his leg. Just before D.J. came into sight, though, he straightened up. No one needed to know about his leg, not even his friend.

"Since you're not dead, I assume they are." D.J. glanced past Devlin to the empty passage behind him. "How many?"

"Two." He shook his head. "I swear they keep getting younger."

D.J. shrugged. "At last count, we've cleared out another half a dozen."

They started back down toward the rendezvous point near the elevator. Just as Devlin expected, there was no sign of anyone else nearby. His gut instinct wouldn't let him shake it off, though, and he owed it to the others to warn them to be more careful than usual.

"D.J., I have to ask you something about the last time I died. Did you or any of the others notice anything strange about it?"

D.J. stopped walking. "You mean other than finding your sword stuck in the barrier?"

"Yeah, other than that."

"No one has mentioned anything specific, but that alone spooked us more than a little."

"In what way?"

"Well, was someone trying to cut their way into the Otherworld, or trying to permanently damage the barrier?"

His eyes were bleak. None of them wanted to think about the horror such a disaster would cause. The Others crossed the threshold heavily armed and ready to kill, and the few who escaped the Paladins reacted to their new home in one of two ways.

The worst ones went on a killing spree until they were brought to bay and destroyed. The second group learned to adapt to the new life in which they found themselves. They quickly lost the unnatural, sickly pallor that came from living in the darkness. Over time their eyes became more accustomed to the bright sunshine, making it all but impossible for the Paladins to track them down. But as they became more human, the negative energy from their origins sloughed off and was absorbed into the land around them. If enough of them crossed in a short time, the damage to the ecology of the planet might very well be irreparable.

Devlin lowered his voice to a hushed whisper, pitching his words so they would carry no farther than D.J.'s acute hearing. "Someone followed me into the passage."

D.J.'s hand strayed to the hilt of his sword and his steps slowed. "We missed one?"

Devlin shook his head. "It didn't feel like an Other. The movement felt human, but I was too busy to check for certain. Did you see anyone that didn't belong down here?" Then he remembered the missing guards at the elevator. "The guards? Did they come back?"

"They're dead." D.J.'s eyes filled with anger. "They weren't Paladins. Evidently Kincade sent some of the guards down as reinforcements before we could get here. They didn't stand a chance against half a dozen heavily armed Others. The only thing that saved the situation is that the elevator had been sent up for us."

"Are they all accounted for?"

"We haven't had a chance to find out."

If one of the guards had managed to avoid the slaughter, he might have become lost in the maze of corridors. And if he'd stumbled onto the battle between Devlin and the two Others, he could hardly be blamed for turning tail and running. Yet the explanation didn't ring true. Even if the man didn't want to confront a Paladin whose need to fight was in full force, that didn't explain why he hadn't sought out one of the others for help.

"Let's get back to the others and do another sweep through the area. Then we'll call Colonel Kincade to come collect his dead." Not that the bastard would dirty his hands with such grim work himself. No, he'd send some other poor fool to take care of that little chore. As long as Kincade didn't have to face direct evidence of his incompetence, he'd go right on sending his men to do the dying while he collected the glory.

"Rescind that order, D.J. We'll see they're taken care of. They died doing our job. It's the least we can do."

Laurel's back ached and if someone didn't show up soon to relieve her, she wasn't going to be held responsible for her actions. Two of her patients had walked out of their own accord a few hours ago, leaving her just one to care for, but that one was almost more than she could handle.

"Let me up, Doctor."

She ignored the command, as she had for the past twelve hours. Instead, she concentrated on catching up on all the paperwork she'd let slide for the past two days while she'd dealt with the deluge of injured Paladins. Most had needed only rudimentary first aid.

Unfortunately, the one who needed the most care was Trahern. He wasn't pleasant to be around when he was healthy. Injured and hurting, he was a real bastard.

"Let me *up*."

From the sound of rattling chains, he was pitting his strength against his restraints even though he was in no shape to break free. Even in top form it was unlikely he could prevail against the chains, since Dr. Neal had ordered new ones made of a stronger alloy for the older, more violent Paladins. Still, her breath caught every time Trahern marshaled his considerable strength and gave it another try.

She gave up on the paperwork. It was time to check her patient's vitals again. He hated being touched even more than she hated having to touch him. But she'd taken a vow both as a doctor and as a Handler to see to it that the Paladins received the best care she could give them, even if they didn't want it.

"It's about time." Trahern's ice-colored eyes glared up at her in impotent fury. "Let me go."

She ignored him as she reached out to take his pulse. The monitors showed a slight increase in temperature over the readings from an hour before. Paladins weren't prone to infection, but it wasn't unheard of. It could also be due to Trahern's progression toward becoming Other.

And right now, with the way he was acting, she wouldn't advise him to make any long-range plans.

"Get your hands off me."

"Mr. Trahern, we've had this discussion before. I make the decisions regarding your care, not you."

He waited until she placed her stethoscope against his chest, then made another attempt to break free. She jumped back out of reach, almost stumbling to the floor. His laughter was nasty and mean.

"That's enough, Trahern."

She hadn't heard the door open. Devlin Bane was standing just inside the lab door, with poor Sergeant Purefoy trying to block his way. Obviously Devlin had come charging in without waiting to be announced. Under other circumstances she might have protested, but right now she was relieved to see him. Devlin had a reputation for being the biggest and baddest around. If anyone could intimidate Trahern into behaving, it was Devlin Bane.

Amazingly, Sergeant Purefoy stood his ground. She had to admire his gumption, since Devlin could slap the man aside like a gnat if he wanted to.

"Sergeant, it's all right. Mr. Bane is here to help me." She deliberately let the guard think that Devlin was there at her request. "I should have said something earlier, but I didn't know exactly when he was coming."

Devlin arched his eyebrow at her lie, but didn't say anything. The guards relaxed their stance and backed away. Sergeant Purefoy was still not happy, but he jerked his head toward the door, telling the others without words to leave.

"If you need help with these two, call me." He shot Devlin a dirty look on his way out of the lab.

"My, my, Doctor. Your guard dogs are showing their teeth," Devlin said, sauntering closer to where she stood.

"No need to gloat, Mr. Bane. They're just trying to do their jobs." She turned back to her unpredictable patient. "I was just explaining to Mr. Trahern here that I need to complete my examination. The sooner we get it done, the sooner he stands a chance of getting out of here."

"Let me up, and I'll let you touch me anyway you want to." Then Trahern made kissing noises at her, his face contorted in a travesty of a leer.

"Damn it, Blake, cut it out." Devlin loomed closer, his own temper showing in his stance and clenched fists.

"Get screwed, Bane." Trahern turned away and in a burst of fury, he began jerking on the chains until his wrists bled.

It was time for drastic measures. Laurel headed for the drug cabinet. She always kept a sedative drawn and ready when Trahern was in the building.

When she turned around, Devlin had literally

taken matters into his own hands. They were around Trahern's throat, forcing the injured Paladin to look him in the face.

"Damn it, Trahern. Do you *want* them to put you down? Because if that's what you're pushing for, just say the word and I'll take you out right now." The words were all the more frightening because of his calm tone, as if he didn't much care which answer he got.

"I'm waiting, Blake. What do you want? If it hurts too much, we'll end it. But I can tell you that I don't need this right now. I need you to get my back."

The three of them waited: Devlin with that almost unnatural calm, Laurel with her heart in her throat, and Trahern, his eyes wide and wild. She didn't know if she could bear to see Devlin ease his friend's obvious pain permanently, but a guilty little part of her would be relieved that she wouldn't have to be the one to decide.

"I hate this." Trahern's words had lost their fury, but the grief was almost harder to hear.

"We all do, Blake, but it's how it is for us. Let the doctor help you sleep some more." He released his hold on Trahern and stepped back, the crisis past for the moment.

Laurel quickly swabbed Trahern's arm with alcohol and injected a powerful sedative. His wary eyes met hers for a few seconds as they both waited for oblivion to carry him away.

"I'm sorry," he whispered.

She managed a shaky smile for him. "So am I, Blake. So am I."

His eyes rolled back and his face went slack. She knew she shouldn't, but she brushed the hair back from his face and then pulled the blanket up higher on his chest.

When she stepped away from her slumbering patient, Devlin was staring down at his friend with bitter sorrow etched in the harsh planes of his face. He looked as if he would shatter into a million pieces.

"He's getting close to the limit."

It wasn't a question, but she answered anyway. "The readings are worse than last time, but he isn't there yet. It helped that you were here to pull him back. He doesn't respond well to me or Dr. Neal, but he seems willing to listen to you. The next time he comes in," she said, wishing they didn't both know the next time might very well be Trahern's last, "it might help if you were nearby when he wakes up. Just in case."

Devlin nodded but didn't move. She needed to get him away from Trahern. "Look, I could use a cup of coffee. I'll get someone to relieve me now that he's asleep. That shot should give him a good night's rest."

She reached for the phone and made a quick call. A few minutes later, her favorite technician came through the door. Kenny looked like a prizefighter who'd lost more than his fair share of bouts. But despite his rough appearance, he had a gentle touch with his charges. She trusted him to see to it that Trahern slept undisturbed.

"Page me if he starts to wake up or if there are any problems."

Normally, she would have added an explanation about where she could be reached. But leaving the building with a Paladin, especially Devlin Bane, wasn't something she was ready to share with anybody. It was bad enough that the guards would see them go out together. She was never sure how much they reported back to Colonel Kincade, or Dr. Neal, for that matter.

Kenny merely nodded and reached for the chart. If he thought it odd that she was leaving with Devlin Bane, he gave no indication.

As she gathered her jacket and purse, Devlin caught her by the arm. "I'll meet you somewhere."

That was a good idea. Yet why risk being seen in a local coffee shop? She surprised them both by saying, "How about my place in thirty minutes?"

"That's not smart." He nodded in the direction of the scan room.

The memory of how close they'd come to disaster brought a blush to her cheeks. "Fine. I'm hungry. How about that Italian place off Pioneer Square?"

"I'll be there. Now call in your watchdogs so I can get out of here."

A grin tugged at the corners of her mouth even as she tried to show her disapproval.

"Sergeant Purefoy, Mr. Bane is leaving now. He has promised to behave. Let me know if he gives you any trouble, and I'll make sure the next needle I use on him is rusty and dull."

The guards filed in and then filed out with Devlin walking meekly in their midst.

She straightened her work area, giving Devlin enough time to leave the building. On the way out, she stopped in the women's room to run a brush through her hair and touch up her lipstick. She needed all the help she could get after the kind of day she'd had. If she could catch up on her sleep later, she'd be better able to face Trahern in the morning.

But for now, she was going to have lunch with a fascinating, handsome man. If Dr. Neal found out, she would simply tell him that she and Devlin had needed to discuss Trahern's situation, which was true. If Trahern found it easier to maintain control with Devlin there, perhaps that would hold true for others, as well. Anything that would help a Paladin make the transition was surely worth discussing.

Maybe she was only fooling herself about her reasons for being so excited about a simple meal, but with luck it would also fool everyone else—including Devlin Bane.

chapter 5

Devlin found a spot in a back corner and watched the door from behind the questionable cover of several large potted plants. He had no business seeing Laurel outside of her lab, but the need to be with her, away from the prying eyes of cameras and microphones, was riding him hard.

The memory of her gentle treatment of Trahern bothered him more than he cared to admit. He doubted his friend would appreciate knowing the good doctor had tucked him in as if he'd been a toddler who'd collapsed after throwing a temper tantrum.

There had been nothing sexual in the way she'd tugged up the blanket or brushed Trahern's hair back from his face, but the episode had left Devlin feeling edgy and raw and so damn jealous he hurt. What kind of bastard begrudged a suffering friend a simple, comforting touch? And damn, Trahern was so close to crossing over to the horror of becoming Other. He knew he'd shocked Laurel when he had offered to put Blake out of his misery, but he'd meant it. No one deserved to see the last of his soul slip out of his grasp. He only hoped that D.J. or Cullen showed him the same kindness when his time came. He'd hate like hell to know that Laurel, with her gentle manner and kitten posters, would be forced to end his life.

The bell over the restaurant door jarred him out of the downward spiral of his thoughts. He stood up briefly, just long enough so that Laurel could spot him. She gave him an unsure smile before starting forward. Something about her looked different. Just before she reached the table, he realized that other than that one day in the scan room, this was the first time he'd seen her without the armor of her lab coat on.

His memory of how she'd looked with her blouse open was vague because the room had been so dimly lit. But he remembered all too clearly the silky smoothness of her skin and the taste of her mouth, and how it had felt for a few burning seconds to feel her underneath him.

Laurel's steps faltered, reminding him that she read his thoughts and moods better than most. He tempered his rising desire and leaned back into the corner of the booth, trying to look relaxed and harmless.

"Nice try, Mr. Bane." She gave him an impudent grin as she dropped her jacket and purse on the seat and slid in across from him. "I know you too well to buy the innocent act."

"Can't say I didn't try."

He reached for the menu and pretended an interest in how many different sauces and pastas the restaurant offered. The rich smell of basil and oregano scented the air, reminding him that it had been too long since he'd last eaten. Maybe this wasn't such a bad idea after all.

He noticed Laurel had closed her menu and set it aside. "Already made up your mind?"

"I always have the same thing—the pizza with artichoke hearts and mushrooms."

"No meat?" He should have known.

"Nope, I like my pizzas strictly vegetarian."

He dragged his eyes back to the menu, but tucked away that little bit of information about her. Was this what a schoolboy crush felt like? He wouldn't know because he could barely remember ever being that young.

The waitress appeared at their table and he handed her the menus. "I'll have the spaghetti and meatballs. The lady will have the artichoke pizza."

"Anything to drink?"

He pegged Laurel for a white wine drinker, but she surprised him again. "Bring me a dark ale."

"Make that two."

"I'll be back with your salads and a basket of breadsticks."

Silence settled between them. He had no idea of how to carry on a casual conversation, so he settled on business instead.

"Thanks again for your patience with Trahern. He has a tougher time of it than most."

She kept her hands busy tearing a paper napkin into neat little strips. "I know he does, and it's worse every time. I just wish I knew why."

"That's how it is for us. I'd think you'd know that as well as we do."

Her eyes snapped up to meet his. "Of course I know that, Mr. Bane—but I don't have to accept that it can't be changed. I am a physician *and* a scientist: it's my job to figure out what makes you and the others tick."

He kept his voice low but didn't try to keep his temper from showing. "I don't want to be an interesting specimen in your laboratory. If that's what you want from me, then I'm out of here."

She actually laughed and rolled her eyes. "Devlin, if I were into lab rats, I'd be at a university biology department playing with rodents. I chose to work with human beings because that's what I wanted to do." The smile faded. "And I never forget for one minute that's what you are. Sometimes I think I am more aware of that than you and some of your friends are."

She leaned forward. "And that's exactly my point. *Why* do you change? And why do you change at different rates? For example, you're decades older than Trahern, but if he continues at current rates, his readings will soon pass yours."

She leaned back in her seat. "Forget I said that. I can't believe I just discussed another patient's case with you—but I care about Trahern, despite his less-than-charming personality, and I feel like I'm running out of time to save him."

As if anyone could, and Trahern would be the first to admit that. He'd never been particularly friendly, even with the other Paladins. Over the past year he'd become totally withdrawn, hardly speaking to anyone. And on the occasions when the barrier was quiet enough that the Paladins could kick back and relax, he rarely joined the others for a drink.

It was the way of their kind. As their connection with their humanity diminished, their tolerance for the company of others disappeared. All that remained was a sense of duty and the desire to kill. As long as that need was directed at the Others, a Paladin could function. Eventually, however, he would turn rabid, killing indiscriminately. It was the Handler's job to cull the rogues before they slaughtered those they'd been born to protect.

Which brought him right back to Laurel Young, with her earnest desire to make life easier for the Paladins under her care. The very idea should have been laughable. Generations of Paladins had lived out their lifetimes knowing that when the end came, it would be in a rage of madness. They asked for no quarter and deserved none.

And his Handler, with her gentle eyes and gentle touch, had no business being around them.

"Devlin? Are you all right?"

Those very hands came across the table to touch his, bringing him back to the moment. He studied the contrast between Laurel's slender fingers and his callused hand. Soft versus hard. Hands meant to heal reaching out to hands meant to kill. What kept her from being repulsed by him? Did she have any idea of how many had died at the point of his sword?

He suspected that knowing wouldn't change anything. Considering how many Paladins she'd stitched up and revived, she had a better idea than most the cost of the ongoing war they fought to protect their world.

Since she was looking as if she really wanted an answer, he lied. "I'm fine."

Before she could call him on it, he spotted their waitress heading toward their table. "Our food's here."

Laurel accepted the diversion, but the way she looked at him warned him that she hadn't abandoned the discussion. Giving in to the temptation to spend time with her had been a huge mistake. Here, among the ferns and the heady aroma of Italian spices, he could almost pretend theirs was a normal relationship. The kind where two friends shared a simple meal. Or better yet, two about-to-be lovers savoring the last few moments before they crossed that line, exchanging heated looks and promises of what was to follow.

He wanted her with the same ferocity as his need to protect the barrier, as if it came from the very depths of what made him a Paladin. He didn't know what to make of it. Paladins never married and rarely had relationships that lasted more than a few weeks. For one thing, women had an uncanny way of sensing when a man was a bad risk. Men with the primitive instincts of ancient warriors might prove entertaining in the sack, but they weren't likely to stick around for the long haul.

And if he thought carrying Laurel off to his bed for a few nights of hot sex would cure the problem, he'd be up for it, pun intended. He shifted uncomfortably in the seat, the direction of his thoughts having had a predictable effect on his anatomy.

"Stop it, Devlin."

"Stop what?" He set his fork down, curious to know what she was talking about.

"Stop looking at me as if you were a big cat about to pounce on a mouse."

He couldn't help but grin, something he rarely did. "Can I help it if you'd make such a tasty little morsel?"

She blushed but met his gaze head on. "Devlin, I'm your Handler. We shouldn't. We can't."

She was right. It didn't seem to matter, though.

He tossed his napkin down on the table, then enough money to pay the bill at least twice over. "Let's get out of here and take a walk."

She nodded, her eyes huge. "All right."

Outside the sky had clouded over in the short time they'd been in the restaurant. That was fine. Gloomy fit his mood. Without speaking they turned north and then west, away from Pioneer Square and down toward the waterfront.

The silence was only slightly more comfortable than the dangerous conversation they'd been having in the restaurant. He was acutely aware of her. The breeze played with her hair, the short dark curls calling out to be touched. Her long legs matched his, stride for stride.

If it were only this intense physical desire, he could ignore it. But he also liked the way she stood up to him and the ferocity she brought to the care of her patients. He knew without question she'd bring that same intensity to bed, and he wanted to experience that firsthand. She warmed him in places that had been cold for far too long.

"I'll walk you home."

"Not yet. I didn't get to finish my pizza, so you owe me an ice cream."

She was offering him a few more minutes in her company. Maybe he was weak-willed, but too damn bad. Maybe they could be just friends for the duration of an ice-cream cone. Then he'd take her home, before one or both of them lacked the strength to walk away.

"Fine. One scoop or two?"

"It's definitely a two-scoop kind of day. And I want the good stuff, the kind that will clog your arteries but tastes so good that you don't care."

Then she surprised him by looping her arm through his as they searched the piers for an ice-cream stand.

Laurel loved her condo, with its view of Elliott Bay and the Seattle skyline. But at that moment, she wished she lived miles away from the city, someplace that would take her far longer than the next few minutes to reach. But there it was, just ahead of them at the end of the block. She would key in her security code, her door would open, and she'd cross the threshold by herself. Devlin would walk away, back to his own place, both of them alone and hurting.

But she wouldn't let that ruin the last few minutes of what had been an amazing escape from her normal life. After they'd had ice cream, they'd wandered the shops along the piers, looking at everything from expensive artwork to the tackiest souvenir stands. She'd seen it all before, but this time everything seemed brighter and more beautiful because she was sharing it with Devlin.

"We're here."

"Which one is yours?"

She pointed to the brick building on the corner. "That one on the right."

"I should have guessed it, with all those flowers." He stopped walking and looked around.

"What's wrong?"

"Your front door is too exposed." He grabbed her hand and tugged her toward a nearby alley between two old buildings.

"Too exposed for what?"

Devlin stopped abruptly and gently pushed her back against a brick wall, protected from the view of the street by a stack of boxes. "Too exposed for this."

Then his mouth found hers. He tasted of chocolate mint and heat. This was what both of them had been wanting since leaving the lab behind. She felt crushed between the rough brick and a powerful male body, but it was so incredibly good and right.

Feeling daring, she wrapped one leg around his, depending on his strength to keep her from falling. He surprised her by lifting her other leg and wrapping it around his hips, settling the center of his need in the cradle of her own heat.

She whimpered.

He thrust his tongue in and out of her mouth with the same rhythm he rubbed his body between her legs, telling her without words what he'd really like to be doing. When his hand slipped between them to squeeze her breasts, she lost all control as a climax hit her without warning.

She felt Devlin smile against her mouth. "Damn, I knew you'd burn like this in my arms."

The wave of passion left her boneless and shaken. Devlin made no move to set her down, his face buried in her hair, his hands soothing.

"Did I hurt you?" he murmured near her ear.

"Right now, I couldn't be better."

"We'd better get you home. I'm due back at the Center early in the morning." He eased her back down to the ground, holding on to her in case her legs weren't ready to support her yet. "I'll walk you to the door."

He stepped back, putting a little distance between them, as if that would be enough to temper the passion that still shimmered between them.

Knowing he was going to walk away, even though he should, made her feel wronged and bitchy. "I'm a big girl, Devlin. I can make it that far by myself. Besides, as you said, it's too exposed."

"Fine."

His easy capitulation made her even madder. She turned on her heel, intent on showing him that she could play hardball, too. Before she'd taken a second step, his hand clamped down on her shoulder and spun her around. Then she was right back where she wanted to be, in his arms and kissing him for all she was worth. There was a bit of temper coming through from his side, as well.

Gradually his touch gentled; his kiss coaxed rather than demanded, and they both eased apart. Laurel did her best to ignore how much it hurt. They walked in silence to the door of her building. Neither of them seemed to know what to do next.

"You'd better go." She allowed herself the small privilege of reaching up to straighten his collar.

He flinched, but stood his ground. "Do you want me there in the morning when Trahern wakes up?"

"I can handle Trahern." She could, too, even if he did his best to scare her.

Devlin's mouth softened into an almost smile. "I know you can, tiger. Hell, most of us live in mortal fear of you. But if you want me there, say so."

She was tempted but decided against it. "I appreciate the offer. But I don't want him to feel like I need backup again, or that we're ganging up on him."

"Good night, Laurel."

"Thanks for a wonderful time, Devlin."

He nodded, his face settling back into its normal harsh lines.

Then he was gone, disappearing back into the shadowy world that seemed to be so much a part of who he was. She knew without asking that she wouldn't see him again until they carried him across the threshold of her lab, broken and bleeding. A tear burned down her cheek, but she made no effort to stop it or any of the others that followed in its path.

Some things in life were worth crying over, and her heart told her that Devlin Bane was one of them.

The night had passed in fits and jerks, peaceful sleep always just beyond his reach. His dreams had been filled with images of Laurel—of what might have been if he'd been invited into her condo, into her bed, into her. Hell, it didn't help that he already knew firsthand the sweet taste of her kiss and the smooth feel of her skin. And the memory of those deliciously long legs wrapped around him, holding him next to the damp heat of her body, wasn't going to fade in this lifetime. Or the next.

He'd given up on sleep long before the first rays of sun broke over the mountains to the east. A pot of coffee and two-day-old pizza for breakfast did little to improve his mood. Neither did using up every drop of hot water in the tank trying to scrub off the last bit of her scent from his skin. If only the memories were as easy to rinse away. With any luck, there'd be a crisis needing his attention when he went into work early.

Although there were closer entrances to the Center than the one down near Pioneer Square, he needed to walk off some of his mood—even though no one ever expected Paladins to be cheery and fun to be around. They were all loners at heart, although some of the younger ones still had friends, both inside and outside of the Paladins.

He didn't miss it. It took too much effort to guard every word he spoke, to keep up the lies about what he did for a living and why he disappeared for long stretches of time. After he had a few deaths under his belt, he could no longer tolerate large crowds for extended periods of time without risking losing control of his hair-trigger temper.

Funny, he'd felt none of the usual irritation with Laurel despite all the crowded shops that she'd dragged him through. For a few hours, he'd forgotten who and what he was. He suspected that he would continue to pay dearly for that lapse in the dark hours of the night when he was alone with his memories. But all things considered, he couldn't regret a single second of the time he'd spent with her.

One of the side benefits of being a Paladin was an underdeveloped conscience. Remembering that cheered him considerably. Just in time, too, because Penn was on his feet and waiting for him outside the Center's entrance.

"They were about to send out search parties." Penn's teeth shone whitely against the dirt on his face.

"Why?" It couldn't be the barrier. He would have felt that himself.

"I don't know, but Cullen and D.J. said if I heard from you that I should tell you to hustle your ass." He settled back down in his usual spot and tugged a ragged blanket up around his shoulders. "And before you ask, they seemed more excited than worried."

"Thanks for passing along the message."

As soon as he was inside, he went in search of his friends. Cullen was at his desk reading a book; he had a passion for dark fantasy novels. Devlin didn't care for them himself. They came a little too close to the life he actually lived, and he read to escape reality.

"I hear you were looking for me."

Cullen stuffed a torn envelope in the book to mark his spot and set it aside. "Actually, it's D.J. who has something he wants to show you. He's probably at his computer, hacking into another classified site."

Devlin shook his head. D.J. was an electronics genius and he got his kicks playing cat and mouse with cyberpolice. So far, he was ahead a zillion to none. The other Paladins had a betting pool going on how long it would be before he slipped up and got caught. Not that anyone would ever put D.J. behind bars for his not-quite-harmless pranks; the Regents, who ran and controlled the Center and therefore the Paladins, had too much clout for that. They protected their own, even from themselves.

Sure enough, D.J. was sitting cross-legged on his chair, his keyboard in his lap. His fingers were a blur as they danced over the keys as he laughed and taunted the screen.

"Too late, you careless bastards! Next time you'll

make sure to close any back doors into your system."
After the CPU processed his last command, he hit
the delete button, then turned to face Devlin and
Cullen and grinned. "That was fun."

"We do *not* want to know."

"I wasn't going to tell. Let it suffice to say that the
military will be upgrading their security procedures
shortly."

He managed to make it sound as if he'd just done
them a favor by slipping around in their files. Who
knows, maybe he had.

Cullen leaned against the wall and crossed his
legs at the ankles. "I assume you showed them the
error of their ways just in time for our new software
to hit the market."

Clearly insulted by that suggestion, D.J. gave his
friend a disgusted look. "I'm being patriotic, not mer-
cenary."

Neither Cullen nor Devlin bought that one. D.J.
played tag with other computer geeks because it was
a cyber pissing contest, one that D.J. always won.

"Penn said you wanted to talk to me."

"I left something on your desk."

"Don't make me guess. I'm not in the mood."

D.J. stood up and stretched. "It's a nice puzzle for
you to figure out."

Devlin led the parade into his office. A bunch of
small, wadded-up rags were piled in the middle of his
desk. "What the hell are those?"

He picked one up. It looked like a small drawstring bag that had been slit open across the bottom.

The fabric was thick and soft, but other than that unremarkable.

"Where did they come from?" He suspected he already knew the answer. If they didn't have something to do with the Others, D.J. wouldn't be bothering him with them.

"We found them under one of the guards who was slaughtered." Cullen held out his hands for Devlin to toss him one. "We've already run some preliminary tests on a couple of them."

"And?" He wasn't going to like the answer. He just knew it.

"They came from across the barrier."

Devlin dropped the bag as if he'd been burned. Feeling foolish, he poked at the pile to show that he wasn't really afraid of any possible contamination. After all, when they collected the bodies of the Others, they all came into contact with their clothes without injury. Maybe. No one really knew what factors caused the Paladins to become more violent. It might come from their frequent exposure to the aliens and their artifacts.

"Anything else special about them?"

"They were all slit open with the same knife—standard guard issue, by the way. We found the knife, but no fingerprints or identifying marks."

Devlin untied the knot that held a bag tightly closed. It took a little effort, but it was possible. Cutting them open meant whoever wielded the knife was in one hell of a hurry.

"Any residue inside the bags?"

D.J. nodded. "A couple had some crystalline dust

in them. It's nothing we recognized, although that's no surprise. Research is repeating the tests. They promised to have the new results back to us by tomorrow."

No one had ever been either brave enough or stupid enough to cross the barrier to check out the world on the other side. Considering how much the Others risked on a chance to escape, the place had to be the stuff nightmares were made of.

Something about the bag nudged at a memory, but it wouldn't quite kick loose.

"Any idea what these things might mean?"

Cullen ticked off his ideas on his fingers. "First, they're not from here, so the Others must have brought them across. Second, they must have held something of value, because the Others normally only bring weapons and the clothes on their backs with them. And third, someone on this side must have agreed about the valuable nature of the items, or they wouldn't have killed the guards to get their hands on the stuff."

The fourth, unspoken possibility was that it hadn't been the Others who slaughtered the guards. That didn't bear thinking about, but it tied in with the attack on Devlin himself. A human had gone rogue. If Cullen wasn't willing to bring up the possibility, he had to.

He turned away from the pile of bags to face his friends. "There's something about my latest death that you should know. We were on a routine check of the barrier when a portion of it came down with no warning. Luckily, only a dozen or so of the Others managed to get across before we got it repaired. While Trahern and a couple of his men stayed behind to make sure it didn't happen again, the rest of us took off after the escapees. I tracked two of them who were heading up toward the surface."

He closed his eyes, trying to recapture even the smallest of details, but most of the rest was clouded by remembered pain. Cullen prodded him.

"What happened to the Others?"

"We fought. I remember killing one about halfway up the north tunnel, but the second one disappeared while we were fighting. I had started to search for him when from out of nowhere, he came flying at me swinging an ax. I don't know where the hell he got it, because he didn't have it with him when he crossed over." Of its own accord, his hand reached down to rub the ache in his leg. "I managed to hold him off for a few seconds, but then someone else came out of the darkness. He was the one who gutted me."

"Did you get a good look at him?"

"Not his face, but I remember his hands." He held one of his own out in front of him. "His skin was this color, not pasty gray. I was killed by a human, not an Other."

"The hell you say! We'll kill the son of a bitch twice over!" D.J. glared around the room, as if their unknown enemy might be lurking in a corner. His quick temper had him pacing like a caged lion.

Cullen, always the calm one in the group, shook

his head. "No, we won't. Retribution will have to wait, because we need him to talk first. There's obviously more going on here than just an attack on Devlin." He laid it all out for them. "Devlin gets killed—nothing special about that. But judging by the fact they'd brought along an ax, I suspect they meant for it to be permanent."

Devlin's breath caught in his throat. He'd been thinking the same thing, but he didn't like hearing that he was right. No one came back from dismemberment. "Then what stopped them?"

"You hadn't been dead long, maybe only a few seconds, when we found you. Chances are they heard us coming and panicked." Cullen frowned. "Come to think of it, there were two dead Others by your body, but I don't remember either of them having an ax. If you didn't finish the second one off, then your killer must have."

D.J.'s smile was chilling. "Their partner was tying up loose ends. Can't trust anybody these days."

"Then there's the little matter of my sword being found stuck in the barrier," Devlin said. "With all the power shimmering along that stretch, the bastard's lucky he didn't get fried." And too damn bad that he hadn't, although Cullen was right. They needed to question the son of a bitch before exacting any revenge. He'd have to content himself with being the one who convinced the traitor to start talking. His hands clenched into fists in anticipation.

"Too bad you never saw his face. Any of the guards have it in for you?"

Devlin walked over to his weapons and ran his thumb along the edge of a knife. It was already sharp, but he needed something to keep his hands busy. He picked up a whetting stone. "None of them are fond of us. But, no, not that I know of. I make a habit of cooperating with them. I might not like to be herded around at gunpoint, but it's their job."

And their vigilance kept Laurel safe from a potentially rogue Paladin. For that reason alone he would put up with Purefoy and his buddies. Devlin stroked the knife slowly over the stone, letting his mind move down different pathways. "I think you are right about it being a guard or someone else in Ordnance. No one else could access the tunnels without setting off an alarm. Besides us, there's no one else who would know the tunnels well enough to pull off something like this."

"Do you think it was planned, or spur of the moment?"

"We don't know enough yet to make that guess. I could have walked in on something without realizing it." He poked at the bags with his knife. "I'd bet my favorite sword that someone has made a deal with the devil. Those were made to hold something small, something valuable enough to kill for."

D.J. picked one up by its strings. "The material is thicker than you'd expect—maybe to cushion the contents. Or could be to muffle sound."

"We're just playing a guessing game now." Devlin set his knife down. "D.J., I assume you can slip in and out of the Regents files without being caught."

His friend's smile was feral. "Who do you think designed their security system? Of course, they don't know that." He laced his fingers together and then pushed them out to arm's length in a knuckle-cracking stretch. "What are we looking for?"

"I'm not sure yet. Start with the guards' schedules the night I was killed. We might not be able to pinpoint our culprit, but we should be able to eliminate a few names. Those on duty at Research, for instance."

"Will do. I'll also check out financial records. If someone is dealing with the other side, there'll be a money trail somewhere." He dropped the bag and headed for the door.

"I'd better go with him," Cullen said. "He's good, but not infallible. Once he gets on the scent, there's no turning him back without someone there to jerk his leash." Cullen followed his friend out of the office. "Watch your back, Devlin. They've come after you once. They're likely to do so again."

What kind of fool would form an alliance with those bastards?

The shrill ring of his phone cut off his thoughts, as he grabbed the receiver and snapped, "Bane here."

"You're late for your appointment."

Laurel was the last person he wanted to see. "I'm canceling."

"No, you're not. Dr. Neal rescinded your release until you finish up the tests he ordered. You can come quietly like the good little soldier you are, or I can send the guards."

"Keep those watchdogs of yours away from me, Doctor, and your needles, as well. I'm busy."

She had her own fair share of stubbornness. "They are not my watchdogs, Devlin." The use of his first name was deliberate, a less than subtle nudge that there was more between them than just the patient-doctor relationship.

His bad mood wasn't her fault. He pinched the bridge of his nose, trying to ward off a headache. "I'll come back when I can, Laurel. There's something going on here that requires my attention."

"Devlin, I know your job is important, but you can't do it if you don't take care of yourself. Now get over here before I send in the troops." Her voice dropped to a whisper. "Please."

With the mood his men were in, the last thing he needed was a bunch of armed guards showing up to drag him away. It didn't bear thinking about.

"Fine. Give me a couple of hours."

"Do you want me to send a car?"

"No. I said I'd be there and I will."

He slammed the phone down, effectively ending the discussion. Picking up his knife, he stared at it for a long second. Then with a flick of his wrist and a string of obscenities, he sent it sailing through the air to stab the wall across the room. He stomped over to yank it free, wishing he had a living target for his anger.

There was no use in trying to get any work done with the mood he was in; he might as well go to the Armory to repair the edge on his sword. Though the

Regents employed arms masters to keep the Paladins' weapons in top condition, Devlin preferred to do the job himself.

Most of the Paladins found some way to temporarily forget the war they fought each and every day. For Devlin, the hours he spent honing his blades brought him some peace. Repairing his sword would ease some of his anger before he had to report back to Research. The last thing he needed was for their damn tests to be skewed because of his bad mood.

On the way out, he caught Cullen's eye. "Dr. Young called. Seems Dr. Neal has ordered more tests to make sure I'm fit for duty. It's bullshit and we both know it, but if I don't jump through the hoops, there'll be hell to pay."

His friend gave him an odd look and then nodded. "Watch your back. We know some of the guards might be involved, but that doesn't mean they're the only ones."

Which meant he was probably a fool for walking the streets of Seattle alone, but he'd be damned if he'd let some sniveling guardsman scare him into hiding. Besides, it was broad daylight. If someone was going to come after him, it would be more likely under the cover of night. He left the building and slipped down the alley past Penn.

"Keep your eyes wide open, Devlin. You want me to shadow you for a while?"

"No."

"I figured as much." Penn settled back into position. "Cullen said for you to check in when you get to Research."

Damn Cullen. He should have known his friend would have put the word out as soon as they suspected there was a problem. He could take care of himself, and they all knew it. The only reason he didn't go charging back in to pound some sense into the man was that he would have done the same if the situation had been reversed.

"Okay—this time. But tell him I don't need a baby-sitter."

"Will do."

chapter 6

$\mathcal{T}$he minute hand crept toward the twelve. In another sixty seconds, Devlin would officially be late. He took perverse pleasure in making them wonder if he'd show up. Once he was inside the building, he tossed his knife and throwing blades on the counter as he sailed past the guard station.

"I'm here. Let's get on with it."

Three of the guards snapped up their rifles and scrambled after him to form an escort. Damn, he hated incompetence. If they were under his command, he would have kicked their asses for being so slipshod. He didn't bother to wait for clearance into Laurel's lab. He shoved the doors open and let his ragtag companions follow as they would.

Inside, Laurel was nowhere to be seen. He turned on the corporal at his side. "Okay, where is she?"

Before the young soldier could sputter out an answer, Dr. Neal appeared from behind some filing cabinets. "Dr. Young isn't here right now. I'm filling in for her." He nodded at the guardsmen. "Thank you, gentlemen, for showing Mr. Bane in."

After they were gone, Dr. Neal looked up at him over the top of his glasses. "Mr. Bane, I know how frustrating it is for you to have to follow our protocols, but I would appreciate your making some effort in that direction."

"Doctor, if I had gone rogue, I'd have had time to kill the whole bunch of those half-trained buffoons before any of them got off one shot. Shaking them up once in a while helps keep them on their toes."

"That's not your responsibility, although I will mention the incident to Colonel Kincade. It would seem that some of the newer recruits are a bit lax. And in light of what happened earlier, you'd think they'd know better."

A sick feeling settled in Devlin's stomach. "What happened?"

"Nothing of concern to you. Have a seat and roll up your sleeve."

While Dr. Neal wrapped a tourniquet around his arm and patted the inside of his elbow to raise a vein, Devlin looked around the lab for any clues about what had happened earlier.

There was a good-size dent in the side of a filing cabinet that hadn't been there before, and one of Laurel's potted plants was definitely looking a little worse for the wear. What had gone on in the two hours since he'd talked to her?

Dr. Neal noticed that Devlin was looking everywhere except at his arm. "Still hate needles, I see." There was a wicked twinkle in his eyes as he applied a small bandage to the wound. This one had kittens on it. No doubt they'd been on sale, too.

"I want another X-ray on that leg. It was a worse-than-usual break, and I know it's still bothering you more than you will admit. You've been favoring that leg, especially after taking over the fighting in the tunnels."

"My leg is fine." And how would Dr. Neal know a damn thing about how he felt after fighting those two Others? Were the tunnels wired for cameras, or had one of his friends been talking behind his back?

"Then the X-ray will show that, won't it?" Dr. Neal calmly pushed the button on the intercom. "Please escort Mr. Bane to Radiology. You'll need to wait to bring his films back to me."

Devlin left without a word. If Dr. Neal didn't want to talk about what had happened, maybe one of the guards would. It didn't take a genius to know that he was making them more nervous than usual. What the hell had happened? If something had gone wrong with one of his friends, he would have heard about it before he'd left the Center.

The technician in Radiology was new. She positioned Devlin's leg on the table and then scurried behind her shield to take the X-ray. That was the last he saw of her until she practically shoved an envelope containing his films at him.

"Tell Dr. Neal that I'll pick up the X-rays later. No need for you to bring them back. No need at all."

Then she disappeared back into the warren of

hallways and exam rooms. Damn, if she was that skittish around him, she wouldn't last long working for the Regents. He and the others were unpredictable at the best of times. At their worst, it took cool heads and steady hands to keep them under control.

At their worst.

Aw, hell, had somebody crossed the line? Kincade had brought in some reinforcements from other sectors to help out while Mount St. Helens was throwing her weight around. If one of them had been too far gone to save, he wouldn't have necessarily heard about it. Son of a bitch! Maybe he was jumping to conclusions, but the explanation felt right.

Every Handler knew the day would come when they would have to put down one of their charges. Most of the time one of the more experienced doctors would step in to assist, but what if Laurel had been alone? If a Paladin had a reputation of being close to the edge like Trahern, she might have had another doctor on standby just in case. But with an unfamiliar patient, she may not have had any warning. No one knew what pushed a Paladin over the edge to becoming Other.

He stepped up the pace back to the lab, forcing his escort into a trot to keep up. Inside the lab, Devlin tossed the films down on the counter in front of Dr. Neal.

"Who was it?"

The older man looked up from the chart he'd been reading. He took off his glasses and rubbed his eyes. "I doubt that you knew him. He was a recent transfer from another of the Pacific Rim sectors."

Devlin felt a little guilty for feeling relieved that the dead Paladin wasn't one of his friends. "How did she handle it?"

Once again, Dr. Neal didn't pretend to misunderstand. "She took it hard. No surprise there." His dark eyes filled with grief. "We all do, you know. It isn't easy to hold the power of life and death over a man, especially one who has spent his life keeping the rest of us safe."

"Where is she?"

"I sent her home."

She shouldn't be alone, but Devlin didn't say so. The last thing either of them needed was for her boss to get suspicious about Devlin's interest in her. He nudged the envelope to bring Dr. Neal's attention back to the matter at hand.

The doctor picked up his glasses and put them back on. "Well, let's take a look at those X-rays. I'm sure you have better things to do than hang around here all day."

It didn't take a trained eye to see the difference between the films. In the first one, his femur had been splintered by the blow from the ax, with bits and pieces of bone going every which way. In the second, there was just the barest hint of line where the bone had knit back together.

"I'd say you were a lucky man, Devlin. If that ax had been swung with just a wee bit more force, you'd have lost that leg altogether. I've read about cases of Paladins surviving an amputation, but not many. Of course, an injury of that magnitude would have ended their fighting career."

Which probably hastened them on their way toward insanity. Part of being a Paladin was an inborn need to fight. Being unable to swing a sword would be impossible to live with.

"I'll sign your full release and send it on to Colonel Kincade."

"Thanks, Doc."

"And do your best to stay away from here. We don't give out bonus points to frequent customers, you know."

Devlin laughed at the old joke because he was expected to. "If you'll buzz the guards, I'll leave."

As he reached to do so, Dr. Neal gave him a serious look. "I mean it, Devlin. I don't want you back in here anytime soon. Be careful."

The guards marched through the door in a tidy formation almost before Dr. Neal had taken his finger off the button and Devlin allowed them to escort him to the front door. Not for the first time, he had to wonder at the logic of keeping Paladins under armed escort inside the Research Department only to turn them loose on the general public. Maybe they figured if one lost control outside, his actions would be lost among all the other violence that took place out on the streets every day.

Out in the sunshine, Devlin turned back toward the Center, although he had no intention of going there. He had only one destination in mind, but he wasn't about to let anyone inside Research know that.

He wasn't going to tell Cullen or D.J., either, for that matter, but he had to give them some excuse for not returning to finish his shift.

He pushed the speed dial on his cellphone, and lucked out when he got Cullen's voicemail.

"Cullen, it's Devlin. Look, I'm beat, and I've got some personal business to take care of. So unless all hell breaks loose, I'm checking out for the day. I'll have my cell if you need me."

The need to check on Laurel was riding him hard, but he needed to take a circuitous route to get to her condo. It was unlikely anyone would be foolish enough to follow him, but neither of them could afford the risk. Still, each step he took in the wrong direction was an agony. How could they have just sent her home alone?

Finally, after twenty minutes of wandering in and around the area, he caught a bus that would carry him back to Laurel's home. She might not want him bothering her, but he didn't give a damn. Once he knew she was all right, he'd leave.

Devlin sat back in his seat and begrudged every stop the bus driver made.

That damn Paladin was a slippery bastard, he had to give him that. From the way the man had been acting, he could have sworn that Bane knew he was being tailed. When he'd first left Research Bane had headed back down toward the Center, only to veer off to the east at the last minute. If it had been anyone other than Devlin Bane, he'd have thought the man had lost his sense of direction.

It had taken a couple of turns around the block to pick up his quarry's trail again, this time leading west toward Puget Sound. Finally, the man had run to catch up with a northbound bus, effectively ending the chase for the day. He couldn't really say he was disappointed, though. Taking on a Paladin in the middle of a crowded city wasn't the best plan of action; too many eyewitnesses and complications.

But where was Devlin Bane heading? The only person he knew of who lived in that direction was Dr. Young. That thought brought him up short. She'd gone home early today after putting down one of the out-of-town Paladins who had gone Other. He shuddered at the memory of the crazed killer, loose in the lab until they'd managed to corner the bastard long enough for Dr. Young to kill him. Although he rather liked the doctor, she was too wrapped up in her patients to give much notice to a lowly guard.

Paladins rarely had any weaknesses that could be exploited. If Bane had developed a soft spot for the doctor, that information could prove to be useful.

If he could beat the bus to the other end of town, he could find out if his suspicions were correct. Feeling better about his chances to bring down Bane, he flagged a cab and told the driver to floor it.

Laurel hurt, a deep-down, inside kind of hurt that burned and chilled at the same time. One of the guards had driven her home and waited until she was inside before pulling away from the curb. She'd told Dr. Neal that she was fine, that she could make it through the rest of the day, but not even she had believed it. There was some pride to be taken in the fact that she didn't break down until after she'd done her job, though.

She'd killed a man today because it had been her duty as a doctor and a Handler. If he hadn't turned into a ravening monster, he probably would have thanked her for easing his passage into the afterlife. For playing God and deciding that it was time for him to die.

Tears burned like acid down her cheeks as she squeezed her eyes shut. He was one of the transfers from Japan, here to help while the mountain was acting up. Had he boarded the plane in Japan thinking he might never return? Did he leave anyone special behind? He deserved to have someone to mourn his passing, to hold him safe in their memory. The man had been a hero.

And how had she repaid his service? With a needle full of toxins. Some retirement plan *that* was. She pulled an afghan up around her shoulders and shivered. Today she would allow herself to grieve, not just for the Paladin who died that afternoon, but for all the others who would follow. Trahern, so close to crossing that threshold himself. D.J. and Cullen. And Devlin Bane. What if it had been him looking up at her with no humanity left in his gaze?

She would have reached for the needle, because

the Devlin Bane she knew would no longer exist.

Her doorbell chimed, once, twice, three times, but she ignored the summons. She was in no shape to deal with anyone. After a few seconds of silence, she decided they had given up and left. Then the pounding began.

She squeezed her eyes shut and wished as hard as she could that her uninvited guest would just go away and leave her alone. Finally, blessedly, the noise stopped and she could go back to being miserable without interruption. Sinking down lower on the sofa, she tried to empty her mind of everything that hurt. Ten seconds later, the pounding started up again.

Obviously ignoring the problem wasn't going to solve it. Slowly, she made her way to the front door and looked through the peephole. One very angry-looking Paladin was glaring right back at her. He was poised to hit the door again just as she opened it. Without a word, he pushed past her and then slammed the door shut himself and threw the lock.

"Why didn't you answer when I rang the damn doorbell? Hell, half of Seattle probably heard me out there. So much for keeping my visit a secret." He glared at her, his hands on his hips.

She did not need this, especially from him. "Any rational person would have assumed either I wasn't home or that I didn't want company. It's not too late for you to leave."

Rather than get into a stare-down contest, she walked away, not caring if he followed her or not. He did. Before she reached the couch, he caught up, planting himself in front of her. It would have taken more energy than she had to go around him.

"What happened today, Laurel?" His voice was gentle, as was the hand that reached out to cup the side of her face. "Talk to me."

Anger she could have disregarded, and demands were made to be ignored, but his concern proved her undoing. The tears were back in force as she stepped forward and he enfolded her in the strength of his arms.

"I killed him, Devlin. He was fine when they brought him in to be stitched up. Then, just as we undid his straps, something happened. One minute he was answering my questions, and the next he was trying to choke one of my technicians. It took six of the guards to get him back under restraint."

It had all happened so fast, but she could see every detail in her mind, as if it were a movie playing in slow motion. "His eyes changed color, and he was screaming and screaming."

"Go on, let it all out." She could feel the rumble of Devlin's words through his chest.

"I knew I had to end it. There was no going back for him."

Devlin's arms tightened. "No, there wasn't, Laurel. The man he used to be was long gone. You didn't kill the man, but the monster."

"When I gave him the injection, it took longer than I thought it would, much longer than they told me it would." The horror of those moments between the time the needle pierced the skin and the last breath he'd drawn had been a nightmare for all who had to watch. "I killed him. I'm a doctor. I swore an oath to heal, not to kill."

He pressed a handkerchief into her hand. "You put down a rabid animal, Laurel, not a man. There was nothing left of the man or he wouldn't have turned Other. You have to believe that, because it's the truth."

She wanted to believe that. She *had* to believe it, or she wouldn't be able to live with her decision. There hadn't been time to bring in Dr. Neal or another more experienced doctor. Still, she sobbed until her eyes were swollen and Devlin's shirtfront was soaked.

Somehow they'd moved to the couch without her being aware of it, and he held her cradled on his lap. His hand moved in slow strokes up and down her back, his touch soothing her wounded spirit. Finally, she surrendered to sleep.

His arm was killing him, but he'd chew it off before he disturbed the woman sleeping in his arms. Laurel needed the slumber more than he needed to ease the cramp in his muscles. If she slept until doomsday, he'd sit there and hold her. It was the least he could do to repay her for the act of mercy that had eased the passing of one of his kind.

And if there were a God in heaven, it wouldn't be Laurel Young who jabbed that last hated needle in his arm. She deserved better.

Laurel stirred slightly, signaling her return to consciousness. "How long have I been asleep?"

"Long enough for the sun to go down."

"You should have awakened me hours ago." Her voice sounded as rumpled as the rest of her looked. She was adorable with her cheek rosy where it had lain against his chest and her dark eyes blinking sleepily. He wanted to kiss her, starting with her bare feet all the way up to her forehead and then back down, lingering at all his favorite spots in between.

Another part of his body became damn uncomfortable when she stretched, her thin T-shirt accentuating the curves of her chest. It was a good thing he'd lost all feeling in his arm because that was all that kept him from sliding his hand up underneath her shirt to test the weight of her breasts. He clamped down on that idea. He was too old, too jaded, too everything to be thinking such thoughts about her.

"You needed the rest." Though it had been his choice to hold her close rather than carry her down the hallway to her bedroom. If he ever crossed the threshold of that room, it would be by invitation only and neither of them would be leaving it soon.

"Thank you." She managed a small smile as she kissed him on the cheek. "That was sweet of you."

He had to laugh. "No one ever accused me of being sweet before."

"Then they don't know you very well." Her chin took on a stubborn tilt, as if she were ready to do battle with anyone who would challenge her opinion.

The sadness was still there, though, in the depths

of those gentle eyes. Maybe now she'd understand
why he thought she was so wrong for the job she
held, even if it meant he'd never see her again.

"I know what you're thinking, Devlin, and I'm not
quitting. Period, end of discussion." She sat up
straighter but made no effort to move off his lap. "I
think he deserved someone's tears, don't you?"

Killing that poor bastard had all but torn her heart
out. What would happen to her if she'd actually
known and liked the man? One of these days it would
be Trahern or D.J. or Lonzo or, God forbid, him. He
needed to get away from her, to put some physical
distance between them until this need to touch her
faded.

He started to lift her off his lap, but she stopped
him with a touch. "Don't push me away, Devlin.
Please, I need this. We need this. I'm just asking for
tonight."

They *both* wanted a hell of a lot more than just
one night of hot sex. But before he could marshal any
reasonable arguments, she brushed her lips across
his, teasing them into parting with darting little licks
of her tongue. Each flicker left heat burning in its
wake, until he could stand it no more. He plunged
his tongue into her mouth, slipping and sliding,
learning the flavor of her need.

She moved to straddle his lap without breaking
off the kiss. He retained enough sanity to pull away
long enough to ask one question. "Are you sure you
want this?"

She pulled her shirt off over her head and tossed

it on the floor behind her. Her hands shook a bit when she tried to undo the clasp on her bra, but she smiled when it finally slipped free. She shrugged the bra down off her shoulders and sent it flying to join her shirt. He was doomed and he knew it. When her hand started to slide down between them, right to where the combined heat of their bodies all but set the air around them on fire, he caught her wrist.

"Not here." He mustered enough strength to muscle them both up off the sofa. "Which way?"

"Down the hall to the left."

They made it halfway down the hall before he had to stop and kiss her again. Then he pressed her back against the wall as he lifted her high enough to be able to pay homage to her breasts. He tried to be gentle, licking each nipple into a firm peak, but she would have none of it. When he sucked hard on one sweet breast, she moaned her approval. Damn, she tasted good.

If they didn't get to her bed soon, they'd end up making love on the floor; he was in grave danger of losing control. Once inside her bedroom, he freed a hand long enough to flip on the lights and to rip the blankets down before tossing Laurel onto the middle of the bed.

He stripped down to his boxers, hoping leaving those on would help him stay in control longer. For the same reason, he prevented Laurel from removing her drawstring flannels by the simple means of trapping her hands over her head.

"Kiss me."

"Where?" He kept her trapped with one leg thrown over hers. "Tell me."

"My mouth." Her smile transformed her into a temptress. "To begin with."

He did as she asked. When he figured he'd done a thorough enough job, he whispered, "Where else?"

She blushed. "My breasts ache."

"Can't have that, can we?" He let go of her hands, wanting her touch as badly as she needed his. Her fingers tangled in his hair as she pressed him against the sweet firmness of her breasts. He licked and suckled his way from one to the other, paying special attention to each of them.

Her fingers dug into the muscles of his shoulders, urging him onward. Finally, he allowed himself the pleasure of sliding his hand down between her legs as he kissed his way down to the gentle curve of her waist. The soft flannel did little to disguise her damp heat. He squeezed slightly, causing her legs to clamp together in an effort to increase the pressure.

She was so ready for him, but he had a few other ideas he wanted to try. He dragged his hand back up to the waistband of her pants and teased her by slipping his fingers in only an inch or two before withdrawing them again. After the second time, she pleaded with him.

"Now, please, Devlin. Now."

He pleased them both by sliding his hand all the way in, feeling her readiness with one finger and then two. She arched up in a mute request for more. He turned his attention back to her breasts, tugging on them with his lips and tongue as he stroked her with his hand and fingers.

Finally she could take it no more. "Devlin Bane, take me now!"

He stripped her pants and panties off with one swift motion. Then he shed his boxers and pulled a foil packet out of his wallet. She held out her hand. "Let me."

He knelt on the edge of the bed while she slipped it in place. Then she leaned back on the mattress and waited with a smile that was all woman and temptation. He wanted to go slow, to memorize each moment, each taste, each scent, but they'd gone too far to slow down now. He lifted her knees slightly and settled himself in the cradle of her body. With one quick thrust he was deep inside her, a sanctuary he'd only dreamed of finding in this life.

Laurel was on a roller-coaster ride like nothing she'd ever experienced before. She'd never felt so cherished in her whole life. Sensations washed over her as his hands taught her that the touch of a warrior could be gentle. It was tempting to lie back and let Devlin control this dance they were sharing, but he deserved to be pleasured by their passion as much as she did.

As he drove deep inside her body, she gasped with the impact and pleasure of being stretched taut and filled with the hard length of him. She smiled up at him as he strained to maintain some semblance of control while her body learned to accommodate his.

She brushed his hair back off his forehead and

then tugged him down for a heart-stopping kiss. "Ride me hard, Devlin. Don't hold back." If this was going to be their one time together, she wanted it to be everything they had to give.

"Hold on, Laurel . . . hold me!"

Then he started moving, slowly at first but then picking up speed. The world around them narrowed down until it was no bigger than the bed they shared. Nothing existed other than the heat their bodies generated as he pulled her legs up high around his waist, allowing him to penetrate harder, deeper, faster.

She dug her nails into his strong back, knowing she would leave marks and not caring. Then he reached between them, brushing his thumb across the center of her need once . . . twice . . . three times before he triggered an explosion deep within her. She begged for mercy, but he gave her none. Instead, he withdrew and slid down her body. Before she could protest, he cupped her bottom in his hands and held her prisoner as he kissed his way up the inside of her thighs to where her body still trembled in the aftermath.

He showed her no mercy, forcing her toward the edge again with his lips and tongue. When she came a second time, he gave her a satisfied smile. Then he suddenly flipped her over on her stomach and pulled her hips back toward him, entering her again. The new position felt primitive, as if the two of them had been transported to an earlier time when the strongest male laid claim to the female of his choice.

She knelt before him, her forehead pressed into

her pillow. No one had ever taken her with such passion, such intensity. And never had she welcomed a lover with such total abandon. It pleased her to know his control was slipping, as his belly slapped against her bottom, each parry and thrust stripping away the last bit of rational thought she had. There was nothing but Devlin and the way he made her want and feel and need.

Devlin slipped his hand down around the curve of her hip to urge her to join him, and their bodies shuddered and shivered in shared ecstasy.

Then gently, with the sweetest of kisses, Devlin settled her at his side, and they slept.

Circling the building, he slipped from shadow to shadow. The reek of the Dumpster offended his nose, but it afforded the best position to watch Dr. Young's condo without being seen by passersby. Cursing that last cup of coffee he'd had, he used the privacy of two large bushes to relieve himself. If he'd known that damn Paladin would be staying for so long, he'd have come better prepared for a stakeout.

He was hungry, he was tired, and he was sorely disappointed in Laurel Young. Despite her dubious choice of professions, caring for those animals they called Paladins, he'd always thought well of her. But the light in her bedroom had just come on and Devlin Bane was still inside. The thought of her taking that murderous bastard as a lover made him physically ill.

And jealous.

The light stayed on for a damn long time, another reason for him to hate the Paladin. It was one thing for the good doctor to take a quick roll in the hay; he could understand a woman being tempted by all that testosterone. Even the guards got some of that kind of action; some women found it hard to resist a man in a uniform.

But it was obvious that she'd not only spread her legs for the bastard, she was letting him share her bed for the night. The image of the two of them, naked and sweaty, snuggling in for the duration, pissed him off. For that, he hated them both.

He decided to set off on his long walk home. He'd finally found the Paladin's weak spot, a weapon he could use against him. With all of the other Paladins guarding Devlin's back in the tunnels, he didn't have a chance to bring the man down there. But he could lure him into a trap alone, using Laurel Young as bait.

For the first time since accepting the contract, he smiled.

chapter 7

*T*he scent of coffee slowly brought Devlin back to consciousness. He couldn't have had more than a few hours of sleep because he and Laurel had made love multiple times in the tangle of blankets. But instead of being tired, he felt pretty damn great as he sat up on the side of her bed. He found his boxers where he'd kicked them under a chair and retrieved his jeans from a corner across the room. He needed a shower and maybe some of that coffee he smelled.

Then he and Laurel needed to face the music.

Not ready to deal with all the implications of what they'd done, he buried his body and his conscience in the stinging hot spray of the shower. It didn't help that the bar of soap smelled like her skin, something flowery and feminine. He used her pink razor to scrape his face clean of whiskers, wondering if he'd left beard burns on her breasts or on the tender skin between her legs. She hadn't complained, but then she had definitely been a bit distracted.

He grinned. Who would have guessed that their sweet, innocent Handler would turn out to be such a passionate lover? Judging from her reactions, some of what they'd done had been new experiences for her. That pleased him. He might not have been her first lover, but he'd been her best. He'd made damn sure of that.

Which was going to make it even harder to walk out of her door and not look back.

After toweling off, he dressed and ran his fingers through his hair. He'd have to stop by his place to change clothes first. But before any of that could happen, he needed to talk to Laurel. Though hot sex had helped her get past yesterday's events, the two of them had to come to terms with today and the future.

He picked up his shoes and padded down the hallway to the kitchen, and it hit him that the condo was very quiet. Too quiet. Unless he was mistaken, he had the place to himself. Son of a bitch, she'd left without telling him! He'd accuse her of being cowardly if he wasn't feeling more than a little relieved himself. Nothing like the morning after to ruin a good night of sex.

Especially if it had been far more than just good sex.

He stepped into the kitchen and looked around. How considerate. She'd left the coffee on for him. There was even a box of cereal sitting by a bowl and spoon. He wanted to slap the stuff off the counter and kick the stool across the room. Instead, he poured himself a cup of coffee, adding two spoonfuls of sugar and a splash of milk. Then he spotted a folded piece of paper with his name written on it, stuck to the fridge with a magnet.

Yanking it down, he sent the cutesy magnet clattering to the floor. She'd had an early morning meeting that she couldn't miss? Maybe, but that didn't explain why she'd snuck out without a word. And as lightly as he normally slept, she must have crept around as quiet as a whisper to keep from waking him up.

The scalding coffee went a long way toward stabilizing his mood. His cup went into the dishwasher, his towels into the hamper, then his cellphone rang. He snapped it open. "Bane here."

"You're needed." There was a note of excitement in Cullen's normally calm voice.

"What's up?" Either the mountain was restless or the pressure along the tectonic plates had reached the breaking point. Let the Others come—he'd be ready, sword in hand.

Cullen confirmed his suspicions. "The readings along the fault are climbing. We're going in."

He glanced at the clock on Laurel's mantel. "Be there in thirty."

"We'll be waiting." The phone went dead.

Devlin looked around the apartment with regret. The chances of him ever being there again were pretty slim, and it was a damn shame. But as long as his mind was his own, he'd cherish the memory of spending the night in Laurel's bed, in her arms. He turned the lock and pulled the door closed on his way out, wishing it didn't hurt so much.

In just under twenty minutes, he turned into the alley where Penn sat guard.

"Lonzo and the others have been pouring in. They must be expecting a bad one." Penn looked envious. Given half a chance, he'd abandon his post to follow them down into the tunnels to fight. But a couple of months before, he'd suffered such a severe wound to his sword hand that it weakened his grip. The Handlers were hopeful that given enough time he'd return to full strength. Until then, he did what he could to keep busy.

"Cullen said the readings are climbing quickly."

"Give them hell for me." He flexed his hand. "Tell them I'll be coming back soon."

Then he sniffed the air as Devlin walked past. A wicked grin spread across his face. "Nice perfume. I hope the lady was accommodating."

Devlin clenched his fists as he fought a powerful urge to kick the shit out of the unsuspecting Paladin. His comment wasn't anything that hadn't been said before to Devlin and any other number of their compatriots. The difference this time was that Laurel deserved better. Hell, the other women he'd known over the years probably did, too, but still, Laurel was different.

He headed for the entrance. With luck, he'd soon have a more suitable target for his temper. The thought of pounding a few Others into dust pleased him.

Inside, he headed for his office to retrieve his weapons. His sword still bore the burn mark from the barrier, but otherwise it was in prime fighting condition. He strapped on the sheaths for his throwing blades and then slipped a small revolver in the back of his waistband where it wouldn't interfere with his mobility. Guns worked just fine on Others, but they couldn't be used near the barrier itself. A careless shot could bring an already unstable barrier down.

His friends were waiting at the elevators that would carry them to the tunnels below the city. The barrier wound along the major fault lines throughout the world, and in most areas it remained stable for years at a time. But along the Pacific Rim's string of volcanoes, the barrier was more susceptible to attack. The Regents deployed their supply of Paladins accordingly. Every time that Mount St. Helens sent up a plume of ash and steam, they took up position along the barrier and waited for the attack to come.

"Glad you could make it." D.J.'s fingers flew over the keypad next to the elevator. Immediately, a soft hum signaled its approach.

Devlin stepped to the back of the crowd, to allow the others to load first so he could take his accustomed position at the front of the elevator. A soft *beep* sounded as the doors started to slide open. Before they could enter, however, the march of footsteps caught their attention. The Paladins were all too independent to make orderly soldiers; marching in neat formations was out of the question.

That's how Devlin knew that it was a squad of Guardsmen approaching. The Paladins all turned to face the newcomers, each jockeying for position to defend himself if necessary. Cullen and D.J. moved up on either side and slightly behind Devlin. Their unspoken support felt good.

The Guard turned the corner with Colonel Kincade leading the parade. What in the hell was he doing there? He carried his usual sidearm but otherwise didn't look ready to do battle. His men, on the other hand, were in full riot gear.

"Mr. Bane." Colonel Kincade held up his hand to bring his men to an abrupt halt.

"Colonel Kincade." He kept his tone of voice neutral. None of the Paladins had much use for the man from Ordnance, but he wielded considerable power in the organization.

"These men will join you in the tunnels." He stepped to the side as if Devlin and the others hadn't yet noticed his escort.

"Why? The barrier hasn't failed yet. You can always send down reinforcements after we've assessed the situation."

Down in the tunnels, the Guard was sometimes more of a hindrance than a help. Few of them had the same hand-to-hand combat skill as the Paladins. When they got into trouble, it was up to Devlin and his friends to get them out of it. A fair number of Paladins had been gravely wounded or killed outright trying to rescue their lesser companions.

"I don't want to risk waiting. Too many Others can

escape the tunnels if we aren't prepared. If my men are not needed, Sergeant Purefoy here will relay that information to me." He shot Devlin a knowing look. "These men are trained to fight the filth that comes across, Mr. Bane. They are not here to guard elevators or to run errands for you. I'll be looking forward to your report on today's activities."

Then the conceited bastard walked away, having effectively set the two groups at odds.

Now someone would have to take charge of deploying both the Paladins and the Guard so they wouldn't get in each other's way. Make that *two* someones, so they could watch out for any unexpected attacks from a Guardsman.

Devlin said, "We'll take the first elevator, Sergeant. Send half of your men in the second, the rest when our elevator returns." Without waiting for a reply, he turned to his friends. "D.J., get that elevator door open. We've wasted enough time."

As soon as the doors glided closed, sealing the Paladins inside and out of hearing, he turned to face the others. "I don't want Kincade's men down here any more than you do, but most of them are brave, good men. Against any other enemy, I wouldn't hesitate to march into battle with them. But today I don't have any choice in the matter and neither do you. I assume you've all heard that I was killed by a human down here in the tunnels."

He held up his hand to stave off any comments. "We don't know if the sneaky bastard is going to try again, but I don't want anyone fighting alone today.

Pick a partner and stick with him. Spread out to the far ends, both north and south. Cullen and I will deploy the Guard here in the middle. Keep your radios open. If anyone needs help, yell and we'll all come running."

One by one they nodded and began pairing off. Just before the door opened, they all pulled down their eye goggles to protect their eyes from the superbright lights in the tunnels that were designed to put the Others at a greater disadvantage. Two by two, they spread out to do as they'd been told.

Devlin watched them go as he and Cullen waited for the Guard. His friends weren't easy men to be around, but they would get the job done. And maybe, with luck, the barrier would hold and no one would have to die today.

Just as the elevator *ping*ed to announce its arrival, a rumble shook the ground and a ripple of dark energy slithered up the length of his spine. Hell, so much for luck. The barrier flickered, and then failed right in front of them.

Devlin drew his sword, stood shoulder to shoulder with Cullen, and waited to draw blood.

The fighting went on for hours and hours. The bodies were piling up, making it almost impossible to move without tripping over Other wounded, as well as far too many of his own men. He had to admit that the Guard had made a good showing. The Others fought to the death, because the battle could have only two outcomes for them. Either the Paladins would drive them back across the barrier to the darkness of their homeworld, or they would die trying to cling to this one.

At least the barrier was back up in full force, so no more Others would come screaming across. Earlier, every time the Paladins thought they had the situation under control and could start mop-up procedures, the barrier would flicker and they'd find their backs to the wall with a fresh onslaught of Others, armed to the teeth and ready to die. He'd seen Lonzo go down when he'd tried to stop half a dozen from reaching the elevators. Devlin and a handful of the Guard had fought their way to him, but it was too late. Laurel would have another Paladin to revive as soon as he could spare the men to start treating the wounded and the dead.

"Hey, Devlin! Where the hell are you?"

He turned in the direction of Cullen's voice, keeping one eye on the tunnel to his left. Trahern and D.J. had circled around to the south, to herd any escapees down toward where Devlin and the Guard were waiting for them.

"Over here!" He watched to make sure his friend spotted him. Cullen headed straight for him, stepping over bodies. There was dried blood on his sword arm, but Devlin couldn't tell if it was Cullen's or someone else's.

"Have you got things under control down this way?" Cullen leaned wearily on his sword as if it were a cane.

"Trahern's making one last sweep. There's no telling how many made it across that last time, so we don't know if we got them all." Poor bastards. How bad was their homeland, that facing almost sure death at the end of a Paladin sword was an improvement?

"Once I hear from Trahern and D.J., we can start sorting things out. Why don't you have the Guards start moving the wounded into the elevators?" He didn't have to say that the dead could wait, even the Paladins. They would start reviving even without their Handlers' help. They'd get them to the lab in plenty of time before they actually woke up.

Lonzo was another one of Laurel's caseload. As far as Devlin knew, Lonzo was in no danger of crossing the line. It wouldn't hurt for Laurel to be reminded that the majority of the time the Paladins made the transition back to living without incident.

He was about to ask if Cullen knew how many others went down when the sound of running feet brought his full attention back to the tunnel. Planting his feet wide, he raised his sword into attack position, ready to deal with the four Others heading straight for him. Cullen moved beside him, prepared to do battle yet again.

Three adult males with their strange, pale gray eyes came out of the tunnel and spread out, weapons at the ready. Behind them stood a lone female, her face calm as she met Devlin's gaze and then Cullen's. She brought up her own sword and touched it to the center of her forehead in salute. Then she called out something in their guttural language. The males echoed the words and surged forward.

Just that quickly, Devlin was fighting for his life against three experienced swordsmen. Unfortunately, they were in the one area where there was room enough for all three to engage him at once. The woman ran full tilt toward Cullen, keeping him from coming to Devlin's aid. When a couple of the Guard moved to join in, he waved them off.

"Get back. Get the wounded out of here. And for God's sake, stay out of Cullen's way."

In a flurry of double-handed slashes he went on the attack, drawing first blood, wounding one of the Others badly enough to force him to withdraw from the fight—a definite improvement in the odds. The remaining two males fought in tandem, a sign that they had trained together. The taller one feinted to one side, drawing Devlin in that direction. At the same time his partner went left and then spun quickly to fling a circular blade right at Devlin. He managed to get his arm up in time to deflect it away from his neck, taking the injury in his forearm instead. Though painful, it was unlikely to prove fatal if he could dispatch his opponents soon.

He noticed that they were slowly retreating toward the barrier, where the woman was clearly giving Cullen a run for his money. She moved with the grace of a dancer, one with lethal moves. A trickle of blood ran down her cheek from a small cut, but it didn't interfere with her concentration. She yelled something at the men, who immediately backed away, careful to keep Devlin and Cullen from reaching their wounded comrade.

Just then, almost as if they'd been expecting it, the barrier flickered, going down only long enough for the four of them to escape. Devlin dropped the tip of his sword, his arm tired. He and Cullen stood staring at the restored barrier, too tired to feel anything but relieved.

A movement out of the corner of his eye demanded his immediate attention. Cullen was slowly sinking to the ground. A deep gash along his rib cage was bleeding badly.

"Guard! Get a stretcher!"

He supported his friend until they could get Cullen strapped onto a gurney. His own wound was hurting like hell, but he couldn't do anything about it until D.J. or Trahern showed up to take over the mop-up campaign. His radio was missing, so he grabbed Cullen's before they wheeled him away.

"Trahern! D.J.! Phone home."

The reception was full of static, a common problem so near to the barrier, but he could make out D.J.'s voice. "We're on our way back." He mentioned a time frame, but the noise in the background made it impossible for Devlin to make out whether he'd said it would be twelve or twenty minutes. Either way, he figured he could hold up that long. It seemed likely that the fighting was done for the day. He hated that he was going to have to admit to Colonel Kincade that he'd been right to send the Guard along in support.

Had Sergeant Purefoy survived the day? If so, he could make the official report to the colonel, saving Devlin the hassle. He headed over to where the Guard's medics had set up a triage station to see what he could do to help.

Laurel's back ached and she was seeing double from exhaustion. They'd been bringing in the wounded since midday with no end in sight. She had started with two Paladins who required surgery to stop the bleeding. Half a dozen more had major wounds that needed to be stitched up. She'd ordered fluids and antibiotics to speed them to recovery.

At least her patients would all recover. Dr. Neal was tending to the wounded Guardsmen; one of the nurses had told her that several of them would never fight again.

She was afraid to ask how many more Paladins were waiting before they started bringing in the dead, and she constantly wondered where Devlin was. By all reports the fighting had been brutal, with almost no one escaping unscathed. The most severely wounded had already been brought in, leaving only those who had very minor injuries, and the dead. She'd give anything to know which group Devlin was in.

Her feet were killing her, so she sat down while there was a slight lull in the flow of patients. Had it only been half a day since she'd awakened next to Devlin in her bed? She knew she'd been cowardly by leaving without waking him, a decision she now regretted. Chances were he would survive the day, but maybe not. She could have simply said good-bye, or "the coffee's on," or even coaxed him into making love one last time. Instead, she'd written a note that was a stupid lie to avoid admitting how much the night in his arms had meant to her.

But when she'd awoken, her body sated and a bit sore from the night's activities, she'd come face-to-face with a truth she wasn't ready to deal with. Somewhere along the line, she'd tumbled head over heels in love with Devlin Bane. The sex had been phenomenal, but it was far more than that. In his arms, she felt cherished and safe. He was a hard man, one with problems that might prove insurmountable, but there had been a gentleness in his touch that had brought her peace of mind.

"Dr. Young?"

The tug on her sleeve jerked her attention back to where it should have been. Judging by the puzzled look on Kenny's face, it wasn't the first time he'd called her name.

She offered him a weary smile. "I'm sorry, Kenny. I was somewhere else. It's been a long day."

"And about to get longer. They'll be bringing in the dead next. Time estimate is twenty minutes."

Her stomach lurched and dropped to her feet. "Any names yet?"

"Lonzo Jones for sure. Maybe a couple more." He looked as tired as she felt.

"Why don't you take a ten-minute break? I'll get

set up." She pushed herself to her feet. When he hesitated, she made shooing motions with her hands. "Go on, and take anyone who hasn't had a chance to drink some coffee or sit down for hours. We'll need everyone back to peak form when that door opens again."

"You sure?" Kenny asked.

"Yes, go on. The tables have been set up; there's nothing else to do until we know how many are coming in." She prayed that Devlin wasn't one of the mortally wounded. She tried to push the idea out of her mind; it didn't bear thinking about.

To keep herself busy, she restocked the trays and double-checked her supply of the special drugs necessary to aid in reviving a Paladin. Most of them could come back on their own, but medications hurried that process along.

Kenny and the others returned, still looking a little worse for wear, but she had no doubt about their ability to care for their charges. She put on a fresh lab coat and made one final check to confirm that the tables were ready.

Two Guardsmen came through the doorway pushing a gurney with Lonzo Jones on it. Her team went into action, transferring him to the closest table and stripping him down, cleaning his body and cataloging his wounds. She began suturing a large gash on his thigh just as another gurney came through the door.

It was Devlin. She couldn't see his face, but she recognized his shirt. She'd worn it last night when they had raided the kitchen. Kenny and two of the nurses left Lonzo's table to take charge of Devlin and the Paladin on the third gurney just coming in.

Was he dead again? Last time they'd been terrified that he wasn't going to make it back. She forced her attention back to Lonzo. The others would get things started for Devlin and the other one. Someone mentioned Cullen Finley's name. She couldn't remember a time when this many from one group had been taken down.

As she snipped off the last suture, she sent a prayer skyward that the barrier would hold long enough to get these men healthy and back on their feet. She picked up a new suture pack and started on the next wound, this one on Lonzo's shoulder. Once the major wounds were cleansed and closed up, they could start his meds and move onto the next patient—Devlin.

Then she heard his voice, complaining loudly about something. Miracle of miracles, he was only wounded! Greatly relieved, she finished the last of Lonzo's stitches and turned him over to a surgical nurse to bandage his wounds.

Her hands were shaking as she washed and disinfected them. Kenny handed her Cullen Finley's chart, meaning the triage team thought he was the more critical of the two.

She smiled down at her newest patient. "Well, what brings you here?" She flipped through the notes from triage. Cullen looked too pale and his skin had a clammy feel to it. No doubt shock, brought on by trauma and blood loss.

"Check his blood count and get a unit of blood started. Get me the results stat." She gave Cullen a pat on the arm to reassure him. "You're just a bit low on oil, Mr. Finley. Once we get your tank topped off and get that nasty gash stitched up, you'll be on the mend."

"Told them it was nothing serious, Doc." Cullen's voice was faint, but if he was talking, he'd be walking soon enough.

"I'm going to check on your friend here while they get your wound ready for closure."

She wrote her orders in his chart and handed it off to Kenny. She drew a deep breath and then turned to face Devlin, who was watching the flurry of activity surrounding Lonzo. There was pain in his eyes that she suspected had nothing to do with the jagged cut on his arm.

"He'll be fine, Mr. Bane. Lonzo is in good hands."

Angry green eyes snapped back to glare at her. "Right now he's dead, Dr. Young. Don't sugarcoat it."

She lowered her voice. "I know you're hurting and you're worried about your friends, but don't take it out on me. I've been the one picking up the pieces and stitching your friends back together." She gestured toward the cluster of medical staff surrounding Cullen and Lonzo. "Those people have been ankle deep in blood since the first gurney rolled through the door. We need support, not attitude right now."

For a brief second she thought his expression softened, but it was gone so quickly that she couldn't be sure. He looked past her to where Kenny stood, waiting with yet another suture tray. "Fine. Later." Then he closed his eyes and turned away.

The gash along Cullen's ribs took her a long time to close, but with the infusion of blood and fluids, he was already looking better. As long as infection didn't set in, he should be fully recovered soon.

"Kenny, please move Mr. Finley into the ward." She mustered up another smile for her patient. "You're already responding to the treatment, and I've given you something to make sure you rest easily. I'll be by to check on you after I see to your friend here."

"Don't let Devlin scare you, Doc. He's all bark and no bite." Cullen gave her a ragged smile as they wheeled him away.

He was wrong; Devlin *did* bite. She had the mark to prove it, but not where she was willing to show it off. The memory brought a smile to her face and gave her the courage to deal with her last patient.

"Let's see that arm." She gently tugged at the edge of the temporary bandage that triage had applied. Between the adhesive and the dried blood, it was stuck tight to the skin. "This is going to hurt unless we soak it off."

"Rip it off, Doc. It's going to hurt any way you do it, so just get it over with."

"Brace yourself."

Devlin gripped the side of the gurney with his other hand while she drew a deep breath and yanked. On the second pull it came free, breaking open the wound again. She let it bleed clean for a bit. What would have caused such a wide, deep cut? It was the wrong shape for a knife wound and too fine for a sword.

"What did this to you?" She deadened the area and held pressure on the wound until the local anesthetic took effect.

"Throwing blade. They were aiming at my neck." His matter-of-fact tone only made the image more horrific.

"Glad you managed to block the blade." She began the slow process of bringing the two sides of the wound back into alignment with small, evenly spaced stitches.

"I don't think you bled enough to need a unit of blood, but I want to give you an IV with antibiotics in it. Once that's done, we'll feed you and then see if you're up to going home."

She started to turn away, but his hand snaked out to catch hers, his grip firm but gentle. "Laurel."

Slowly she turned back to face him.

"I was out of line earlier."

If he could apologize, then so could she. "And I shouldn't have run out. I'm not used to . . ." She looked around to make sure no one was within hearing. "I don't often have guests for breakfast."

She was afraid she was blushing. She knew it for certain when Devlin's mouth quirked up in a small grin that came and went in a heartbeat. The wicked gleam in his eyes was still there, though. "Maybe you need more practice, Dr. Young."

They were playing with fire, flirting within

earshot of the others. "Maybe you're right, Mr. Bane. I'll be sure to keep you posted on my progress."

"Get back!" The shout came from across the room where her team was still working on Lonzo Jones. He was thrashing about, and she ran to help subdue the dead Paladin.

"Damn it! Get those restraints in place before he hurts himself or one of you!" She used her full weight to hold down his left leg while one of the others leaned on his right. The sudden fit was over just as quickly as it had begun. It took the last little bit of Laurel's courage to lift Lonzo's eyelid to check the color of his pupil.

"His eyes are still brown."

At least half a dozen people, herself included, sighed with relief at the same time. That struck them all as funny. Their laughter may have had a touch of hysteria to it, but it still felt good.

"Keep him isolated for now and keep those restraints in place twenty-four/seven until further notice. I'll want reports every fifteen minutes for the next two hours and then we'll reevaluate."

"Yes, Doctor."

She made the necessary notes in his chart and handed it back to the nurse, intending to check Devlin's vitals one more time. Her footsteps faltered when she saw that his gurney was empty. Where had he gone?

She looked toward the door. He was on the other side, watching her through the small square window. Turning his head slightly, he focused on Lonzo briefly before meeting her gaze again. His face turned stony and his eyes jade cold, as the distance between them stretched so much farther than a few feet. He shook his head and then turned and walked away.

Hurt made her feet leaden as she tried to cope with the loss. Someone was bound to notice if she stayed rooted in one spot, numbly staring at the doorway, but neither could she face her coworkers. Rather than risk embarrassing herself, she caught Kenny's attention and nodded toward the door. She hadn't taken a real break in hours; no one would question her disappearing for a few minutes.

Outside of the lab, she took a quick look around. There were half a dozen or more armed guards stationed along the hall, but there was no sign of Devlin. No doubt he'd either charged past the guards or else lied and said he'd been released. With all the commotion around Lonzo, they probably had believed him or were too busy to notify her of his departure.

On any other day, she would have reported them for the lapse. But they were dealing with the loss of several of their own compatriots, and she didn't want to add to their burden. If Devlin had left the building there wasn't much she could do except to change his chart to cover for him. She had a feeling that Colonel Kincade wouldn't take kindly to having a Paladin waltzing out of Research without proper clearance.

"Can I help you, ma'am?" The closest Guardsman, looking impossibly young, stepped away from the wall to catch her attention.

"Did Mr. Bane go this way?" She stuffed her

hands in her lab coat pockets to hide how shaky they were.

"Yes, he did. We escorted him out the front door about three minutes ago." Then he frowned. "He was cleared, wasn't he?"

She hated lying, but short of calling out reinforcements to drag Devlin back, she really had no choice. "Everything's fine, Corporal. I just forgot to tell him something. I'm going out for a breath of fresh air. Maybe I'll be lucky and catch up with him."

The sun was just setting to the west, painting the scattering of clouds overhead in shades of peach and orange as she stood on the top step and looked in both directions.

Devlin was gone.

Her shoulders slumped in defeat. Seeing Lonzo go through the throes of death and revival had clearly hit too close to home. That could have just as easily been Devlin they were strapping down, and his eyes they had been afraid to look at, for fear they'd turned Other.

And he'd known that if so, she would have reached for the needle and ended it for him, just as she had that poor Paladin who had died yesterday. What kind of relationship could they have, when she held the power of life and death over him?

The answer was obvious: no kind of relationship at all. Not if it was going to mean more than the occasional dinner together. Although she didn't regret what they'd shared, it only made it harder to face a future without Devlin. He'd shown her a side of himself she bet few people had ever seen.

She turned abruptly to return to the lab, and ran smack into Blake Trahern. He reached out to steady her when she backed up too quickly and almost tumbled down the steps. He looked down at her, his silvery eyes expressionless, making it impossible to guess what he was thinking or what kind of mood he was in.

He wouldn't have been her first choice to ask a favor of, but he could track down Devlin and make sure that he was all right.

"Mr. Trahern, can I speak to you for a minute?" She tugged him over to the side and out of sight of the doorway. "Mr. Bane has left my lab without permission."

"So? He's a big boy." He started to walk away, but froze when once again she put her hand on his arm.

"I just need to know that he's all right. Lonzo died in the tunnels today. When my staff was working on him, he reacted adversely."

"You mean he lost control." Just as Trahern had, it went unspoken.

"He hasn't revived yet, but we had to restrain him, yes. He wasn't consciously trying to hurt anyone, and his eyes are still human." Unless she was mistaken, there was a lessening in the tension in Trahern's stance.

"When I went to finish Mr. Bane's care, he was gone. I know he's a big boy, as you say, and he should heal just fine without the antibiotics I would have given him."

"But?" Trahern stared down at her as if she were

some new species he'd never before encountered.

"But I just need to know that he's all right. Can you check on him and let me know?"

"Will do, Doc. He won't like it, though." Surprisingly, Trahern smiled, for an instant bringing warmth to those icy gray eyes. "But even Devlin Bane needs to get shaken up a bit once in a while."

Her jaw dropped open in amazement. To add to the surreal experience, Blake crooked a finger and pushed her chin up to close her mouth. "Don't want you to catch flies, Doc."

Then he stepped around her and disappeared up the street, leaving her stunned and speechless.

chapter 8

*H*e was being followed and didn't like it one damn bit. His arm hurt like hell, leaving him in no mood to put up with Ordnance's games. If they wanted him back in Laurel's lab they could damn well ask. Then he could tell them all to go to hell and be done with it.

He marched through the Seattle waterfront, daring all comers to bring it on. He was running on adrenaline and sick fury, but still had enough strength to take down a handful of guards if necessary. In fact, he was looking forward to pounding something or even someone.

But even if he could escape his shadow, he couldn't walk fast enough to escape the image of Lonzo being subdued and strapped down like some rabid animal. And Laurel had joined the throng to lend her strength to the others until once again Lonzo was no longer a threat, naked and vulnerable on that steel slab.

He'd been through it and seen others go through it before, of course. But never before had it been his lover who had tightened that last strap, who decided to allow Lonzo to continue in his struggle to revive. What if he'd had to stand there helpless as Laurel injected the toxins that ensured that Lonzo breathed his last?

He admired her courage and willingness to take on the burden at such a cost to her own soul. He wanted to wrap her in his arms and protect her from such horror. Yet, he also wanted to curse her for making him care again, knowing that each day took him one step closer to the end of *his* humanity. And here he was, wanting desperately to spend every night of eternity in her arms and in her bed, losing himself in the sweet heat of her body, not in the insanity of becoming Other.

Son of a *bitch*, he needed a fight. Rather than trying to elude his unwanted company, he sidestepped onto a staircase that led down to some basement-level shops. He kept his back to the near side wall and waited. It didn't take long before a familiar figure strolled by. Devlin climbed the stairs and fell in behind his unsuspecting victim, then charged forward and dragged Trahern into a handy alley.

In less than five seconds he had Blake shoved against a wall, his hands on the man's throat. Trahern refrained from fighting back, leaving his arms slack at his side. His lack of resistance enabled Devlin to regain control of his temper. He slowly backed away, still itching for a fight if Trahern made one wrong move.

"Why are you following me?"

Trahern shrugged. "It's a free country. I wasn't aware you owned this particular stretch of sidewalk."

"Damn it, don't toy with me. You've been trailing me since I left Research, and I don't like it one damn bit."

Trahern came to full attention, like a wolf that had scented prey. "No, I haven't. I spotted you just before you went down those steps back there. Before that, I'd been heading straight for your place." He sneered. "Your woman wanted me to check up on you."

Devlin's fist connected with Trahern's jaw before he was even aware of taking a swing. Blake stumbled back into the wall but made no move to retaliate. As Devlin flexed his sore hand, he couldn't decide if he was disappointed or relieved.

"Don't call her that."

"Not saying it doesn't make it less true." Trahern spread his stance, his fists clenched as if bracing for another attack.

"I didn't deny it. I just said don't say it. She deserves better." Even if it damn near killed him to admit it.

"I'd guess that is up to her, don't you think?" Trahern relaxed a bit. "But you've got bigger problems than you and the delicious Dr. Young having the hots for each other. I meant what I said before you punched me. I wasn't the one dogging your footsteps."

Devlin believed him. Trahern was many things—sarcastic, easily riled, and bitter—but he was also brutally honest, because he didn't give a damn if he offended anyone or not. If he said he wasn't Devlin's ghost, then he wasn't. So who else might have been trailing him?

"You heard that the last time I was killed it wasn't by an Other." Cullen or D.J. would have made sure that all the Paladins closest to Devlin knew what had happened.

"Yeah. That's a bitch. It's bad enough we have to fight those Otherworld fuckers without having to worry about getting backstabbed." Trahern looked past him toward the street, as if he expected another attack to come boiling down the alley.

"Well, this isn't the first time I've had an itch; someone's been breathing down my neck ever since I revived. The other day in the tunnel, I fought and killed two Other males. While I was tracking them, I knew someone was behind me. The coward never showed himself."

"Probably waiting to see if the Others took you down so he could move in for the permanent kill." Trahern's eyes were cold enough to freeze the evening air.

"That's what I thought at the time." This was no time to keep secrets. "Yesterday I left Research to go to Dr. Young's condo to see how she was dealing with putting down her first Paladin."

"I heard about that." Trahern shook his head. "She's got backbone. She put the poor bastard out of his misery and still showed up for work today."

"Yeah, well, I had to see for myself that she was all right." It was none of Trahern's business how hard Laurel had cried or that Devlin had spent the night in her bed. "I took a circuitous route from Research to her place. I never saw anyone trailing me, but something was driving me to keep doubling back."

"So there's no way to know if you shook your tail or not. And if he managed to stay with you . . ."

"He would have found out that I went to Laurel's place. Damn."

The urge to hit something was riding him hard again. How could he have been so stupid? He wasn't anyone's idea of a white knight, and yet he'd gone charging off to rescue Laurel yesterday with no thought to the fact that someone was out to kill him. He might very well have led the bastard straight to her door.

"I don't particularly want to get punched again, but I'm guessing you didn't just share a cup a tea with her and leave." The sympathy in Trahern's normally cold eyes was a surprise.

"No. I was still at her place this morning when Cullen sounded the all-call." And he was about to go charging right back there unless he could come up with a better idea. "Want to bet my shadow stuck around long enough to know that I didn't leave?"

"Shit, that sucks."

The succinct comment startled a smile from Devlin. Trahern always did have a way of cutting straight to the heart of the matter. He considered the possibilities.

"Someone needs to watch her place." He didn't want to ask more of Trahern than he was able to give, but he hoped he'd volunteer to share the job. If he asked any of the other Paladins to share in guarding her place, they'd start to wonder why he cared so much. It wouldn't take them long to figure out that there was something going on between Devlin and Laurel. She didn't need the whole bunch of them looking at her and wondering about the nature of their relationship. And he didn't have enough time or energy to go around beating the hell out of any of them who even so much as looked at her wrong.

"Leave that to me."

"Thanks. I owe you."

Trahern snorted. "I'm not doing it for you." He walked away.

Devlin stared after him until he disappeared into the shadows. Very little surprised him anymore, but Trahern always had been an enigma. He didn't need to understand what made Trahern tick to know that he could trust him to keep his word, though. Evidently the man wasn't as immune to Laurel's gentle treatment of her patients as he'd like everyone to believe.

But for now, Devlin had a mission. He needed to draw his opponent out into the open, though not yet. Too many of the other Paladins were in no condition to fight, and his own arm was screaming with pain.

But in a day or two, there would be a reckoning. He'd see to it personally.

"He's all right."

Trahern, never one to waste words, had already hung up the phone before Laurel had a chance to thank him. The knot of worry in her stomach relaxed. She knew the recuperative powers of a Paladin, but it helped to know for certain that Devlin was on the mend. She would have to repay Trahern for his kindness. Chocolate chip cookies, maybe? The meals the kitchen prepared for him always included some cookies.

The small weakness made her smile. The big, tough Paladin had a sweet tooth.

The door to the lab opened, and Dr. Neal entered the room with Colonel Kincade at his side. She quickly stood up. The man from Ordnance found it harder to intimidate her if she was looking him straight in the eye. She joined them beside Lonzo's bed.

"How is he?" Dr. Neal asked as he picked up the chart and started flipping through it.

"About as you'd expect. He hit a rough patch earlier, but he's been quiet for several hours now. I ordered a new scan and tests for the morning."

Kincade stepped closer to the table. "When will I get him back?" He turned his cold gaze toward Laurel. "I must point out how shorthanded we are right now. The mountain is still rumbling, and our manpower is down by at least a third. I'm not asking you to risk his health, just for an estimate of when I can reasonably expect him to be returning to duty."

As much as she disliked the man, his request wasn't out of line. "Based on his previous revivals, I would estimate another two days, three at the most. The wounds are already starting to close, and his CPK levels have dropped. All of the other indicators seem to be on track, as well. I'll know more in the morning. I'd be glad to e-mail you an update after the results are analyzed."

"See that you do." He immediately dismissed her, turning to Dr. Neal. "Shall we visit my men then, Doctor?"

"Of course. I'm sure a visit from you will cheer them all greatly."

Dr. Neal winked at Laurel as he led the pompous ass out of her lab. She wondered how her boss managed to maintain such a sunny disposition around such an irritating man. Well, he wasn't her concern. Her still-unconscious patient was.

"Lonzo, don't worry about the colonel. You'll be here until I know that you're completely healed. It wouldn't be to anyone's advantage to have you return to full duty too soon." She patted him on the arm and then placed her stethoscope on his chest. Closing her eyes to hear better, she listened for a heartbeat. It was faint, but there. For the next twenty-four hours, his pulse would gradually speed up until it reached a normal rhythm. By then, his lungs should also be back up to full capacity. A Paladin's recuperative powers were truly amazing. "You're doing fine. Just be patient."

It was getting chillier in the lab now that night was upon them. Maybe she was fooling herself, but she liked to do what she could to make her unconscious patients more comfortable. A blanket straight out of the warmer had to feel good on some level to these men as they struggled to return.

Having done all she could for Lonzo, she returned to her desk and the mountain of paperwork that always followed an influx of new patients. The majority of the Paladins would be discharged by the next afternoon. She wouldn't be surprised to have only Lonzo left. That was fine with her.

Maybe she'd let her dictation wait until morning. Her eyes burned with fatigue and her back was aching. After dimming the lights, she kicked off her shoes and took off her lab coat and laid it on the counter. After brushing her teeth and running a brush through her hair, she stretched out on her cot. She fell asleep wishing she were back in her own bed with Devlin's arms wrapped around her.

He had an excuse all ready if anyone were to question why he was sneaking into Dr. Young's lab. Someone had to make sure that the Paladin was strapped down tight. Everyone had heard about his sudden eruption before they had gotten him under restraint. To give truth to his alibi, he crept closer to the bed, wishing that it was Devlin Bane lying there, literally dead to the world. It would have made his job much easier.

Instead, Bane had been discharged or else left on his own. He'd heard both versions when he'd reported for duty after returning from the bloodbath in the tunnels. He shuddered. He'd backed up the Paladins before, but never in anything like this. Blood had run freely, pooling in sticky puddles to make the floor slippery as more and more Others kept appearing from across the barrier.

He'd killed his fair share, but nowhere near the number that any one of the Paladins had. Blake Trahern and Devlin Bane, especially, were two scary sons of bitches. The rest of them were bad enough, but Bane and Trahern killed without hesitation and without remorse, as if they were mowing down hay instead of living beings. God forbid they ever turn those cold eyes and sharp blades in his direction.

Which made it all the more important that he find some way to take down Bane without incurring the wrath of all the others. He eased closer to the cot where Dr. Young lay sleeping. No doubt she was exhausted. Any other time, he would have felt bad for her. It couldn't be easy working on dead bodies like that Lonzo fellow, not to mention stitching up all those others. But he didn't pity her, not anymore. Associating with Paladins because it was her job was one thing. Fucking one was another.

He'd thought better of her. In a way, he was glad it had happened, though, because it made it easier for him to use her as bait to lure Bane into a trap.

The bastard was just noble enough to trade his life for hers.

Dr. Young stirred in her sleep, forcing him to retreat until she settled into deeper slumber. She seemed to be smiling, no doubt enjoying a happy dream about rolling around naked with her lover. The images that filled his head made him sick. He'd already decided that she would have to die with Bane because of the very real possibility that she'd recognize him, and she would bring the fury of all the Paladins down on his head. Yes, she had to die.

He savored the heady taste of power, knowing it would be up to him whether she died the same quick death he had planned for Bane, or if he would take his time with her. Maybe he'd make an example of Dr. Young, to show everyone what happened to sluts who chose Paladins over real men.

Yeah, he liked that idea.

He sidled back closer to her cot, wishing he dared touch her skin. Instead, he looked around for a pair of scissors. With a quick snip, he stole a lock of her hair to take with him. He held the small curl up to his nose and breathed deeply. His body's reaction to the feminine scent was immediate and almost painful in its intensity. Oh yeah, if he played his cards right, this could be fun.

He tucked the strand of hair inside a tissue and tucked it in his pocket. Now wasn't the time to get caught prowling; his time would come soon. The man with the money wouldn't be patient much longer.

Outside in the hall, he returned to his post. For

now, he would take advantage of the quiet night to make his plans.

Laurel fumbled for her key in the depths of her purse. The day hadn't gone badly, but she was exhausted. Most of the Paladins had been discharged with instructions to check back with her or Dr. Neal if they needed anything. Lonzo had made solid progress over the past twenty-four hours. She fully expected him to be awake and alert within the next twelve hours.

Along with the reinforcements that Colonel Kincade had ordered in from other sectors, they'd requested another three Handlers. The carnage had been too much for Dr. Neal and herself to handle, so tonight, one of the outside Handlers was watching over her patient. Laurel hated knowing that there was a good chance that Lonzo would awaken with a stranger by his bed, but it couldn't be helped.

She was so tired that she didn't trust her own judgment, and she'd headed home to recuperate. There was nothing wrong with her that about twelve hours of uninterrupted sleep wouldn't cure.

If only her bed wouldn't seem empty without Devlin curled up behind her, spoon style. It had been less than two days ago, but it already seemed like forever.

She turned the key in the lock and pushed the door open. Before she'd gone two steps inside, a man's arm appeared from nowhere to yank her inside. Before she could scream for help, he clamped his hand over her mouth.

"Laurel, it's me."

As soon as she recognized Devlin's voice she slumped back against his chest, convinced her pulse was pounding hard enough to bring on a heart attack. Then she got mad and kicked his leg.

He immediately let go of her. "Ow! Why did you do that?"

As if she could have really hurt a big, tough Paladin like him! She rounded on him and ticked the reasons off on her fingers. "First of all, you just scared ten years off my life. Secondly, I've been worried sick since you escaped from my lab yesterday. Thirdly . . . I'm too tired to fight with you right now."

"We need to talk, Laurel. It's important." He took her coat and tossed it over the back of a handy chair.

"Nothing is that important. I've got plans for the evening, and even you aren't going to spoil them for me." She pushed past him on her way to the kitchen.

He tagged along behind her, so she set out two bowls and pulled out two boxes of cereal. One was whole wheat, filled with fiber and nutrients. That was for him. She filled her own bowl with a brightly colored cereal that was full of sugar.

"Hey, I want that, too." He shoved aside the box she'd set by his bowl.

She shoved it back. "Nope, this one is all mine. If you insist on staying for dinner uninvited, you get what you get."

She'd never seen Devlin sulk before. It was cute,

but not cute enough for her to share. When he tried to sneak a spoonful out of her bowl, she rapped his knuckles with her spoon.

"Back off, big guy. When it comes to these beauties, I don't share." Feeling better than she had all day, she sat down on one of the stools at her kitchen counter and relished every bite.

When they were done, Devlin put their bowls in the dishwasher.

"Now can we talk?"

"No, now I'm going to take a hot shower and go to bed."

She slid off the stool and walked away. Before she reached the bathroom, she looked back over her shoulder to where Devlin still sat as if he had the right to take up residence in her home. Just as he had in her heart. Maybe she should order him to leave, but she couldn't muster up the strength or the desire.

He met her gaze head on. "I know I scared you, but I couldn't wait outside where someone could see me."

She wondered how many times in his life Devlin had felt compelled to apologize. Not many, she'd bet. "You're forgiven." Wearily, she walked away.

Once inside the bathroom, she turned the shower on hot before she peeled off her clothes. The sting of the hot water felt sinfully good to her sore muscles and aching bones. A blast of chilly air gave her goose bumps when the bathroom door swung open. The man was making a habit of opening doors without permission.

She opened the sliding shower door far enough to glare at him. "Now what?"

"I'm staying." He didn't bother to hide the fact that he was getting an eyeful of her naked body through the rippled glass and liking what he saw.

"I'm still too tired to talk." That much was true.

"Then we won't talk."

His voice slid over her skin like silk as he started to pull his sweater off over his head. Then he reached for the fly of his jeans.

A stronger woman would have ordered him out of the bathroom, maybe even out of her life. A weaker woman would have swooned at the sight of all that lovely masculine flesh. But she was a woman who needed this man, so she moved back and gave him room in her shower and in her heart.

He stepped inside the shower and slid the door shut behind him, closing out all the worries and pain that existed out there. For now, it was only the two of them with water-slicked skin and mouths that hungered for deep kisses. She loved the feel of her breasts crushed against his chest as their tongues tangled and danced.

Then she broke off the kiss to savor the taste of his skin, starting with the strong line of his jaw and working her way down and down and down until she was kneeling at his feet. She took him gently in her hands, stroking and tugging until he groaned and threw his head back and braced his hands on the wall behind her.

She tasted him with little flicks of her tongue, taking satisfaction in pleasuring her man. He shuddered as if struggling for control and then hauled her back up for another heart-stopping kiss. He picked up the bar of soap and her washcloth, worked up a lather on the cloth, and then turned her to face away from him.

His touch was gentle fire as his hand traced a circular pattern down to the small of her back and then back up again. Over and over he repeated the caress, each time sliding lower. He spent a long time on the curve of her hips. Then he knelt behind her to pay special attention to the back of her knees and thighs. When he was satisfied with the back of her, he turned her around.

That washcloth took far too long to slide up the inside of her legs. She spread her legs as wide as the tub would allow, and he stopped at her knees. Frustration made her want to howl, but then he reached up to circle her breasts. When her nipples beaded with achy need, she leaned forward, begging wordlessly for him to do something about it.

His tongue traced the same paths around her breasts, first one and then the other before suckling her nipples. The man had wicked, wicked ways with his tongue and teeth. Then he went back to work with the washcloth until she trembled. One slow stroke rode up the inside of her thighs to her nest of curls and the hidden center of her body.

Oh Lord, if he did that again, she was going to shatter into pieces. Then he dropped the washcloth and ran a hand up the back of her legs to cup her bottom, and tugged her closer.

"Hold on to me, Laurel, 'cause I'm not going to stop until you see stars." He slipped one finger deep inside her as he began tasting her heat with his tongue. She clung to his broad shoulders for all she was worth as his fingers and mouth stroked and plunged in unison to shatter what little control she still had left.

When the first pulse rippled through her, she whimpered, not sure she could take any more and remain sane. He slipped a second finger inside her, this time brushing her with his thumb. Once . . . twice . . . and then the world exploded into colors there were no names for. When her legs gave out, he eased her down onto his lap and cradled her gently.

After a bit, he kissed her forehead and tried to rouse her. "Uh, Laurel, the water's getting cold."

She giggled and snuggled her face into his neck. "I don't care."

He'd created a monster. "I know, but I don't want you to catch a chill."

When she made a halfhearted effort to stand, he lifted her off his lap and rose to his feet. As Laurel looked up, the evidence of how much he still wanted her stared her right in the face.

"Let's take this discussion to your bed," he suggested. "It'll be a lot warmer and more comfortable there."

He held her hand to steady her as she climbed out of the tub. She tossed him a towel and they both dried off, stopping periodically to kiss. Then she led him to her bed, right where he most wanted to be.

They slid between the covers to meet in the middle.

Her hand strayed down below his waist, but he captured it and brought it back up and held it over his heart. "That can wait a bit."

She frowned at him. "You're not back to wanting to talk, are you?"

Stubborn woman. "Not as long as you promise to listen to what I have to say in the morning."

She nodded. Now that he had her promise, he let go of her hand. It took a second or two before she realized that she was free to do as she pleased. She thought she was being sneaky as she eased her hand down a little bit at a time, but if she didn't hurry up, he might just lose his mind. When her hand finally found its target, he lifted his hips in approval.

"Kiss me, Laurel." He threaded his fingers through her dark hair, loving the silky feel of it.

"Gladly."

She climbed up on his chest, settling her body over his, open and welcoming. He thrust against her, liking the sensation, but not daring to do more until he put on some protection. Their lives were complicated enough without risking pregnancy.

"Hold that thought, honey."

When he threw back the covers to get up, she stopped him. "There's a box in the drawer."

He sat up and reached for the box and realized it had never been opened. That pleased him, even though he knew he had no right to feel that way. More than anything he wanted to stake his claim on this woman, but that could only lead to disaster in the long run. They might have tonight and maybe a few others just like it, but that was all.

"Don't think about it, Devlin." She pressed her sweet breasts against his back and slid her arms around him. "Don't let what might happen ruin this for us."

He closed his eyes and let the comfort of her touch soothe him. She was right. They may not have a future, but they had tonight. He sheathed himself and then rolled back onto the bed, taking her with him. Once again, she welcomed him with her smile and body.

And it was enough.

This time she was right there next to him when morning came. In all the long years of his life, he couldn't remember a single moment that had felt this good. If only the world would stay outside—but at best, he could only hold it at bay another hour.

"It's too early to be thinking that hard." Laurel pushed up to brace her head on one hand while the other moved in small circles on his chest. "I know I promised to listen this morning—and I will—but at least wait until after my first cup of coffee."

He kissed her fingertips. "Actually, I was trying to decide if I needed another shower."

Her eyes, the color of extra-dark chocolate, drifted half closed. Her lips parted in a smile that was pure temptation. "I never shower until after my morning workout." And that wicked, wandering hand drifted down and down and down.

Damn, he knew they shouldn't. But when it came to Laurel Young, it seemed that he was a pushover.

In a well-planned maneuver, he trapped her beneath him. Judging from her smile, it was right where she wanted to be. He nuzzled her neck, drawing in her scent.

She giggled. "Don't! That tickles." Her own fingers dug lightly into his ribs, trying to give as good as she got.

He'd never had a lover who was playful, and he liked it. It felt good to laugh in the morning, especially with a beautiful woman underneath him. Her smile was enough to melt his heart.

Then the shrill ring of a cellphone from the other room shattered his concentration. He rested his forehead against hers. "Is that mine or yours?"

"Mine, I think. It's in the side pocket of my purse."

He rolled off her and padded naked into the living room, pulling the irritating electronic device from her purse. On his way back to the bedroom, a second chirp joined the chorus. So much for their morning plans. One call might not signify anything; two could only mean bad news.

Laurel stood wearing a short robe when he walked back into the room. He tossed her the phone and then stepped back out in the hall to answer his. It wouldn't do for anyone to hear her talking in the background.

"Bane here."

"Good morning, Devlin. Hope you've had your first cup of coffee." D.J. sounded irritatingly chipper.

"Why?"

"Colonel Kincade has called a ten o'clock meeting. Thought you'd appreciate a heads-up. He didn't say what it was about, but we're assuming it's about coverage, with so many of us down right now."

There was no use in taking his sudden bad mood out on D.J. "Thanks. I'll be there. Call everybody you can. A show of strength never hurts."

"Will do." The phone went dead.

He had almost two hours to get to the Center. Maybe they still had time for that shower. And then they'd talk.

Hours later, he was in a foul mood and didn't give a damn who knew it. While they all stood around waiting for the meeting, no one had been either brave enough or foolish enough to ask what had him pacing the small confines of his office. He almost wished someone would; a down-and-dirty brawl would be just the ticket to blow off the temper that simmered right below his skin.

The talk he had with Laurel had not gone as planned. Why that should surprise him, he didn't know. Nothing about her was predictable. Those innocent-looking eyes and sweet smile were a disguised stubborn streak a mile wide. She definitely had a mind of her own, something he would normally admire in a person, but it was damn inconvenient at times.

What he couldn't figure out was where he'd gone wrong. Yesterday, when he had planned his strategy, his arguments about why they shouldn't see each other anymore made perfect sense. From the start, they had both known there was no future for them. He was more than three times her age, even if no one could tell by looking at him. He wasn't really human any longer and would become less so as time went on. Then there was the little matter of someone wanting to kill him. If his unknown assailant grew more desperate, anyone near Devlin could be caught in the fallout. He hadn't shared that particular point, instead reminding her that his calling was a dangerous one and that his luck could run out any day.

He'd even told her that she deserved better than a man who lived to kill, although the very thought of someone else sharing her life or her bed made him want to punch something.

She'd calmly responded with a few points of her own. Seeing him outside of work was a clear violation of a normal patient-doctor relationship. Any emotional attachment she might develop for him could very easily cloud her professional judgment. Besides, if any of the Regents who ruled over both Ordnance and Research found out that she was seeing Devlin, her job would be in serious jeopardy. Certainly, they would make sure that she never saw him again.

And although she didn't say the words, the look in her dark eyes made it clear that she was worried about the possibility that she would eventually have to kill him herself.

Yes, it had been all so logical. They were both adults who had given in to the temptation of playing with fire—but the woman knew a little about strategy and tactics herself. Before he could do the noble thing and walk out her door, she'd untied the sash of her short robe and let it slide to the floor. He'd taken her right there on the floor with little gentleness or finesse, but lots of desperate need. It had left them both shattered and still poised on the edge of disaster. There had been no good-byes, no resolution.

And selfish bastard that he was, he had no regrets.

chapter 9

Devlin waited until the last possible minute to enter the meeting room. Maybe it was petty of him, but he didn't like being at Kincade's beck and call. He also had asked Trahern, Cullen, and D.J. to walk in with him. The Paladins all towered over Kincade and Devlin figured he hated that. When the four of them walked in and stood side by side, it was bound to irritate the man from Ordnance.

That pleased Devlin to no end.

Just as he expected, Kincade stood in the front of the room. He glanced up at them and frowned before turning his attention back to his watch. Devlin gave his friends a slight nod, signaling that their little display of power was done. The others found seats and waited for Kincade to start. Devlin, however, leaned against the wall near the door, as if he might walk back out any second.

Kincade worked hard to ignore him, dividing his time

between staring at the door on the other side of the room and his watch. A look of pure disgust crossed his face as he turned his attention back to his unwilling audience and took his position behind the podium. He stared at them, waiting for the room to fall silent. Most of the local Paladins and a good number of the reinforcements ignored him until Devlin cleared his throat. One by one, the men fell silent, acknowledging Devlin with their eyes before Colonel Kincade. Judging from the expression on his face, the united gesture had sent the colonel's blood pressure soaring.

"I've called you here this morning—"

Before he could finish his little speech, the door he'd been watching finally opened. Devlin had to laugh. The little bastard had worked so hard to get their attention, and just that easily, it was gone. His good humor was short-lived when every Handler in the area came filing in with Dr. Neal and Laurel in front. Right then, the only person in the room who looked happy was Colonel Kincade. Devlin straightened up and tried to catch Laurel's eye.

No dice. In fact, she positioned herself so that she stood facing the other side of the room. Son of a bitch, what was going on? From the smirk Kincade shot him from across the room, he wasn't going to like it one bit.

Kincade tapped the microphone to signal that it was time to get down to business. "The command here at Ordnance has expressed some concern over the current mental state of the Paladins under our command."

"What the hell is that supposed to mean?" The question came from one of the imported Paladins seated near the back.

"It means that each and every one of you will have a condition scan performed within the next forty-eight hours." The bastard was clearly enjoying himself.

"Like hell!" Trahern rose to his feet and stood with his arms crossed over his chest. Several of the others followed suit.

The whole situation was about to get out of hand. There wasn't a man among them who would willingly submit to a brain scan on a whim. "Is this because of Dr. Young's patient turning Other with no warning?" Devlin asked.

Kincade ignored him, and Dr. Neal had the good sense to realize that Colonel Kincade was handling the situation badly. He stepped forward, drawing all the attention to himself. Most of the locals knew him to be a fair and caring man; he'd brought most of them back from the edge at least once.

"Mr. Bane has asked a legitimate question, one that deserves a fair answer." His calm voice carried easily to the back of the room. "Yes, there is some concern because of the incident the other day."

"That's a nice, sanitized way of looking at it, Doc. Why not call it what it is? Dr. Young made the decision to execute one of us," Blake said.

Laurel flinched. Damn it, she didn't have anything to apologize for, Devlin thought. If she hadn't put the poor bastard down, someone else would have. It was the way things were. They all knew it.

"He wasn't one of you any longer, Mr. Trahern. He'd turned Other, almost without warning. We've received his medical records. For some reason, he hadn't had a scan in almost a year." There was no mistaking the genuine regret in Dr. Neal's eyes. "All of us in Research feel that we need baseline scans on everyone to prevent such a tragedy, if we can."

Devlin wished he could see Laurel's expression. This couldn't be easy for her. "Scans won't cure the problem, Dr. Neal. At best they might give you a bit of a warning, but that's all."

"That's true, Mr. Bane, but we'd like to find out more about why some of you progress so much faster than others. The last scan on the deceased was normal." He consulted his clipboard. "In fact, it was on the low side of normal. There was no reason to think that he was so close to the edge."

"What happens if we refuse?"

Naturally Trahern would ask that question. The tension level in the room jumped to a new high. If someone didn't step in and take control, the situation would get ugly damn fast. They couldn't afford to resort to lash out in violence. Ordnance would bring in the Guard in enough numbers to take them down. Knowing the colonel, he probably had them on standby out in the hallway. Then Kincade would ensure that those tests were run, and anyone on the edge—like Trahern—would no longer get the benefit of the doubt when they revived angry and out of control.

"I'll take the scan." Devlin walked to the front. "All of us will."

Dr. Neal nodded his approval. "I've got a schedule printed out here. I would appreciate it if you'd each pick a time slot before you leave the room." That they wouldn't be allowed to leave until they did went unspoken.

Cullen and D.J. more or less dragged Trahern with them to sign up right after Devlin. Maybe if the four of them went together, it would reduce the stress the test always caused.

Devlin made his way to Dr. Neal, who gave him a welcoming smile. "Thank you for your assistance, Mr. Bane. I have a feeling if we'd left it up to Colonel Kincade, things might have gotten a bit dicey."

Devlin didn't want the man's thanks; he wanted his scan over and done with. "I'm first on the list, Doctor. Can we get it over with now?"

"Certainly. I'm sure Dr. Young will be able to take you right away. We calibrated the machines before coming down to Colonel Kincade's little gathering. That's why we were late."

"I'd rather *you* did the test, Dr. Neal."

He crossed his fingers and hoped the man wouldn't ask why, since Laurel was his official Handler. A movement across the room caught his eye. She was walking out of the room with Trahern, D.J., and Cullen trailing in her wake. His first reaction was jealous anger, but he reeled it back in. As edgy as he was feeling, he didn't need to be closed up in that dark little room with Laurel.

God knows how it would affect his readings, and with Colonel Kincade on a crusade to weed out anyone skating on the edge, he couldn't afford to take any unnecessary risks. Besides, if his unknown assailant *was* one of the Guard, it was best that he spent as little time as possible in Laurel's company, especially in public.

He drew Dr. Neal's attention to the situation. "Seems Trahern has decided to cooperate. I wouldn't want to crowd him right now."

"Very well, Mr. Bane. I think you have the right of it. Let's go to my lab."

"This can't be right." Dr. Neal's voice carried more than a trace of frustration as he twisted a few dials and pushed a couple of buttons on the console. "I'm sorry this is taking so long, Devlin, but I'm going to have to repeat that last series."

"What's wrong?" Were his scores that much worse than before?

"Apparently nothing is wrong, at least not with you. We just recalibrated all the machines, but this one seems to be a bit off, even though the control test scores are right on the button."

"Then what's the problem?"

"Your scores don't correlate very well with the scans that Dr. Young ran the other day."

"So maybe her machine is off."

"No, we made sure that both machines get the same readings on the control samples." He paused to study the printout and then flipped through Devlin's chart and frowning. "I'll be damned."

He pushed another button, causing the machine to spew forth another couple feet of paper. "You're finished for now, Mr. Bane, but I may need to have you back again. We'll get those electrodes off, and then I'll show you what has me puzzled."

Back out in the lab, Devlin leaned over the doctor's shoulder to study the last three scans he'd done. Once Dr. Neal had them lined up side by side, the pattern became clearer. Normally a Paladin's scans showed a steady increase in the brainwaves that rendered them less and less human. In Devlin's case, the pattern was reversed. The change from the oldest scan to the one Laurel had run was slight, but definitely toward the better.

But the change in the newest one was dramatic, to the point of being unbelievable. Such a thing was unheard of in the long history of Paladins. Although the ability to track the changes with scans was a relatively recent development, the Regents had kept records of Paladin symptoms and behavior patterns for centuries. They all got worse—no exceptions, no reprieves.

"I don't know what to make of this, Mr. Bane. I'll have to discuss it with Dr. Young to learn her thoughts on the subject. If necessary, I'll contact my colleagues in other parts of the world to see if they can shed any light." He turned to face Devlin. "Have you noticed any changes in how you feel? Are you doing anything differently than you used to?"

"No, my life is pretty much as it has always been." Besides sleeping with his Handler and harboring some pretty strong feelings for her.

"Well, if you think of anything, let me know. Maybe after I scan a few more of the others, I'll be able to figure out if it's the machine or if it's really you." He gathered up all Devlin's readings and shoved them back in his chart. "Would you send in the next man on your way out?"

"Sure thing."

Cullen was waiting in the hall. If he was surprised to see Devlin coming out of Dr. Neal's lab instead of Laurel's, he didn't say so. "I assume it went well since you're still walking around."

"Yeah, so far. Dr. Neal said to send you on in." He glanced toward Laurel's door. "Any word on Trahern yet?"

"No, but at least he wasn't fighting her on it. When she said she'd take him first, he went along meek as a lamb. I swear, that woman must have some serious mojo if she can charm a hard-ass like Trahern."

She had some serious mojo, all right. "I think I'll wait around for a while."

"Good idea." Cullen drew himself up to his full height. "Wish me luck, Devlin. I'd hate to give that bastard Kincade the satisfaction of finding one of us too close to the edge for comfort."

"Don't sweat it. If I can pass the test, you can for sure." He slapped his friend on the shoulder. "Stop by my place when you're done. I've got a couple of cold ones with your name on them."

"Will do."

After Cullen disappeared into Dr. Neal's lab, Devlin sat on a nearby bench. A couple of guards shifted their positions, probably to keep a wary eye on him. As long as he made no sudden moves, they'd leave him alone.

Hell, they should be smart enough to figure out that he was still fine. If there'd been any doubt about his stability, Dr. Neal would have pulled the plug on him back in the lab. He closed his eyes and stretched his legs out in front of him and tried to get comfortable.

What if those readings turned out to be right and he was becoming more human again? How could that even be possible? The only change in his life was his new relationship with Laurel. What would she think when Dr. Neal showed her the results? He let his eyes drift closed and settled back to wait for his friends.

"Blake, I don't mean to complain, but you're crushing my wrist." She managed to get the words out between clenched teeth.

He loosened his grip a little, enough so that her circulation could be restored. Normally she was careful to keep her professional distance from her patients, especially one as prone to angry outbursts as Trahern. But ever since he'd checked on Devlin for her, she had found him less intimidating. Experience might prove her wrong, but she was determined to give him the benefit of the doubt.

She'd thought Devlin dreaded the brain scan, but his worries were nothing compared to Trahern's. He had to know that he was one that Colonel Kincade was targeting for close scrutiny. She wished she could have told the man from Ordnance that he was wrong, that Trahern was stable and doing fine. The tests were never meant to be a weapon for Ordnance to hold over the heads of the Paladins, but that was how Kincade was using them.

The other day, when she'd run the scan on Devlin, his scores had improved. She had no proof that holding his hand helped, but she'd been unable to account for the anomaly any other way. If it worked for him, maybe it would for Trahern. She wished she could have seen the expression on his face when the lights went down and she'd all but ordered him to hold on to her wrist for the duration of the scan.

"Talk to me, Mr. Trahern." If she could keep him focused on something other than the needles scribbling endless wavy lines on the paper, maybe he would relax a bit.

The silence dragged on for several long seconds. Finally, he stirred slightly and said, "What about?"

Must she think of everything? "I don't know. The weather, books you've read, even your childhood."

"I thought you people in Research had us all cataloged down to the number of freckles on our asses." There was no humor in his voice at all.

She tried again. "All right, where did you grow up?"

"On the streets."

If she hadn't been looking right at him, she would have missed the quick twitch of his lips that indicated he was jerking her chain and enjoying it. That was okay with her. As long as Blake concentrated on thwarting her, he wasn't thinking so hard about the scan.

"On the streets where?" She shook her forefinger at him. "I promise not to go screaming down the hall shouting your deep, dark secrets to anyone who'll listen."

"St. Louis." He paused again. "I grew up in St. Louis, Missouri. I was transferred out here when I turned eighteen."

That was about the longest speech she'd ever heard him make. Certainly the most personal. "Do you have any family left back there?"

"No."

How could the man make one word sound just like a door slamming in her face? Maybe it was time she did the talking. "I'm from the Midwest, too. My whole family still lives in one town."

"Why aren't you there?"

"Because I'm here." Two could play the game of cryptic answers.

"Do your parents know what you do for a living?" Trahern let go of her arm, seeming more relaxed.

"They know I'm a doctor and that I do research." She leaned back in her chair. "My parents love me, but they'll never understand how I can be happy living so far away. If they had their way, I would be married with a herd of children by now. Sometimes I think they want grandchildren more than they want me to be happy."

Shock had her sitting upright again. She'd never admitted that before, even to herself, and here she was confessing all to Blake Trahern. "Forget I said that."

The machine beeped to signal that the test was done. "Let me take a quick look at the printout before we disconnect you."

Just that quickly the silence was heavy with tension as Blake waited to hear the verdict. She tried to hurry, but not so fast that she'd miss something important. As far as she could see, his readings were holding steady—an improvement over his usual pattern.

She smiled down at her patient and started gently removing the electrodes. "Well, Mr. Trahern, I'll take readings like these from you anytime. Most are exactly what they were on your last scan; a couple have even dropped slightly."

He swung his legs down off the bed. "Thanks, Doc."

"You are most welcome. I'll forward the results to Colonel Kincade when we finish running all the scans."

He started out the door. Just before he stepped across the threshold, he turned back. "You know, sometimes those who are closest to us have the hardest time seeing who we really are."

Then he was gone, leaving her wondering who

had looked at Blake Trahern and not seen the real
him.

Devlin opened the door and stood back as half a
dozen Paladins filed into his living room. Most had
been there before and made themselves comfortable
on his oversize leather sofa and chairs. He'd had the
devil's own time getting the furniture through the
door when he bought it, but it had been worth the effort. Like most of the Paladins, he was several inches
over six feet.

"Beer's in the fridge, and the pizzas should be
here in a few minutes."

He was about to close the door when Trahern appeared on his porch. Devlin hadn't been expecting him,
since he rarely chose to hang out with any of them.

"Blake, come on in."

"I can't stay." He looked past Devlin toward the
others. "I wanted to tell you something. Can you
come outside for a minute?"

"Sure. Just let me tell the others where I'll be." He
walked into the living room. "I'm going to watch for the
pizza. Try not to drink all the beer before I get back."

Cullen came out of the kitchen carrying a tray full
of cans and a bowl of chips. "I wouldn't stay gone too
long if I were you."

"Save me one, at least."

He followed Trahern a short distance down the
street, out of hearing and sight of the others.

"What's up?"

"I passed my scan. Thought you might want to know."

"That's real good news, Blake. I bet that'll piss off Kincade."

"I hope so." Trahern smiled but kept his eyes focused over Devlin's shoulder.

"You didn't come all the way here just to tell me that." He could have phoned that in.

"I wanted to tell you that I've been watching Dr. Young's condo like you wanted. I don't know if it means anything, but I found a pile of cigarette butts behind a Dumpster near her building. If I were going to stake the place out myself, it's right where I'd stand."

"Damn it all to hell. Does it look like the bastard has been back?"

"Difficult to tell. I counted the butts, though. I'll know if he's added to the collection."

"Thanks again, Blake." Devlin meant it. He'd rather take charge of the situation himself, but he wouldn't risk leading his unknown shadow right back to Laurel's doorstep.

"Like I said, I'm not doing it for you."

Then Trahern was gone. No explanation offered and none asked. He watched his friend disappear down the street just as the pizza deliveryman pulled into the driveway. Devlin took the stack of boxes and went back inside to join the others.

The lights in his office were a shade too bright for comfort. Maybe he should have resisted drinking those last two beers last night, but the impromptu gathering had evolved into a major celebration. Not one of the Paladins had run into problems with the mandatory scans. He didn't know exactly what Colonel Kincade had been trying to accomplish, but he'd failed on every count.

Blowing off some tension was worth a headache any day.

D.J. knocked on the doorframe and then entered. He tossed a file down on Devlin's desk, then snagged a nearby chair and flopped down in it. He closed his eyes and leaned back.

"Good party last night."

"How's your head?" Devlin rarely took pain medicine, but he pulled some aspirin out of his drawer and took two with a sip of coffee before tossing the bottle into D.J.'s lap. "Heads up."

D.J. opened his eyes long enough to catch the bottle. After swallowing a couple of the pills dry, he set the bottle back on Devlin's desk. "You'll find that report pretty damn interesting."

"What is it?" Until the aspirin kicked in, he wasn't in any hurry to read much of anything.

"It's the results of the tests that my friends at Research ran on those bags we found in the tunnel the other day." He opened one eye. "They don't know what to make of it. If I'm understanding it right, the dust in those bags shouldn't be there."

Devlin was confused. "What's that supposed to mean? How would they know what those gray bastards carry in their little bags?"

"They said they didn't have enough of the stuff to run every test they wanted to. However, what they *did* get had all those science geeks sitting up and taking notice. If their results are to be believed, the dust comes from a crystal unknown in our world."

"So?"

"Well, blue garnets might not exist in our world, but if they did, everyone and their brother would be fighting to control the market on them."

Devlin's headache was getting worse. "What would they be good for?"

"They weren't completely sure. They want us to bring them a bigger sample. I suggested if they wanted to import stuff from across the barrier, they should set up business down in the tunnels. You know, one free pass above ground for a bag of pretty blue rocks."

The niggling feeling was back, that he'd missed something important. Devlin decided D.J. had the right idea and leaned back and propped his feet up on his desk. Maybe if he closed his eyes and let his mind wander, it would finally come to him.

The two of them sat in companionable silence for several minutes while they waited for the aspirin to kick in. Slowly, the steady pounding diminished.

The blue crystals had something to do with the Others. They had to be valuable, because a handful of Guardsmen hadn't been killed for no good reason. The bags had been slit open and the contents taken. Why take the time, when each passing minute might have meant discovery? Because the bags carried the stench of the Others' world? The stones did, as well, but they had value. And the stones would be easier to hide without the bulk of the bags.

So someone knew about the stones and had made some arrangements to get them. But how? The Others wouldn't be giving the stuff away for nothing, either.

That's when it hit him. He thought back to his first trip into the tunnels after he revived, when he'd fought and killed the two males. One of them had claimed to have already paid. They must have thought they were paying their way across with the blue stones. Son of a bitch—who had the clout to set up a deal like that?

It had to be either Research or Ordnance. The Paladins wouldn't betray their own kind that way. They'd spent too many years and too many lives holding the line against the ongoing invasion.

This was too big to keep to himself, and it was obvious that he couldn't handle it through normal channels. Until he and the others could figure out who could be trusted, they'd have to do this on their own.

First things first. He dropped his feet back to the floor with a thud, startling D.J. back to consciousness. "D.J., tell Cullen and the others to meet me here this afternoon. Keep it casual. I don't want to raise any red flags if we can avoid it."

D.J. leaned closer. "You've figured it out, haven't you?"

"I've got some ideas, but I want to keep this quiet as long as possible."

"Okay, I'll let them know."

Judging by the energetic bounce to D.J.'s walk, either the aspirin had cured his headache or the challenge of a problem to be solved had given him a new surge of energy. Devlin felt a twinge of envy. Hell, he didn't need all of this to break loose now. He had enough on his plate watching his back and trying to keep Laurel safe.

He had no proof, but he'd bet his favorite sword that it was all connected somehow. Whoever wanted the stones also wanted him dead. The chain of events was too close together for it to be otherwise.

He glanced at the clock. If he hurried, he would be able to check on Laurel and still have time to study Research's report on the blue stones. Considering how she'd stared right through him at the meeting on the previous day, he wasn't at all sure about his welcome. But he wouldn't be able to concentrate on anything until he knew she'd made it to work safely. A phone call would be more efficient, but seeing her in person would be far more satisfying.

His headache all but forgotten, he headed out, figuring he could come up with a plausible excuse along the way.

"So you're telling me that they've finally figured out a way to beat the test." Colonel Kincade glared across the table at Laurel, as if it were her fault that all of the Paladins had passed their scans with flying colors. Even Trahern.

"No, that's not what I said." She was tired of his belligerent attitude and obnoxious personality. "What we said," nodding in Dr. Neal's direction for emphasis that she was not alone in this, "is that the scans revealed a great deal of stability across the board. Some had progressed toward the higher-end readings, but none had crossed the line."

Dr. Neal shuffled through a stack of papers until he found the ones he wanted. "We also recalibrated the machines, both before the tests and in between patients, as well. The control readings were right on the mark. I've made you a copy of our report."

He shoved a hefty stack of papers across the table toward the colonel, who predictably ignored it. Dr. Neal smiled but said nothing.

That left it up to her to throw down the gauntlet. "I must say that I find your reaction to our findings to be a bit odd, Colonel. I would think that you'd be relieved to know that your fighting force is ready and able to face the continuing threat of invasion. Instead, you seem a bit disappointed."

Maybe she shouldn't provoke the man, but the whole mess had her teeth on edge. That, and not knowing where Devlin was or what he was thinking. Everything felt disjointed. Yesterday she woke up happily snuggled next to her new lover, only to have him ruin the mood. She should have known that he would equate talking with lecturing and giving orders. Well, she'd shown him when she—

"Dr. Young, what do you think?"

Dr. Neal's quiet voice yanked her back into the

conference, away from the memories of what she and Devlin had done on her living room floor. Fortunately, he repeated the rest of the conversation.

"Colonel Kincade thinks, and I tentatively agree, that we should set up a regular schedule of scans for all of the Paladins. In the past, we've only done them when there was cause for concern." He gave Laurel a sidelong look. "For example, the scan you ran on Mr. Bane when it took so long for him to come back from his last death."

She stared at her hands, examining the idea from several different angles. Her personal dislike for the man from Ordnance was not a legitimate reason to reject his suggestion.

"On the surface, I'd have to agree that the idea may have some merit. It would all depend on what we would be using the data for. These men already feel threatened by the test, which we can all certainly understand." Well, at least she could. "If we are using the scans as a means to better understand the developmental process a Paladin goes through over time, fine."

She fixed her gaze on the colonel. "But if you're going to hold the tests over their heads as a threat, I will not be a party to such a misuse of a patient's medical care."

Kincade's eyebrows snapped together and his face turned an interesting shade of red. But before he could explode, a guard knocked and then stuck his head into the room.

"I'm sorry to interrupt, Dr. Young, but you have a phone call. She said it was important."

The opportunity to escape could not have been better timed. "Gentlemen, if you'll excuse me." She followed the guard down the hall to the front desk.

He resumed his position against the wall, giving her the illusion of privacy. Who would be calling her at work? Her mother would be more likely to call Laurel's cellphone. But maybe not if it was an emergency. Her pulse quickened as she reached for the phone.

"This is Dr. Young."

"Meet me for lunch in ten minutes. Same place as before." The phone went dead as soon as Devlin finished talking.

She gritted her teeth. These men and their dictatorial attitudes. Couldn't he have at least waited for her answer? Instead, she was left standing there having to pretend to carry on a conversation with an imaginary caller, a woman at that. Who had he coerced into calling for him, to keep the guard from recognizing his voice?

"Yes, thank you for the heads-up call. I'll take care of it." She set the phone back in its cradle as she smiled her thanks to the guard. "I'll be leaving the building for a couple of hours. Thanks for coming to get me."

"You're welcome, Doctor."

She returned to her lab to hang up her lab coat and get her purse. Each step of the way, she debated whether she would follow Devlin's rather abrupt orders. If he needed her, all he had to do was ask. No doubt he wanted to keep the conversation short to ensure that no one guessed that she was talking to him and not some anonymous woman, but that didn't excuse his rudeness.

So she'd meet him for lunch, but he was going to get an earful about simple good manners.

She signed out, leaving her expected return time blank since she had no idea how long she'd be with Devlin. If anyone else needed her, they could call her cell. She slipped out the back to lessen the chance of anyone taking note of where she was headed.

The sun was shining brightly, bathing the city with warmth. It felt good to be breathing fresh air and enjoying the sunshine. Too bad Devlin had given her such short notice. Otherwise, she would have taken a more indirect route to the restaurant just for the sheer pleasure of it.

She would like to think that he'd wanted her to join him for lunch because he missed her. No doubt he had questions about the scans or some other Paladin business he wanted to discuss with her away from the prying eyes and ears of Ordnance and the others in Research. She'd help him if she could, but not if it meant compromising her integrity as a doctor.

Before opening the door to the restaurant, she paused to take a casual look up and down the street. The coast appeared to be clear. When a man opened the door of the restaurant on his way out, she slipped inside.

It took a second or two to adjust to the dim light, but she spotted Devlin almost immediately at the same table they'd shared before. From another man, she might have thought he picked it out for senti-mental reasons. But Devlin had no doubt chosen it because it was tucked in an out-of-the-way corner, yet gave him a clear view of the door.

Her heart jumped when his eyes met hers, mak-ing her wish they were someplace a whole lot more private. She wound through the clutter of tables and chairs to where her lover waited. The thought thrilled her, and she stood beside the table until he got up and let her slide in next to him.

He laid his arm along the back of the booth, pulling her close to the heat of his body. Her lecture on manners scattered to the winds when she realized he was about to kiss her, and she met him halfway. His tongue slid into her mouth almost instantly as his hand anchored the back of her head at just the right angle for him to kiss her.

She grabbed on to the front of his flannel shirt and held on for dear life as his tongue slid in and out of her mouth, making her want to pull him on top of her and finish what they'd started. Unfortunately, someone next to their table cleared his throat, re-minding them both that this was hardly the place for this.

Her face flamed bright red as Devlin pulled away, his green eyes sparkling with heat aimed directly at her. It was all she could do not to slink down under the table in embarrassment, but Devlin kept her an-chored at his side as he turned to deal with their waiter.

"We'll have two dark ales and two small pizzas:

one veggie with artichokes and one with the works." He gave Laurel a sly grin. "And you'd better hold the onions."

The waiter laughed as he quickly headed toward the kitchen. Considering how close she came to tossing her glass of water at him or Devlin, it was a wise move on his part.

chapter 10

$\mathcal{H}$e knew he shouldn't have kissed her like that, but it would have taken a far stronger man than he was to resist. She tasted sweet, with a hint of hot temper thrown in for spice. He liked it. It didn't take a genius, though, to figure out that the good doctor wasn't particularly happy with him right now. She definitely hadn't appreciated his abrupt phone call. But if she wanted flowery words and fancy manners, she'd picked the wrong man for a lover.

He gave her hair a playful tug. "So how pissed are you?"

Her eyes narrowed. The dark circles under them reminded him that the past few days hadn't been easy for her, either. Maybe he was a selfish bastard, but he couldn't regret anything that had happened between them.

"Next time, *ask* me if you want something; you'll find I don't respond well to orders. Try this again, and you'll sit here until hell freezes over waiting for me to show up."

She scooted over to the far side of the booth to put some distance between them. Devlin laughed as he hauled her right back to his side and kissed her again. Slowly, her resistance melted. She leaned against him, content for the moment to let him hold her.

"Now that we have that out of the way, why did you order me down here on such short notice?"

"Do I need a reason?"

"Yes, you do, especially when you called me away from a meeting with my boss and your Colonel Kincade."

That caught his attention. "What did that bastard Kincade want? He can't be happy that we all passed your damn tests." If he sounded bitter, too bad.

"They aren't 'my' tests, Devlin. And besides, how did you know that everyone passed?" The temper was back in her eyes.

"Don't worry, Doc. We didn't hack into your medical files." Although now that he thought about it, it wasn't a bad idea. D.J. could do it without leaving any trail. "Most of the locals and a few of the imports showed up at my place yesterday for pizza and beer. It won't come as a surprise that the subject of mandatory scans was a topic of interest to all of us."

"Hmmm. Sounds like you guys had way more fun than I had. I was at the lab until the wee hours, scoring the scans and dictating reports." She eased her head back against his arm and closed her eyes. "I am so looking forward to going home tonight."

He wished like hell that he was going to be there waiting for her, but that wouldn't be wise. Even now he didn't have much time before he needed to be back at the Center to talk to the others. If that waiter didn't hurry up with their order, they'd have to have it boxed up to go. He caught the man's eye, and the waiter signaled that their food was on the way.

"So about Colonel Kincade . . ."

Laurel sighed. "He wants mandatory scans on a predetermined schedule. No decision had been made when I left."

Damn, he'd been afraid of something like that. "Do you think he'll get his way?"

"I don't know. Testing has always been up to Research, not Ordnance, but the man is being pretty insistent. After what happened the other day, the Regents may give in to him. I know you all hate the scans and the tests, but if we can determine what it is about your physiology that brings you back from such horrific wounds, maybe we can learn to control the bad effects it has on Paladins long term."

"We've done fine for centuries without it."

She had the nerve to laugh. "Who would have thought that a big, tough guy like you would be such a stick in the mud? Just because something has always been done one way, it doesn't mean that's the only way or even the best way. What if we found out a way to improve the readings on your scans, somehow slowing down the process? Wouldn't that be worth suffering through a few extra tests?"

Maybe. But what if their scores improved, but

they still turned Other with no warning? And hadn't Dr. Neal said that Devlin's own scan readings were lower than before?

"Did Dr. Neal mention anything about my scan results?"

"No, we barely had time to calculate the results on the ones we each ran, without exchanging reports. I was going to look over all the reports this afternoon. What did he say to you?"

"He mentioned a couple of the readings stuck out, that they'd dropped lower from the scan you did the other day."

Before she could respond, the waiter appeared with a large tray balanced on his shoulder. He set their food on the table and for a few minutes, they concentrated on their meal.

Devlin practically inhaled all his pizza, as well as a piece of Laurel's. He wished that they had time to wander back down to the waterfront again, afterward, but they both had pressing business to see to.

"Thanks for coming."

"You still haven't told me why you called." She wiped her mouth with her napkin and set it down.

"I wanted to make sure you were all right." He'd arranged to have Trahern follow her to the restaurant and back to see if anyone showed too much interest in her activities. He knew he could depend on Trahern to protect her, but it would be a long wait until he got a call saying she'd arrived back at the lab safe and sound.

"Is there a reason to think I wouldn't be?"

How much should he tell her? Enough to make her careful, without sending her screaming back to headquarters to raise the alarm. His Handler was no weakling, but she wanted to see only the best in people. The fact that she thought Paladins were redeemable showed how innocent she really was.

He did a quick check of the patrons in the restaurant to make sure there were no familiar faces. "There's been a lot going on recently that doesn't add up. We're trying to get a handle on the situation, but we've got way more questions than answers at this point."

"Questions about what? I've already explained about the scans."

"No, not about your end of things. There's been some weird shit going on at our end. It's probably nothing, but it has us being extra cautious."

Like not trusting any of the guards or Kincade or even Research. Until they knew who was dealing with the Others, everyone was suspect, except for the Paladins and the woman sitting next to him.

"You're not telling me everything." It wasn't a question.

He shrugged. His woman had a tendency to tilt at windmills. If she thought for one minute that someone within the organization was corrupt, she wouldn't rest until she raised the alarm. Once that happened, he might as well paint a target on her back. "No, I'm not."

She stared into his eyes, trying to ferret out his secrets. "Promise me you'll tell me when you can."

When he nodded, she surprised him by reaching

up for a kiss. The spice of temper had been replaced by oregano and dark ale, but the passion was still the same. Hot and sweet and addicting. She was playing with fire, and they both knew it. Finally, one of them showed the good sense to break it off. He was pretty sure that it hadn't been him.

"I've got to get back to the lab." Her lips were swollen and too damn inviting.

"We should leave separately." Although she wouldn't be alone, but he didn't tell her that.

"Will I see you later?" There was a shadow to her dark eyes, because she already knew the answer.

"No."

She pasted on a bright smile. "Well, then, this has been pleasant, Mr. Bane. Thank you for lunch."

He slid out of the booth to let her out, wishing like hell that he didn't have to. She had obligations, and so did he for that matter. But given half a chance, he'd chuck it all for another night spent in her bed.

Laurel must have sensed something about the direction of his thoughts, because she gave him one of those mysterious womanly smiles—the kind that could bring a man to his knees. He took a half step back before he realized what he was doing, and her smile turned into a big grin.

"Chicken." Then the little minx patted him on the cheek and sailed past him toward the door.

As if that weren't enough, she put a little extra sway in her walk. He tried to convince himself that in fairness to Laurel, he should chalk up their relationship to hot sex and a few laughs and let it go. But when she gave him one more sweet look from the door, he knew that wasn't going to happen.

Cursing under his breath, he yanked his cell-phone out of his pocket and hit a number on his speed dial. "She's out the door. Keep me posted."

Devlin had called for the Paladins he knew the best and trusted. Years of fighting together against a common enemy had made them closer than brothers, each a finely honed weapon against the darkness.

Devlin flexed his sword hand, wishing he had a better idea of what they were up against. One rogue would eventually slip up, and they'd have him. But if the treachery was deeply ingrained within the Regents, who knew how far up the chain of command the problem went?

His office door opened and his friends filed in. Unless Colonel Kincade chose that moment to drop in for one of his unannounced visits, no one would give a damn if Devlin and his friends wanted to hang out together. They frequently gathered in his office just to shoot the bull.

D.J. plopped down in a convenient chair and propped his boots up on the edge of Devlin's desk. Cullen did Devlin the favor of knocking D.J.'s feet back down to the floor. Although he appreciated the gesture, they both knew it was futile. D.J. had no respect for his own belongings, much less other people's property. His scuffed combat boots would be back to scratching the woodwork within minutes.

Trahern was the last one through the door, quietly closing it behind him. As usual, he stood with his back to the wall as far from the others as possible. He wouldn't say much during the meeting, but when he did speak the others would listen. He had a knack for seeing through the bullshit to the heart of the matter.

D.J. raised his hand like a kid wanting the teacher's attention. "Want to tell us why you dragged us in here, Dev? I'd planned on spending the afternoon doing some research."

Cullen snorted. "You mean you were going to hack into some other poor bastard's security system, drumming up business for your new program."

"I prefer to think of it as doing market research." The innocent expression on D.J.'s face didn't fool anybody.

Devlin tried not to laugh but failed. "Sorry, D.J., but you won't have time for recess today. I've got some digging I want you to do."

D.J.'s smile turned predatory. "More on the Guard? I checked out most of the locals and didn't see anything. Bunch of fucking Boy Scouts."

"Expand your search and repeat it every day or so. Something is going to show up eventually." He sat down on the edge of his desk and met the gaze of each of his friends. These were the men who he would trust with his life, and more important, he'd trust them with Laurel's, as well.

"You all know part of what I'm going to tell you, but I'm going to start at the beginning to bring you all up to speed." He closed his eyes briefly to gather his thoughts. "The last time I died, human hands were wielding the sword. That's why D.J.'s been checking out the bank records of the Guard. Someone had to have a good reason to come after me. Since I don't know of any reason that one of the Guard might have it in for me, I'm assuming money is the motivation. I hope so, because that would give us a chance of catching him."

"I'll rerun everything when we're done here." D.J. started to put his feet back up on the desk, but a glare from Devlin stopped him cold. He grinned sheepishly and sat up straighter.

Devlin resumed his explanation. "I haven't actually seen him, but my gut tells me someone has been following me, both down in the tunnels and on the streets."

These men wouldn't question his relying on a gut feeling. None of them had survived this long without having a highly developed survival instinct.

Cullen spoke for all of them. "That takes balls. The stupid bastard has to know that he's a walking dead man. Any one of us would love the privilege of gutting him with a dull blade for what he's pulled."

"That's why I figure there must be some serious money behind the attack. They would have to make it worth the risk. But there's more to this than someone being pissed at me. D.J. got the test results back from his friend in Research this morning. Those bags we found had traces of blue dust in them. Seems the stuff had to come from across the barrier because there's nothing like it on Earth."

"Yeah," D.J. agreed. "He couldn't do a full analysis with the small amount of the stuff he could collect from the bags. He seemed to think it came from some kind of garnet, except they aren't blue in our world. I don't know yet what they'd be good for. We'll need more than dust to figure that out."

Restless, Devlin paced across to his weapon wall and back. "Something has been bothering me since we found those bags, and I finally figured out what it was. My first time back in the tunnels, I cornered a pair of males up near the surface. They seemed damned surprised to have to fight. The older one even asked me why I was there, because they'd 'already paid.' Someone is telling the Others that they get a free pass to the surface if they cough up a healthy bribe. Then the sick bastard turns us loose to mop up his mess. No wonder they've been coming across in such big numbers lately."

The tension level in the room was climbing by the minute. Paladins weren't always likeable men, but to the last man, they were men of honor. To betray the safety of the entire world for profit was unthinkable. Whoever was operating behind the scenes had a lot to answer for.

"Right now the readings are stable, but Mount St. Helens has been venting steam and ash pretty frequently. Next time it looks as if she's going critical, I want us down in the tunnels long before she blows to catch whoever killed those guards and slit the bags, before he has a chance to do it again."

"Do you think he's the same one who has been following you?" asked Cullen.

"No way to know for sure, but it makes sense. It

strikes me that the one doing the dirty work is getting paid for his willingness to kill, not for his brains. Someone else is doing the thinking for him." He crossed his arms over his chest.

"So, what are we going to do about it?" Cullen's eyes narrowed, and his smile was grim. "Besides kill the son of a bitch."

"I want him dead, too, but we need information more." Devlin held up one hand and began ticking off items. "First we need to find the money trail, because that's where we'll find the most answers. Secondly I want to find some of those blue stones to test. Once we know what they are good for, we'll have a better idea of who wants them so badly. Finally I want to get my hands on the little rat bastard who's after me."

He glanced at Trahern in the back. He'd had no intention of bringing up Laurel, yet it was his fault that she was involved. She wouldn't appreciate having her name linked with his, though, not in front of the other Paladins.

Trahern understood what he was asking and shrugged. "So, do you want me to tell them the rest or do you want to do it?"

No, goddamn it, he didn't. "Maybe you'd better, since you're the one who found the evidence. I'll fill any holes when you're done."

Cullen and D.J. twisted around to look at Trahern. "The rest of what?"

"Someone has been spying on Dr. Young."

"How do you know?"

"I found a pile of cigarette butts behind a Dumpster. The spot gives you the perfect view of the front door of her place." Trahern's light-colored eyes darkened to the color of sword steel. "I found some of the same brand on the other side of the street, by one of those bus stop benches—too many butts for someone waiting for a bus that runs every half an hour."

Cullen went right for the heart of the matter. "And you just happened to be hanging around her place because why?"

Trahern kept his eyes on Devlin, his expression carefully blank. "The day she pulled the plug on that Paladin, Devlin went to her place to see how she was handling it. We think he was followed. Now, maybe some poor homeless SOB sleeps there every night and the cigarettes belong to him, but we doubt it. Devlin and I both think the guy is really after Devlin and hopes to catch him coming out of Dr. Young's place."

Cullen swung his attention back to Devlin. "You've gone back to her place? How many times?"

Devlin bit back the urge to curse loud and long. Cullen had managed to convey several levels of questions in those few words, the answers to which were none of his damn business.

"That doesn't matter. She doesn't deserve to be collateral damage just because she knows me."

"So what do we do next?"

"We can't do much about the blue stones until the pressure builds up on the barrier again. The way it's been flickering lately, that could be any minute. As

far as my own problem, Trahern and I plan on leading the sneaky little bastard on a merry chase."

D.J. sat up like a hunting dog on point. "And what
about Doc Young? I'd be glad to keep her safe. Hell,
if she doesn't mind you sniffing around, maybe she'd
let me console her, too."

Devlin's temper flashed hot and furious. He
hauled D.J. up out of his chair by his shirt and put all
his strength into a punch straight to his friend's gut.
"SHOW HER RESPECT OR I'LL KICK YOUR
WORTHLESS ASS OFF THE NEAREST PIER."
Then he shoved D.J. back, who dropped to the floor
in a puddle of pain.

He stepped back to look at Cullen. "Any questions you want answered?"

"Ah, that would be no."

Trahern's laugh sounded rusty as he held up his
hands in mock surrender. "You've already given me
that particular lecture."

"Okay, back to business then. I haven't told Dr.
Young about our concerns, because every thought
she has runs across her face like a fucking billboard.
If we told her to be careful around the Guard, she'd
get all twitchy around them and warn the bastard off.
And I can't start showing up to carry her books home
every night like a lovesick schoolboy without causing
all kinds of complications."

"So where does that leave us?" D.J. had managed
to sit up, his words ragged with pain.

"As much as possible, she should have an escort.
She just won't know it." Devlin offered D.J. a peace

offering with a hand up off the floor. "I figure we can take turns, working in pairs. Trahern will stake out her place late this afternoon. I'll trail her home. You two can do the same tomorrow."

"Fine by me," Trahern said. "And if you don't mind, I'm going to call in a couple favors from someone to see what he can find out."

Devlin frowned. "You're sure you can trust him?"

"With my life." Trahern met his gaze head on and didn't blink.

"That's good enough for me."

"Okay. If you don't need me for anything else, I'm out of here." Trahern disappeared out the door with D.J. hobbling after him, still rubbing his stomach.

Cullen hung back until they were both gone.

"What?" Devlin knew he sounded belligerent, but Cullen was used to it.

"I'm thinking Doc Young isn't your usual type."

"What the hell is that supposed to mean? I wasn't aware I had a type." He prepared to punch another friend.

"We usually limit our choice of women to those who've been around the block a time or two and don't expect more than a good time, especially in bed. Laurel Young isn't like that. She's too good for the likes of us."

Devlin knew that and even agreed with it, but that didn't mean he appreciated Cullen shoving it in his face. "Keep your opinions to yourself." He widened his stance. "What's between her and me isn't up for discussion, not even with you. Maybe especially with you."

What Cullen lacked in size, he more than made up for in sheer cussedness when it came to fighting. They'd sparred together before, but never got down and dirty enough to hurt each other. Devlin had a feeling that was about to change.

Cullen backed away to give himself room to maneuver. "That's bullshit, Devlin, and you know it. You get in her pants, and she's going to be hearing wedding bells and dreaming about little babies with your ugly face."

"Shut up, Cullen. You don't know what you're talking about." His face flushed hot.

His friend's jaw dropped. "Oh hell, you two have already done the dirty."

That did it. Devlin's left fist shut Cullen's mouth for him, sending him stumbling back a few steps. Devlin followed, but before he could land a knockout punch, Cullen got in a few good licks of his own. The little bastard was as slippery as a snake, combining martial arts with down-and-dirty street fighting. It didn't take long before Devlin had blood streaming down his face from a cut above his right eye. Cullen wasn't faring much better, but he was still dancing from one foot to the other.

"Come on, you can do better than that."

Devlin charged, sending Cullen crashing into a chair that cracked and splintered under the impact of the two men. They both went down onto the floor, taking a lamp and a small table with them. When Devlin got Cullen pinned and was about to pound him into the floorboards, something that felt suspiciously like the tattered remains of his conscience stayed his hand.

Breathing heavily, he rolled to the side and tried to bring his temper and pulse back under control. Cullen lay where he was for a few seconds and then slowly sat up.

"Got it bad, huh?" He grinned and wiped a dribble of blood off his mouth with his sleeve, then checked to see if his teeth were loose.

This time Devlin didn't bother to deny it. "She's got me tied up in knots that would make a sailor proud, but I don't want to talk about it. It's going nowhere and we both know it."

"Fair enough. Well, I've got to go help D.J. with his hacking."

Devlin slowly climbed to his feet, wincing when a couple of bruised ribs protested. At least they didn't feel cracked. He laughed when Cullen spat out a string of colorful curses as he tried to move slowly enough to avoid pain. It didn't work.

"While you two are playing cybergames, see how hard it is to get into our medical files without leaving a trail."

The fight already forgotten, Cullen smiled. "You forget who you're talking to. I have a modest talent for sliding in and out of tight places online, but D.J. is a fucking genius. Do you want anything in particular?"

"No, I just want to know if we can do it. Colonel Kincade can't be happy about our scans and I wouldn't put it past him to try to alter a few. Might pay to keep an eye on them." He dropped his voice. "Especially Trahern's."

"Will do. Take care, Devlin. And let me know if there's anything I can do to help." He limped to the door. Just before he left the room, he looked back, his eyes full of sympathy. "I think I'm jealous, you lucky bastard. Keep her safe. And if you hurt her, we'll pick up where we just left off."

"Fair enough." If the situation were reversed, he'd be the first in line to start swinging his fists.

He looked at his desk and the stack of paperwork piled on the corner. Then there were all the e-mails he needed to answer. Rather than deal with either one, he decided he had time to check in on Lonzo before it was time for Laurel to leave work. Besides, it gave him a legitimate reason to be in the area. Satisfied with his plan, he walked out and locked the door behind him.

He had to do something and soon. Every time the phone rang, he about jumped out of his skin. The man had been patient up until this point, but he wouldn't stay that way for long. He hadn't mentioned a deadline, but no one offered that much money for a job without expecting that it get priority.

Luckily, he'd finally come up with a plan to take down Devlin Bane. If Laurel Young were taken captive, Bane would walk straight into hell to try to save her, even if it meant this time when he died, he'd stay dead.

His cigarette had burned down to a stub. He dropped it at his feet and then ground it out with the heel of his shoe. It was getting too dark to risk lighting another one. Before he could lure his bait out of her home, he had to take care of one little problem. He didn't know how Trahern had come to be standing guard outside of her home, but the last thing he wanted was for that half-crazy bastard to come after him with death in his eyes.

So, he'd arranged a little distraction for Trahern. It wouldn't fool the man for long, but it should force him to reveal his current position. Although he couldn't compete with a Paladin like Trahern, he was a damn fine shot. Trahern would be unlikely to recover from a head shot. But even if he did, he'd be out of the picture long enough for the rest of the plan to succeed.

He checked his rifle and sights. His night gear gave everything an unnatural glow, allowing him to pick out far more details than normal eyesight. From his position on the roof across the street from Dr. Young's condo, he had a clear view of every possible approach. His cellphone vibrated, telling him that the next step in the plan was about to be put in motion. He settled himself comfortably and waited for the show to start.

Lord, she was tired. She couldn't remember her last good night's sleep. After locking the door and throwing the deadbolt, Lauren kicked off her shoes and tossed her purse on the closest chair. She also missed Devlin. Of course, if he were there, they wouldn't spend much time sleeping, but that was a sacrifice she'd be willing to make.

He'd told her that she wouldn't see him tonight, and she believed both what he said and the regret in his green eyes. Although she might not be all that experienced, a woman knew when a man wanted her. She could still feel the heat of his gaze when she'd turned back to smile at him.

She padded into the kitchen to pour herself some iced tea. A glass of wine sounded better, but she still had a few things to take care of before retiring for the night. Dinner was due to be delivered in half an hour or so. Until then, she'd change into her favorite flannel boxers and a baggy T-shirt.

Maybe she'd put in a movie to watch while she ate, something romantic and sweet.

Back in her living room, she waited for the delivery car to arrive. Her mother would be horrified to learn that Laurel rarely cooked. She knew how, of course. Her mother had seen to that because a woman was expected to cook for her family. However, working twelve-hour days through medical school and with longer days and sometimes nights at the lab now, she wasted little free time on household chores.

The doorbell rang. She checked out the window to make sure she recognized the driver, then handed him a check in exchange for a bag holding several white boxes. The smell of soy and garlic had her stomach rumbling in cheerful anticipation.

She set the bag on the counter while she got out a plate and flatware. But before she even had the boxes out of the bag, the peace and quiet was destroyed by sudden screams and the shriek of sheet metal crashing against something solid. Adrenaline had her running out of her front door toward the accident before she realized she'd even made the decision to do so. She could render first aid until an ambulance arrived.

From the condition of the small import wedged against the building across the street, she had no doubt that someone was hurt, maybe several someones. She ran back to her condo to grab the medical bag in her hall closet.

It took some quick maneuvering to work her way through the clutter of people. Intent on her goal, she didn't notice she was no longer alone. Just as she passed a Dumpster, a big hand reached out to snag her arm and drag her into the alley. Before she could manage more than an outraged squeak, the hand's partner clamped down over her mouth.

"Don't scream, Laurel. It's me. You're needed."

Devlin's harsh whisper in her ear left her limp and shaking. She nodded so that he'd release her, then she rounded on him, ready to rip into him but good.

"Are you crazy? You scared me half to death! Again!" Then she remembered the accident. "I've got to get to that car."

He blocked her way. "I need you here more."

"Somebody could be dying out there."

Devlin looked grim. "I'm sorry, but the ambulance should be there any minute. Trahern can't wait."

He was right—the sound of sirens was growing louder. "Trahern is hurt? I didn't get a call."

"You wouldn't have. He's back here in the alley." He took her arm and pulled her along with him. "He's been shot. We can't let him die."

She shoved the car wreck to the back of her mind and concentrated on keeping up with Devlin, regretting she hadn't put on shoes before charging out the door. The alley was relatively clean, but rocks and other objects made walking painful.

When she stumbled for the second time, Devlin finally realized what the problem was. Without breaking his stride, he swept her up in his arms and carried her down to the other end of the alley where she could see Trahern's legs sprawled on the ground behind some boxes. Oh Lord! He wasn't moving. Fear for him burned like acid. How many more times could he die and come back human?

Not many.

chapter 11

*D*evlin set her down and then flattened one of the boxes for her to kneel on. She dropped to Trahern's side, fearing for his life. A bright splash of blood had stained the entire right side of his shirt and had pooled on the ground next to him. She checked his pulse and was relieved to find it was steady. His eyes blinked open.

"Doc?" He made a feeble attempt to sit up.

She put her hands on his shoulders and gently pushed him back. "Yeah, Blake, it's me. Try not to move until I see how badly you're hurt."

When she tried to peel up his T-shirt, it stuck in the already thickening blood. She pulled a scalpel out of her bag to cut the material away, but it was slow going.

"Devlin, I need your knife."

A deadly-looking blade appeared in front of her face. "Don't do anything fancy, Laurel. We need to move him out of here before any of those cops pulling up out there decide to get curious. We don't need that kind of trouble."

"I can walk." Trahern tried once again to push himself up off the ground.

"Lie still! Move like that again and you're likely to get cut with this knife. That's not what you need right now."

She managed to cut away enough of the shirt to see the wound more clearly. She generally treated Paladins for blade wounds, but a bullet had created this particular one. It had cut a deep groove along Blake's abdomen.

Devlin looked down over her shoulder. "How bad is it?"

"A bad bleeder, but not fatal."

Grabbing several packs of gauze squares from her bag, she put together a makeshift pressure bandage and used surgical tape to secure it in place. Once they had Trahern somewhere more private, she'd do a better job tending the wound. Right now, both men were tense with the need to get out of the alley. She didn't blame them; she was feeling pretty exposed herself.

"That should hold him until we get him inside." She pushed herself to her feet. Devlin was standing with his back to the wall, a nasty-looking gun in his hand. He always looked dangerous, but this was the first time she'd ever seen him with his game face on. It scared her, even knowing he was guarding her and his wounded friend.

"Uh, Devlin, we can go."

His eyes flicked in her direction and then down at Trahern. "Stay here until I check the street."

The police were still at work on the accident; the last thing they needed to do was carry a wounded Trahern past them with his shirt in bloody shreds. While Devlin scouted out a safe route, she slid her arm around Trahern's shoulders and helped him into a sitting position. None of the Paladins showed much reaction to pain, but his face was drenched with sweat and he bit his lip to keep from moaning.

She both hated and admired their stoicism. "Go ahead and curse if it will help, because standing up is going to hurt even worse."

He didn't waste his breath on talking of any kind until she had him up on his feet. While she gathered up her medical supplies, he leaned back against the wall with his eyes closed. Judging by his pallor, nothing but sheer cussedness was keeping him on his feet. There wasn't anything she could do about the blood on the ground, but she moved the cardboard over it to hide it from immediate sight.

"Shall we try?"

She wrapped Trahern's arm around her shoulder and helped him start shuffling down the alley. They'd gone no more than a handful of steps when Devlin returned. He immediately took Trahern's other side.

"Almost everyone is still congregated at the other end. I didn't mean to be gone so long, but I wanted to check out the situation about the car while I had a chance. Seems there was no one in it. The owner is hopping mad, because the police are accusing him of negligence for not setting the parking brake and leaving the car in neutral. The owner swears he always sets the brake and that someone had to have messed with the car. The cops aren't buying his story because the car was locked up tight. Anyone trying to open the door without the key would have set off an alarm."

Trahern shook his head. "The wreck was timed to hide the sound of the gunshot."

"That's what I'm thinking, too." Devlin angled his body to stand between Trahern and the crowd a block away. "I can't support you like this while we're out in the open. If the bastard wants to try another shot at one of us, I need to be able to move fast."

She felt Trahern shift more of his weight to her shoulders. "Sorry, Doc, but it's you and me."

"Come on, big boy, let's get across the street."

They started forward again, finding their rhythm. His long legs took one step for every two of hers, but they kept at it. Once they reached her side of the street, they turned their backs on the ruckus a short distance away and made their way up to her place.

Devlin blocked their way. "Why is the door standing wide open?"

"I probably didn't close it on my way out. When I heard the crash, I ran out and then went back to grab my medical bag."

"Wait here." Devlin had his gun in his hand as he disappeared inside her home. It didn't take him long to check the place out.

"All clear." He slipped the gun into his belt at the back of his pants and reached for Trahern. "Where do you want him?"

"The guest bedroom. We can lay him down in there."

Trahern snarled, "Quit talking like I'm not here. Take me into the bathroom and leave me alone. Once I get washed up, I'll be out of here." He frowned at Devlin. "I'll need something clean to put on. Walking down the street like this might draw some attention."

There was no use in arguing with Trahern. She knew him well enough to know that he wouldn't give in to an injury that was no worse than this one. "I've got some extra large men's sweats that should fit you. Devlin, while I get them, you make sure he gets that wound cleaned out with antiseptic wash, then slather it with this." She pulled a bottle of Betadine solution and a tube of antibiotic ointment out of the vanity drawer. "Bandages are in the other side. Clean towels and washcloths are in the linen closet."

While the two men handled the necessary first aid, she rooted through her closet to find the sweats her brother had left behind on his last visit. He wasn't quite as big as Trahern or Devlin, but the soft fleece would do until Trahern got home.

She handed them to Devlin and then left them alone again. She went into the kitchen to reheat her dinner. By the time Trahern and Devlin joined her, she had three plates on the table and the food ready.

"Sit down and eat. And before you argue, Blake Trahern, remember this is your doctor talking. I know you are the toughest thing around, but either you eat now, or I call the lab and have you picked up and admitted for observation." She'd do it, too. The adrenaline rush of the crisis was starting to wear off and there were questions she wanted answered before she collapsed for the night.

Neither of the men bothered to argue. Devlin took the seat on her right. "Looks like you ordered a lot of food for one person."

Lord save her from a jealous man. "The sweats are my brother's, Devlin, and I happen to like Chinese food. I usually order enough for two or three meals. Saves on delivery charges."

Both men started shoveling the food into their mouths like there was no tomorrow, probably because they knew the questions were coming and neither one wanted to be the one to answer them. She let them eat in silence, giving herself time to come at the situation from several different angles. What had just happened?

When the eating slowed down, she set her plate aside and leaned forward. "All right, gentlemen. Time for some answers."

"Look, I've got to go while I can still walk." This from Trahern. His color was marginally better, but the pain showed in the lines bracketing his mouth.

"Not until I—"

Devlin interrupted. "Come on, give him a break. Look, I'll call D.J. He can take Blake home and keep an eye on him. But while we're waiting for him, you go pack."

"Pack? What are you talking about?"

But Devlin had turned his back to her as he punched in D.J.'s phone number. Something was going on, something neither one of the men wanted to talk about. And whatever their problem was, it now involved her. After all, how did Trahern come to be shot in the alley so close to her home? Then there was the little matter of Devlin conveniently being there to rescue his friend.

Oh, yes, the man had a lot to answer for, but it could wait until they were alone.

"Hey, Doc, do you have anything you could give me for the pain? Maybe a couple of aspirin?"

She couldn't refuse Trahern's request, but she suspected he was only trying to distract her. "I'll get some for you."

When she returned from the bathroom, the door from the kitchen to the garage was open and Devlin and Trahern were gone. She listened for a couple of seconds and heard them talking softly out in the garage as a car pulled into her driveway. Disgusted that she'd fallen for Trahern's ruse, she took the aspirin herself, figuring that whatever Devlin had to tell her was going to give her a headache.

To keep herself busy, she cleaned up the remains of their dinner and put the leftovers in the fridge. She was stuffing the last of the plates in the dishwasher when she heard footsteps in the garage. Once again, her pulse sped up.

Maybe if she enticed Devlin into her bed, he'd be in no position to duck her questions. The idea pleased her in several ways, although she didn't want to jump him as soon as he walked in. She'd let him shut the door first.

He came in with a determined look in his eye. She stood her ground, resolved to make him come to her and hoped that she wasn't the only one who couldn't wait until they got naked. But one look at the expression on his face told her he had other plans for the two of them. He stopped just short of where she stood.

"Where's your suitcase?"

"I don't respond well to orders, Mr. Bane."

"Look, Laurel, I don't have time for this. We need to get the hell out of here."

His words hit her like a splash of cold water. Nothing much scared a man like Devlin, but there was extra tension in the set of his jaw.

"Why? What aren't you telling me?"

He ran his hand through his hair in frustration. "Trust me enough to do what I ask. I'll explain later, but right now you're not safe here. Go pack enough clothes for several days."

She wasn't about to be run out of her own home without good reason. Crossing her arms over her chest, she prepared to wait him out. "I'm not going anywhere until you tell me what's going on."

Devlin crowded closer to her, using his height to try to intimidate her. "Don't argue, Laurel. Just do it or I'll pack for you and carry you out of here over my shoulder. Once we're settled someplace that's safer I'll explain more, but right now there isn't time."

She had no doubt that he meant every word. "Fine. Be that way."

As she marched past him to her bedroom, he

caught her arm and swung her around to face him. His mouth, so grim and unhappy, crushed down on hers. The wild flavor of a warrior ready for battle mixed with the taste of her anger to form a volatile mix. It wouldn't take much for it to explode out of control. She wanted it to; she *needed* it to. Their tongues tangled and mated, maybe soothing their tempers but fanning the flames of their passion until they both burned red hot. He lifted her up so that the curves of her body fit against the hard planes of his.

"We don't have time to finish this." Not that he moved to put any distance between them as he nuzzled her neck.

"That doesn't seem to matter." She wanted to climb him or throw him to the floor.

"The sooner you get packed, the sooner we can get naked someplace safe."

As bribes went, it was a dandy. She dragged a suitcase out of the back of her closet and opened it on the bed. She started with underwear, making sure to pick out the laciest ones she owned. Since he was going to see them, she wanted to look good.

In the bathroom she loaded up the basics, figuring she could always come back for anything she forgot or buy more. There wasn't much she couldn't live without for a few days.

That left clothes. She packed several pairs of basic slacks and the blouses to go with them, clothes she wore to work every day. She added some jeans and three sweatshirts, her hands shaking enough to make it difficult to fold things neatly.

After one last look around, she tucked in two pairs of shoes and a little jewelry. Finally she was ready, although it took a couple of tries to get the suitcase closed. She pulled up the handle and rolled the suitcase behind her into the living room. The drapes had been drawn and Devlin was standing at the edge of the window, staring out into the now-dark Seattle night.

"I'm ready. Where are we going?"

"My place for the night. After that, we'll be better able to make our plans."

She picked her keys up from the counter. "Do you want to drive or do you want me to?"

He held out his hand. "I will, just in case."

A flock of butterflies took up residence in her stomach. "In case of what?"

He offered her the comfort of his touch. "In case the bastard who killed me once and shot Trahern is still waiting out there."

Goose bumps sent chills up and down her body. "Is he after me, too?"

"I think he wants to use you to get to me, because I'm hard to corner." Devlin picked up her suitcase. "Maybe he figures if he threatens you, I'd walk into a trap bare-ass naked with my hands up."

"And would you do that?" she asked, even though she already knew the answer.

"In a minute and with a smile on my face." Then he planted a quick kiss on her cheek to lighten the moment.

She followed him out to the garage, feeling sick.

If his stalker succeeded in killing Devlin, he'd make sure Devlin stayed dead this time. He'd have to, or else spend the rest of his life running like hell with Trahern and the others on his trail.

She climbed into the passenger seat of her car and buckled up as Devlin drove out into the night. As the door of the garage slowly closed, she looked back and felt as if it was closing on her life, as well.

"Son of a bitch!"

He was tempted to take a shot at the car as it backed out of the garage, but policemen were canvassing the neighborhood, looking for witnesses to the car accident.

He wasn't worried about that. When he'd paid that punk to release the brakes and put the car in neutral, he'd been wearing different clothes and a hat pulled down low over his face. His own mother would have had a difficult time recognizing him. He'd come that damn close to grabbing Laurel Young and failed.

He kicked a trashcan and sent it flying across the alley. He should have known that Devlin Bane wouldn't trust Trahern to watch his woman for him. No sooner had he pulled the trigger than Bane came out of cover to check on his friend.

That should have kept Bane occupied long enough to allow time to kidnap Dr. Young. Instead, she'd managed to walk right into Bane's waiting arms. Now he'd have to go to all the trouble of tracking her

down again. Chances were that it would be days before the canny Paladin let her within spitting distance
of her condo again. And she'd be surrounded by a
bunch of his cutthroat friends the whole time.

So he'd have to find some way to catch her alone
in her lab. Yeah, that could work. But time was running out. If he didn't succeed soon, he'd have no
choice but to make a run for it.

He'd have to leave Seattle one way or the other,
but he'd prefer to leave with a nice chunk of change
stashed away to keep him in good wine and pretty
women for decades to come. With that thought in
mind, he headed back home to make plans and pray
that something would go right for once.

Devlin kept a wary eye on the rearview mirror as
Laurel's condo disappeared behind them. He had
complete confidence that he could evade anyone following their car, but they were still vulnerable to gunshots. As they put more distance between themselves
and the danger behind him, his muscles started to
relax.

"Are you all right?" His superior vision let him see
far more clearly in the dim light of the car than a normal human could. Laurel had leaned back against the
headrest and closed her eyes.

She managed a small smile. "Yeah, I'm okay."

"I want to drive around for a few more minutes to
make sure we haven't picked up a tail, but we're not
far from my place."

"Good, because I'm ready for today to be over." She reached over to lay her hand on his arm. "Almost ready."

The heat of her touch slid through him like a benediction. Oh yeah, he liked the way this woman thought. He accelerated to make the light ahead and then made an abrupt left turn. If anyone was after them, he would have to wait until the light changed again to follow them. Halfway down the block, he cut through a parking lot to change direction. He stopped between two cars parked near the exit to make sure no one was paying undue attention to their activities.

The coast was clear. He drove out of the lot and headed for his place. They should be inside and out of sight within minutes. He headed east and pulled into his driveway a short time later.

Laurel looked more alert, taking in all the details she could. "We're almost neighbors."

"Yeah, as a crow flies, it's no more than a mile to your place."

He parked her car next to his vintage Porsche. After retrieving her suitcase from the trunk, he led the way into the house. What would Laurel think of the place? He was betting she'd like it fine. He spent too much of his life underground, but coming home to a spectacular view of Puget Sound and the Olympic Mountains to the west went a long way toward making up for it. A six-foot-high cedar fence kept his small backyard safe from the prying eyes of neighbors. Like most of the Paladins, he valued his privacy.

He carried her suitcase down the hall to his bedroom. He supposed he could offer her the guestroom, but he didn't believe in playing games. There was nothing he wanted more at that moment than Laurel Young in his bed.

When he returned to the living room, she was standing out on the deck, staring down at the lights reflected on the water in the distance. He walked up behind her and slid his arms around her waist and cradled her back against his chest. The scent of her skin and hair had an immediate and predictable effect on his body.

"Beautiful view."

"I like it." He rested his chin on her head. "It's always different."

"Are you going to tell me what all of this is about now?"

"I said I would." He nuzzled her neck and then traced the shape of her ear with the tip of his tongue. "Afterward."

She arched her neck to give him better access. "Good idea."

He slid his hands up to cup her breasts and gently squeezed them as he kissed her neck. She was still wearing the T-shirt and flannel boxers she'd had on at the apartment. No bra. He liked the feel of the soft cotton sliding over the soft mounds. Laurel moaned softly and twisted slightly to demand a kiss. It was nothing like the one they'd shared earlier in her apartment. The heat was definitely still there, but none of the temper. He could have spent hours doing nothing more than simply holding her, letting her scent and taste fill his senses.

Well, maybe not. The cool evening air was definitely heating up around them. If they continued down this path, it might be wise to move back indoors. He forced himself to step back and hold out his hand. Her smile was all he could have hoped for. She allowed him to lead her down the hallway to his bedroom.

He yanked the bedspread down and out of the way. When he turned back to Laurel, she'd already stripped off her shirt. He grinned. "Thank you, Laurel."

She tipped her head to one side, a teasing smile on her lips. "So how are you going to show your gratitude?"

"I can think of an idea or two." He peeled off his own shirt; a little skin-to-skin was long overdue.

"Nice start, but what else have you got to offer me?" She backed up a step.

She wanted to play, did she? He reached for the zipper on his pants. Her eyes followed his hand as he slid the tab down. When he hooked his fingers in the top of his jeans to yank them down, he could hear her breath quicken. In a few quick movements, he stood before her wearing nothing but a smile on his face.

"Well, there is that, I suppose."

She still had on her boxers, but he was in no particular hurry for her to shuck them off.

Once again, he held out his hand to her. She hesitated.

"Feeling shy?"

"No, I'm trying to decide where to start. The possibilities seem endless."

"I'm open to anything you have in mind." He held his arms out slightly and slowly did a three-sixty, giving her a good look at what he had to offer.

"I think I want you to lie down."

"Yes, ma'am."

He stretched out on the bed, his hands behind his head, and waited to see what she'd do next.

Laurel could hardly take it all in. Devlin's body was a work of art, all strong lines and power. She ran a feather-light touch up the length of his leg and then gently caressed his penis with her fingers. It jumped in response, startling her. Devlin laughed, but she didn't mind. He didn't laugh often enough. Whatever scary news he had to tell her, she was determined to concentrate on driving it from his mind for a while.

She straddled him and felt the power of him centered right between her legs. She wanted him inside of her, but not yet. There was far more territory to explore. Scooting farther up his body, she cupped her breasts, offering them up to his taste and touch.

His tongue flicked over the sensitive tips, making her arch backward to thrust her breasts out more. He used his teeth and lips to suckle her, each tug sending another shiver of heat to pull deep within her. Without being asked, he seemed to know she needed more. He placed his palm on her midriff and followed the curve of her stomach down and down until his hand slipped under the elastic band of her shorts.

He offered up his fingers for her to ride, rubbing them against the center of her need and then inside her slick passage. The sensations were almost more than she could handle.

"Devlin . . ." His name was a plea for him to take charge, to give her what they both needed so badly.

He rolled her off his chest and onto her back. Tugging her shorts down and off, he tossed them over his shoulder. He knelt between her legs, staring down at her with such intensity she would have sworn she could feel his gaze touch her skin.

"I've been imagining you here, just like this." His voice sounded rough as he reached down to stroke her where she ached the most. Her hips lifted in response and in invitation. "Tell me what you want, Laurel."

"I want you to take me, Devlin. I don't care how, just take me."

"Then you'd better hold on tight, honey, because it's going to be a long, hard ride."

He raised her up and slowly eased inside of her. She felt stretched and tight and so wonderfully full. When she thought he'd gone as far as he could, he pulled her up off the bed and settled her on his lap. He lifted up, pressing himself inside her just that much farther. Cupping her bottom with his callused hands, he held her still while he pumped up and down. He seemed to know the exact angle that would give her the greatest pleasure.

"Devlin!" She whimpered as the tension inside of her kept building until she was poised at the edge.

Beast that he was, he froze, refusing to give her that little bit more. Instead, he withdrew and slid down to use his tongue instead. Once again, she felt herself spiraling out of control. This time she climaxed, keening out her release. He immediately lifted her legs high onto his shoulders and entered her, hardly giving her time to regroup before he started them both on a relentless drive to the pinnacle again.

She dug her fingers into the sheets and held on for dear life. For the second time he stopped, holding himself back by sheer will alone. His sweat-slicked body shivered with the need to find his release.

"Why are you stopping?"

"A condom. Before it's too late." He left her abruptly to fish one out of the bedside table. Seconds later, he was back.

Then he took her hard and fast, holding nothing back. She loved the feel of him pounding into her body, making sure that she took as much pleasure from their coupling as he did. Then in a few last powerful strokes, he took them both over the top and was waiting to catch her as she fell back to earth.

They both slept. It may have been minutes or hours later that she felt him stir next to her, dragging them both back to consciousness. It was time to talk. She would have been content to bask in the warmth of his arms, but the night wouldn't hold the rest of the world at bay for long.

"Start at the beginning."

His fingers toyed with her hair as he gathered up his thoughts. "There was something different about the last time I died."

"Other than how long it took for you to come back?"

"Yeah, besides that. I don't know, maybe part of the reason for that was that I was killed by a human, not one of the Others." His voice was calm, but she could feel the tension building inside him. "I didn't see his face, but the hands on the sword were human." He paused. "It's strange, but this is about the fourth time I've told somebody about it, and it still doesn't seem real. That day I came to check on you and again a time or two down in the tunnels, I've felt someone following me. I haven't been able to catch him, but he's there just the same." He looked down at her. "I'm sorry, but I think he followed me to your place that first night I came to check on you and then stayed over."

"So he knows we're involved." She snuggled closer. "And that's why you had Trahern watching my place."

"I was on my way to find out if he'd seen anything when I found him bleeding in the alley. We figure the car accident was staged as a diversion. Trahern was right about the crash covering the sound of the shot, but I think the culprit also planned on using the confusion to make a grab for you."

"He figured I'd come running with my medical bag, and I played right into his hands." She shivered despite the warmth. "Any idea who it might be?"

He hedged his answer. "We're pursuing several lines of investigation."

She lifted her head and propped it up on her hand. "Don't give me that line of hooey, Devlin. Tell me everything. You promised." She poked him in the chest with a finger.

He grabbed her finger and brought it to his mouth for a kiss. "Okay. We think it's all tied in with something going on with the Others. We've found some cloth bags down in the tunnel with a blue residue in them. D.J. had a friend test the stuff. It comes from some kind of gemstone, most likely a type of garnet we don't have in our world. It seems likely that someone on our side is taking bribes to let the Others through."

"Only they aren't getting through, are they?" The double betrayal made her sick.

"No, it's been business as usual for us. If they don't stay on their side, we hunt them down and kill them. Or they kill us."

His brutal honesty made her hurt for him and the other Paladins. And, although she would never admit it to him, she felt some sympathy for the Others, facing the end of a Paladin sword instead of finding the sanctuary they so desperately sought.

"You suspect someone in the Regents or the Guard." It was the only answer that made sense.

"Like I said, we're pursuing several lines of investigation. But starting tomorrow, you won't leave the safety of your lab unless you're with one of us. I've tried to keep a lid on things, so I've only told D.J.,

Cullen, and Trahern. Lonzo knows some of what's been going on, but he's missed out on the most recent stuff."

At last, some good news she could share. "He should be released in the morning, if Dr. Neal didn't already let him go this evening. They were waiting for the last of his blood work."

"That is good news. We're going to need every sword arm we can muster before this is over." He leaned over to kiss her again. "Now get some sleep. Tomorrow will be a long day for all of us."

She rolled over on her side and Devlin curled his body behind her. With his arm across her waist and holding her close, she let the worries of the day slip away and slept.

Hours later the phone rang, loud and shrill. Devlin stirred restlessly and then flung an arm out to pick up the receiver. After hanging up, he grumbled something about somebody being a dead man as he pulled on sweats and left the room. Laurel ignored him and burrowed back into the warmth of the blankets. But before she managed to drift back to sleep, he was back, yanking the covers off her.

"Hey!" She made a grab for the sheet, trying to recapture the warm comfort she'd been enjoying.

"Trahern's here. Get dressed."

Devlin didn't sound at all happy about his friend's early morning visit, but he didn't have to take his bad mood out on her. She sat up and glared at him. "Give me the sheet. I'm naked and cold, or didn't you notice?"

His grin was all male as he tossed her the sheet. "I noticed, all right. And if Cullen and D.J. weren't on their way over, too, I'd be right happy if you decided to stay that way."

She wrapped the sheet around herself, moving slowly to give Devlin the best show. Judging by the gleam in his eyes, he definitely appreciated her efforts. He drew her into his arms for a long kiss.

Slowly, he pulled back. "Trahern and the others want to talk about what's going on. Once we hear what they have to say, we'll make plans."

She didn't like the sound of that. "What plans? What aren't you telling me?"

"I'm not comfortable with your going back to the lab until we know more. If the man behind these attacks is one of the guards, you aren't safe there."

"Neither are you safe, but you keep going right back into the trenches. You're just as vulnerable as I am."

He cocked an eyebrow, reminding her without words that he was a trained warrior, able to defend himself. But they both knew that bullets could bring a Paladin down more easily than a sword. Once they were down and bleeding, they were just as vulnerable as any other man.

Devlin let go of her and stepped back. "We don't have time for this right now, unless you want to serve coffee and doughnuts wearing nothing but a sheet and a smile."

"Then get out so I can get dressed, Devlin. I'll sit in on your meeting, but then I've got to go in to the lab."

Devlin ran his hands through his hair in frustration. "Laurel, I know this is hard for you, but please don't do anything until we talk."

Either she trusted him or she didn't. "All right. I'll wait."

He pressed a quick kiss on her lips just as the doorbell rang.

After he left, she pondered what to put on as she brushed her teeth and ran a comb through her hair. If she wore her work clothes, Devlin might take it wrong. On the other hand, sweats didn't seem right, either. She settled for her best pair of jeans and a short-sleeved shirt. She could change if necessary after Trahern and company left.

Slipping on a pair of sandals, she took a deep breath and headed to Devlin's living room. The others had arrived. A sudden wave of shyness washed over her when she realized that this was the first time she was spending time with them as Devlin's lover rather than as their Handler. Devlin wasn't to be seen, but she could hear him banging around in the kitchen. Please, let him be making coffee. A shot of caffeine would be quite welcome.

Three of the Paladins were sprawled on the living room couch and chairs. Blake Trahern was the first to notice her standing in the doorway. Although he didn't actually smile, there was more warmth than usual in his icy gray eyes.

"Good morning, Blake. How are you feeling this morning?"

"I'm okay." He scooted over and patted the cushion next to him, offering her a place to sit.

When she accepted the invitation, Cullen and D.J. looked at the two of them as if they'd each grown a second head. She suspected Trahern enjoyed the stir. Maybe it would deflect some of the attention from her and Devlin. Either way, she drew some comfort from his acceptance.

"Good morning, D.J. You, too, Cullen."

D.J. shifted restlessly in his seat. "Morning, Doc."

"Sorry to bother you so early, Doc." Cullen smiled at her. "Blame it on Trahern. He rousted all of us out of bed this morning."

"Go to hell, Cullen." There was no real heat in Blake's words.

Before Cullen could respond, Devlin walked into the room carrying a tray full of coffee cups and pastries. "Before you complain any more, Cullen, remember that Blake's the one who brought breakfast."

D.J. chimed in. "It's the only reason he's not bleeding."

Laurel held up her hand. "Sorry, guys, let's not go there. I don't like blood before breakfast. You know how squeamish I am."

That little lie had them laughing. Even Trahern managed a rusty chuckle. Devlin poured her the first cup of coffee, his eyes warm as he handed it to her. Once everyone else was served, he sat down on the couch next to her. Being flanked by two of the most powerful Paladins in the Seattle region was a heady sensation.

Cullen set his cup down on the coffee table. "So, what's so important that we had to miss our beauty sleep?"

Devlin took charge of the discussion. "Somebody staged an accident in front of Laurel's place last night. The noise from the crash accomplished two purposes. It drew her outside, where she'd be vulnerable to attack, and the noise covered the sound of Trahern getting shot."

"So the bastard has taken this to a new level." Devlin stood up. "It's one thing to come after me, but attacking Laurel is another."

"Damn straight!" D.J., always the easiest to rile, was on his feet and ready to fight.

"Sit down, D.J. You make it hard for everyone else to think," Devlin said.

He dropped back into his chair, but Laurel could almost see him vibrating with barely controlled energy from where she sat.

"I want this bastard caught and soon. He came damn close to getting Laurel last night." Devlin slid his hand around her shoulders, tugging her closer. "Obviously watching her place didn't work, but we didn't know he was crazy enough to go after Trahern."

Blake didn't respond, but he didn't need to. They all knew how it would go down if his attacker ever crossed paths with Trahern again.

"I'd like to draw him out of hiding. I figure we'd

stand a better chance if Laurel and I disappear for a couple of days. If she doesn't show up at work and we're not at my place or hers, he's bound to start panicking. Whoever is paying him won't like how long it's taking him to get the job done."

Laurel frowned up at him. "I can't just take off, Devlin. I've got responsibilities."

"You said Lonzo is being released this morning. He was your last patient, wasn't he?"

She clearly did not like being forced to admit that. "Yes, but that could change any minute. You all know that."

"I can't go far, either. We'll hole up somewhere within easy driving distance, so we can get back quickly. You have vacation coming, don't you?"

"Well, yes, but—"

"Fine. Then it's settled. While we're gone, recruit a couple of the others to keep an eye on my place and hers. And if anyone starts asking questions, we'll have our culprit."

Devlin could tell Laurel was about to start arguing, but he squeezed her shoulder, hoping she'd take the hint and wait until the others were gone before exploding. His hands ached to get a hold of the slimy little prick who was behind the attacks, but he needed to keep Laurel safe even more.

"If the two of you use credit cards, you might as well leave a trail of breadcrumbs for him to follow. Even your cellphones aren't secure." D.J. spoke with authority. After all, his favorite pastime was hacking into supposedly secure sites.

Devlin nodded. "Good thinking. I'll buy one of those prepaid phones and call you with the number. And cash will work to hide our tracks."

Cullen was the one shaking his head this time. "They could be watching for any large cash withdrawals from either of your accounts, but we can get around that if a bunch of us take out smaller amounts. Then D.J. can make the transactions disappear or at least change the dates on them. Leave it up to us."

"We don't have long, Cullen."

"I'll be back in a couple of hours with a stack of cash. Come on, D.J. And, Trahern, I'll need your account numbers and debit card."

As his friend reached for his wallet, Devlin looked down at Laurel. "Do you like the mountains or the water?"

chapter 12

They lucked out and got a room on the ocean side of the hotel. Laurel opened the sliding door and stepped out on the small balcony. Drawing a deep breath of the pungent ocean air, she could almost believe that she and Devlin really were on a lovers' getaway to the coast.

He followed her out and wrapped his arms around her, resting his head on top of hers. The heat of Devlin's body felt even better than the sun on her skin. She leaned back into his strength and let her tension drain away . . .

Only to be replaced by a new set of sensations. She tilted her head to one side in invitation to Devlin. Bright man that he was, he immediately nuzzled his way up her neck. He gently bit the lobe of her ear, then kissed it in apology for the small hurt.

"Want to move this inside?" he asked.

His whispered question beside her ear sent shivers of heat up and down her spine. "Why? Got something in mind that might shock the neighbors?"

"I certainly hope so." He turned her around and kissed her soundly. Cupping her bottom, he lifted her up to better fit her body against his.

It felt like heaven. "Take me to bed, Devlin."

"I thought you'd never ask." He carried her inside, leaving the door open to the ocean breeze.

Devlin cuddled her closer, loving the feel of her head on his shoulder and the way she felt stretched out beside him. Her breathing was slow and steady, sleep about to overtake her. That was good.

Neither of them had gotten much sleep the night before, after they'd reached his house. The stress of knowing that there was a killer after both of them was taking a toll on her. He and his friends were doing all they could to remove that danger, but the memories would still linger.

Damn, he loved this woman. It hadn't been easy for her to face D.J. and Cullen early that morning, but she'd faced the situation with the same determined strength as she did everything else. She might not have noticed the jealous looks they'd given him, but he had. All of them knew that Paladins didn't fall in love. Lust was as good as it got for them, but what he felt for Laurel was far more than that.

He wished he could turn his back on his job and marry her, so the two of them could live out their lives as a normal married couple. But that wasn't going to happen because each of them were committed to the lives they were living. Changing that would be impossible. Wouldn't it?

The cellphone they'd bought started vibrating on the bedside table. He grabbed it and pushed the answer button.

"Bane here. Give me a second." He eased away from Laurel and took the phone into the bathroom so he could talk without waking her up. "I'm back."

He listened to Cullen's report. So far, no activity on any of their accounts. Devlin was tempted to ask his friend if he and D.J. would be able to tell if the guy on the other end was as good as they were at hacking. They'd take it as an insult, and right now he didn't need them mad at him.

"Thanks for letting me know. We'll be here tomorrow and head back the morning after that. I've had a hard enough time convincing Laurel to stay gone that long."

Cullen promised to call back the next morning and again the day after unless something urgent came up. Devlin hung up the phone and then about jumped out of his skin when he looked up and saw Laurel standing there. She rubbed her eyes sleepily.

"Who was that?"

"Cullen. So far, all is quiet."

"So can we go back sooner?"

"No."

She wanted to argue. It was there in her eyes, but she didn't try. Instead, she surprised him. "I want to fly a kite. And then I want to ride a scooter."

"What?"

She laid her head on his chest and wrapped her arms around his waist. "If we're here pretending to be a couple, then I want to do all the things couples do here. I want to fly one of those big fancy kites on the beach and then ride a scooter."

"Have you ever ridden a scooter?"

"Nope. It's that or go horseback riding." She tipped her head back as if studying him. "I suspect you're more of a scooter man."

If he was going to ride a bike, he wanted it to be a big, fat Harley. But his woman was looking playful, and he was in the mood to indulge her. Especially if it kept her mind off their problems for a few hours.

"All right. Let's grab a late breakfast and then go from there."

"You've got a deal."

Flying kites turned out to be a little more complicated than he'd expected. He couldn't remember ever flying one before. He'd spent most of his childhood scrambling for extra money to keep food on the table—his mother had meant well, but as a parent she really sucked. And Laurel had picked out one of the most complicated kites the shop carried. She'd chosen a large dragon after looking at it and back at him a couple of times. He kept waiting to hear her say that it reminded her of him.

Personally, he thought it needed a few battle scars to qualify as a Paladin. Once they'd managed to assemble it after much laughter and botched attempts,

Laurel had designated him to be the one to hold the kite while she took off running. Watching her laugh as the kite finally caught the wind and almost pulled her from the ground would remain etched in his memory for decades to come.

He'd finally taken the handle that held the string from her hand and dragged her down to sit in the sand with him. She settled between his knees and leaned back against his chest as the two of them watched their dragon swoop and soar above the blue waves.

"He's rather fierce, don't you think?" Laurel asked, pointing up toward their dragon. "I finally figured out who he reminds me of. He's the same color as Trahern's eyes when he's smiling."

Devlin snorted. "Trahern doesn't smile." And he wasn't jealous that she was thinking of his friend. Not much anyway.

"Sure he does, but usually it's just with his eyes." She tugged on the string, making the dragon swoop down and back up.

"I really don't want to hear about Trahern's eyes."

The little minx giggled. "Oooh, Mr. Big Tough Guy is jealous. Well, I'm not here with Trahern, am I? And that certainly wasn't Trahern I was all over back there in our room."

No, it hadn't been. And the thought of some of the particularly inventive things she'd come up with had him wishing they didn't have such a long walk back to the hotel. Maybe she was having some of the same thoughts, because she took the string from him and began reeling in the dragon. The big reptile fought to stay aloft, but finally it surrendered to Laurel's persistence and came peacefully back to roost.

Then she took Devlin by the hand and led him back to their room.

"Any luck?" Cullen leaned over D.J.'s shoulder and watched the screen.

"He's a slippery little bastard, I'll grant him that." D.J.'s fingers flew over the keyboard as he tried to trace who was behind the backdoor inquiries of Devlin's and Laurel's bank accounts. His hands stilled as he muttered a few choice curse words.

"Did he get away?"

"Not exactly, but he's hiding behind some pretty tough security."

Cullen pulled up a neighboring chair, prepared to await the outcome of the cyberbattle. "You can breach the security codes, though. Right?"

"I should be able to. You and I wrote it for the Regents, so whoever is sneaking around out there is using our software. Damn, I knew we were good, but maybe too good."

If they couldn't trace the attack back to a specific person, they'd be no better off than they'd been before, except they now knew that their quarry was part of the Regents organization.

Cullen's cell rang. He recognized Trahern's number. "Got something for me?"

Trahern's voice sounded hushed. "Someone's

walking up in front of Laurel's place, but he's not being sneaky at all about it. I'm a little too far away to get a good look at his face, but judging by his build, I think it's Dr. Neal."

"I can't believe he'd be involved in anything crooked. Even if he took a sudden dislike to us, he wouldn't hurt Laurel."

"I'm not judging the man; I'm just telling you what I'm seeing." Trahern sounded a little pissed off.

"Well, we're getting a definite nibble on the bank accounts. Twice in the last hour, someone has tried to break through to Devlin's records and then Laurel's. The last time was about five minutes ago."

"That eliminates Dr. Neal. He's been right in my sights during that time."

"Good. I'd hate to think I couldn't trust the man who's responsible for putting me back together."

"Penn is supposed to relieve me soon, then I'll be coming in. Want anything?"

"Yeah, a couple of big greasy pizzas and a six-pack. It's going to be a long night."

"Give me half an hour. And tell D.J. to nail the bastard."

"Will do."

"Oh yeah, that's right, baby. Right there."

Laurel lifted her head up long enough to enjoy the look on Devlin's face. Evidently what she was doing with her mouth and tongue pleased him greatly. She cupped his penis again and ran her tongue up and down the thick length of it before sliding her mouth down over the tip. Her man's immediate reaction left little doubt that he wanted more of the same.

After only a few seconds more, though, he stopped her, and pulled her up for a scorching hot kiss. He lifted her so that she was straddling him. "Ride me."

She moved until he was poised at the entrance to her body and slowly took the length of him inside her. They both groaned at how wonderful their joining felt. Then she rocked forward and back, loving the feel of him deep inside her. His big hands reached up to cup her breasts, squeezing and kneading them as she pleasured them both.

"Lean down."

She did as ordered, whimpering with pleasure as he suckled her breasts. Already she could feel the storm building inside of her. "Devlin!"

"Let it come!" He thrust up, pushing himself deeper as her muscles clenched, holding him tightly inside of her. Finally, she collapsed on top of him, both of them breathing hard with the aftermath of passion.

"Thank you," she panted.

He laughed and kissed her on the forehead. "I won't say the pleasure was all mine, but at least half of it was."

"I'm too tired to laugh." But she did anyway.

"I'm too tired to move." He eased her to his side, once again tucking her in close. A man could get addicted to moments like this.

But tomorrow morning they'd be checking out of the hotel and returning to their real lives. No more pretending that the fun they'd shared on the beaches of Ocean Shores was going to last forever. The idea hurt.

Laurel must have sensed the change in his mood. "What happens when we get back?"

"I'm not sure." And the uncertainty was pissing him off. "Unless Cullen and D.J. can track down whoever was trying to get into our bank accounts, we'll have to go back to plan B."

She ran her fingers up and down his chest. "Which is?"

"We return to work and try to catch him some other way."

All of the Paladins were taking the betrayal within the organization personally. Not only had one of their own been attacked and killed, but their favorite Handler was in danger, as well. Laurel wasn't going to walk out her door without having at least one Paladin shadowing her footsteps.

Inside her lab would be harder, but there was no way for Paladins to hang around; the only reason they set foot in the labs was if they were bleeding. Unless the barrier came down, it would be hard to explain a series of wounds.

She rose up to smile at him. "We still haven't ridden scooters, buster. Get dressed or I'm going by myself."

He grabbed her hand and kissed her fingertips. "Are you sure you want to do that?"

"Afraid I'll outride you?"

"No, I'm afraid you'll leave a good part of your skin on the pavement." He was only half kidding, but he'd take her if she really wanted to go.

"And after that, we'll try out the go-karts. I bet I'm a better driver than you are."

That was it. He sat up and glared down at her. "What makes you think you can beat me?"

She only laughed at him. "I double dare you, Devlin Bane. I can outride you on a scooter and I'll win at go-karts."

"You're on." He reached for his jeans.

A few minutes later, they were walking toward the rental place. Laurel twined her fingers in his and all but dragged him down the sidewalk. He couldn't remember the last time he'd taken the time to play, with or without a woman at his side.

He planned on taking the dragon kite home to hang on his den wall to remind him of these two days. And they were about to build a few more memories against the long days ahead when he waited for the next battle to begin.

"I want the red one. Devlin, I think you should take the green one because it matches your eyes."

He groaned even though she was just teasing him. Ignoring her suggestion, he picked out a black scooter that looked newer than the others, while Laurel tried out the controls on the one she'd chosen. The boy who worked on the lot took a long time explaining things to her, ignoring Devlin—not that he blamed him. With her happy mood and bright smile, she was almost irresistible.

Ten minutes later, they were "roaring" down the street at twenty-five miles an hour. When a car passed by, Laurel slowed even more.

He pulled up next to her. "Everything okay?"

She shook her head. "I didn't realize how big cars looked when you're on one of these things."

She had enough to be scared of these days. After considering their options, he called back to her, "Follow me."

He turned off the main road and soon they were riding on the wide-open beach. Although the dry sand was difficult to maneuver in, once they reached the wet sand that was packed down from the receding tide, they could really let loose.

In no time at all, Laurel was laughing with sheer joy as she raced past him and then circled back to coax him into playing, too. They drove in circles, leaving their mark on the sand in big loops and whooping at the seagulls who flew low overhead. Then they raced a few times, with each of them claiming victory at the end. Finally they rode side by side, content to be together as the sun began to sink down in the sky.

When they returned to the rental store, Laurel dismounted and patted the scooter on the seat, as if it had been a trusty steed deserving of a reward. She surrendered her helmet to the waiting clerk and shook her head to fluff out her hair.

"Now, Mr. Bane, we're off to the go-karts—where you're going to breathe nothing but fumes."

He made a grab for her hand, but she giggled and

danced out of his reach. "What's the matter, big man? Afraid of a little healthy competition?"

He was afraid he'd never have another day like this one in his long life, but he couldn't say that. Not when she was so happy. Tomorrow would be enough time for her to face reality.

For the rest of the evening and the night that stretched out before them, he was simply going to have fun with his woman. And damn if he'd let her win. There'd be no living with her if he did.

Laurel slipped out of the bed and pulled Devlin's shirt on over her shoulders. It hung halfway down her thighs, providing decent enough coverage to step out on the balcony. She should be sleeping after the active day they'd shared, but nightmares hovered and she couldn't seem to push them away.

Moonlight rippled on the ocean waves, giving the night a silvery glow. The air had cooled down since the sun had disappeared beyond the horizon in a blaze of fiery color. As the darkness had claimed the town, she and Devlin had sought out the privacy of their room, all too aware that their remaining hours together were slipping through their fingers like the sand on the beach.

Once again he joined her on the balcony, this time standing off to one side rather than holding her in his arms. Even if she understood his need to distance himself again, the rejection hurt.

Crossing her arms, she turned to face him. "I

would have never thought you a coward, Devlin."

"It's for your own good, and you know it." There was no mistaking the hurt mixed with anger in his voice.

"And who are you to decided what's good for me and what isn't?" She'd lived her whole life with her family trying to pigeonhole her into a nice, neat life they could understand. She wasn't about to let Devlin do the same. "You've never asked me about my family, Devlin. Is that because you don't care, or because that would make me more than a good time in bed?"

The muscles in his jaws worked as he bit back whatever he wanted to say. She prodded him some more.

"Well, let me tell you about them. They are good, decent people who go to church on Sundays and rarely travel beyond the county they live in. My siblings have all married their hometown sweethearts and settled down to produce the next generation. All of them love me, and not one of them understands me. I'm the oddball in the family—the freak, the only one for whom staying there wasn't enough. I wanted something different. I thought I'd found it with you."

"Laurel . . ."

She didn't bother to hide the tears streaming down her face. "No, let me finish. You're the only one who understands how important my work is to me, how much it means to me to fight to save every Paladin who enters my lab. Not only do you respect what I do, but you're proud of what I'm trying to accomplish. I know you and the others think of me as a little sister who needs protecting, but I'm not some weakling who can't face up to adversity."

She used the hem of the shirt to wipe her face. "Damn it, Devlin, I love you and I won't let you deny me that right."

Then there was silence. She waited to see what he would do or say.

It wasn't long in coming. He cradled her in the safe harbor of his arms and held her as if she were all that was wonderful and dear in his life.

"Your love is the best gift I've ever been given, Laurel. It's been a long time since I've let myself care about anyone other than my friends, mainly because they were the only ones who truly understand what I am: a man born to spend his life killing. Then you came along with your bright smiles and gentle touches."

He pressed a kiss to her forehead. "I love you, too, but I won't let you die because of me."

He walked back into the room and left her alone.

That did it! She stormed inside and turned on the lights. Devlin was sitting on his side of the bed and reaching for his cellphone, and the sudden brightness made him stop midmotion.

"Don't you *dare* lay that on me, Devlin Bane. You don't have the right to make choices for me, not without talking to me first. It's hardly your fault that some whacko is after you. Heck, a drunk driver could run me down tomorrow. Would that be your fault, too? How about a terrorist attack on the city? How much blame are you willing to take on, to avoid taking a chance that this might work out between us?"

She marched over to stare down at him, and he tumbled her down onto the bed and pinned her with all his weight. As he glared down at her, she smiled and reached up to cup his face. "So you love me, huh?"

"Damn straight I do." He swiftly freed himself from the confines of his drawstring flannels, and in a few short thrusts, he was inside her. "And you love *me*."

She lifted her legs and wrapped them high around his waist, urging him on. "Yes. And nothing—not even you—is ever going to change that."

chapter 13

*L*aurel was alone, and so was he. This was it! Either he
made his move now, or he might as well grab his packed
suitcases and disappear. He hadn't been home when his
mysterious employer called, and the message on the answering machine had been short and to the point: Get
the job done or prepare to die in Bane's place. The cold,
matter-of-fact tone made the threat all the more scary.

He'd scrambled around for two days trying to find
Devlin Bane, with no luck. If he couldn't find his prey,
then he'd force the Paladin to come to him. He'd waited
all morning for a chance to get Dr. Young alone, but
she'd been in meetings with Dr. Neal and then Colonel
Kincade. He didn't know what had been discussed, but
judging by the expressions on their faces, it hadn't been
good. He hoped it was some bad news about their precious Paladins. Maybe the whole lot of them needed to
be put down like the rabid dogs they were.

He liked that idea except for the problem of the Others. Sure, he and the other guards could handle the situation when only a few of them crossed at a time. But when Others poured past the barrier, it took those crazy bastards to turn back the tide. Maybe the Regents should lock the whole bunch in cells underground and only open their cages when things got really bad.

Of course, who'd be crazy enough to be the one who tried to shove them back in the cells when the fighting was done? Not him; he had no death wish.

He peeked through the window into her lab. Son of a bitch, she was eating a sandwich at her desk. What was up with that? She almost always went out to pick up something for lunch, saying a walk in the fresh air cleared her mind. Often she offered to bring something back for whatever guards were on duty, including him.

She couldn't help but be suspicious that something was going on, after the fiasco the other night. Under other circumstances she might have told Bane and Trahern that they were paranoid if they had tried to convince her that someone was after her. But shooting Trahern had no doubt given their arguments the proof she'd needed. The only question was, had they warned her about trusting members of the Guard? He was pretty sure he'd covered his trail, but Bane may have told her not to trust anyone except himself.

There was only one way to find out. Time was running out on him. Unless he succeeded in taking her now, he might as well put the barrel of his pistol in his mouth and pull the trigger. It would be an easier death than either his unknown boss or Devlin Bane would give him.

His hands were a little unsteady as he braced himself to confront the delectable Dr. Young. Maybe he'd keep her "occupied" for a day or two before letting Bane know where to find her. He figured the last place the bastard would look was in the tunnels below the Center. If he got tired of her himself, he could always leave her in one of the tunnels for the Others to find on their next attempt at crossing over.

Yeah, he liked that idea. They'd kill the bitch without hesitation. And when her lover boy found out, Bane would go berserk. It wouldn't take much to convince Kincade or even Dr. Neal that Bane had crossed the line, making his death a mercy kill. His hands steadied now that the pieces were all falling together.

He checked his gun one last time and pushed open the door.

Laurel couldn't believe her eyes, but she'd been staring at the truth for the better part of an hour. The change in Devlin's scans had been substantial on the scan she'd run after he'd revived and when Dr. Neal repeated the tests as part of the general screening.

Unless she was reading more into the numbers than she should be, his scores had first dropped when she'd reached out to hold his hand. She'd like to think that was significant, but the scientist in her wouldn't let her jump to conclusions. It had to be done right; she'd have to set up controlled experiments to validate the findings.

The trouble was, she didn't know what was triggering the changes. Could it be something as simple as physical contact?

Images of the way she and Devlin has spent the previous evening filled her head. Now *there* was an experiment she'd volunteer to participate in, at least in private. The scenario made her grin.

Her intuition was convincing her that she was on the brink of something important. She carefully packed up the reports in date order and returned them to Devlin's chart. He'd have to be told after Dr. Neal had reviewed the data. No doubt he'd be upset to find out that she'd crossed the line by becoming involved on a personal, not to mention intimate, level with one of her charges.

But she'd willingly take the heat, if it meant they had found a way to help the Paladins escape the endless cycle of death and destruction. She gave into the urge to do a little happy dance—

And came face-to-face with the business end of a revolver. Frozen with terror, it took her a minute to recognize who was holding the gun. His normally friendly eyes looked more like Trahern's now.

"Sergeant Purefoy? Is this some kind of joke?" One look at the cold hate in his eyes burst that particular little dream.

"Yeah, Doc, it's a joke. But I'll be the only one laughing." He motioned toward the door with the barrel of the gun. "You and me are going to find someplace nice and private to hole up for a day or two. I have some special fun in mind just for us."

He focused his gaze on her breasts and then slowly moved down her body from there. Then he smiled, letting her know exactly what he had in mind. She stepped back even as her stomach roiled. It was as if she were staring at a stranger, rather than a man she'd known and trusted.

Her revulsion must have shown on her face because he drew back his hand and slapped her. "Don't give me that holier-than-thou look, bitch. I know you've been spreading your legs for Bane. Hell, he's not even human."

She met his gaze head on, determined not to cower. She glanced at the camera mounted in the corner, hoping that someone was watching this little drama play out. Surely not all of the guards were involved in this mess.

When he noticed, he laughed. "Who do you think is supposed to be monitoring the labs right now? And my partner had a sudden bout of food poisoning and had to go home. Imagine that—such an amazing coincidence. So until the next shift arrives, I'm bravely carrying on alone."

He picked up her cellphone from the counter and tucked it in his uniform pocket, then waved the end of his gun in the direction of the door. "You're going to walk through that door with me and act like everything is just fine. One false move or any attempt to escape, I won't hesitate to shoot anyone we run into."

He smiled again. "You, too—although not to kill, mind you. But a leg wound wouldn't interfere much with my plans for us."

That did it! She wasn't going to go along with his plans like a docile sacrificial lamb. What could she use for a weapon? He must have figured she'd try something because he shoved her away from the counter into the middle of the room. Then he was beside her, his gun pressed firmly against her ribs. He half dragged her down the hall to a flight of stairs that led down to the rarely used lowest level.

She deliberately stumbled, breaking her fall by grabbing on to the railing, and sat down hard. When he immediately tried to drag her back to her feet, she refused to move. "Unless you want me to fall and break my leg, you can hold on for a second." She yanked off one of her shoes and held it up. "Thanks to you, I've just ruined a perfectly good pair of heels."

Before he could stop her, she tossed it behind her and then sent its mate tumbling down the steps. Purefoy yanked her back up by her hair, the last vestiges of civility gone.

"I'm not stupid, Laurel." He ran the barrel of his gun down the curve of her neck. "I know you're trying to leave a trail for your Paladin lover to follow, but it won't work. Even if he finds the shoes, he'll think I'm trying to lead him into a trap. By the time he figures out that I really have taken you down into the tunnels, it will be too late—for you and for him."

He started down the stairs, keeping up his commentary. "At one time I thought about trying out one of the female Others. Once I caught one, though, I couldn't get past the stench of their world. And with that gray skin, she looked like a corpse. But I'm willing to bet that one of their males wouldn't mind getting it on with a human female. Did you know the males sometimes travel in pairs? That would make the experience extra special for you, don't you think? After all, there has to be some reason they keep crossing the line between worlds. Maybe it's something as simple as getting laid by a woman who doesn't look dead."

"Better one of them than you, you sick bastard."

She braced herself for another blow, but Purefoy didn't react to her taunt. He shoved her into the corner at the bottom of the stairwell while he fumbled with the keypad. After he'd entered the code and opened the door, he grabbed her by the arm and dragged her into the storage room beyond.

They were surrounded by a deep silence, broken only by their own breathing. She knew from previous visits that the room was filled from floor to ceiling with environmentally controlled files. As a further protection, the lighting was limited to a small pool of light right at the door. Beyond that, motion detectors were set to switch on the overhead lights as needed, limiting the amount of light. Such precautions were necessary because here lay the heart of the history of the Paladins, carefully written and maintained by the Regents since the misty beginnings of the written word.

"Come on." He headed for the farthest corner,

stumbling along the aisle at the leading edge of darkness as he outran the speed of the detectors.

They skidded to a halt in front of an elevator tucked way back out of sight. Purefoy's fingers flew over the keypad, calling the elevator up from the depths below, and a chill settled over Laurel. She'd never seen an Other except in pictures, and once in an autopsy done to show new Handlers the kind of being the Paladins did battle with.

The thought of being staked out like a goat to attract a predator male made her sick. But would that be any worse than being used by the crazed man at her side? Had the fact that she'd chosen a Paladin lover really driven him to this extreme?

No, that didn't make sense. If he'd ever been interested in her as a woman, he'd never show any sign of it. Their relationship had always been professional but cordial.

What was motivating him to risk certain death at the hands of the Paladins? Surely he had to know that even if he was successful in his attempt to kill her and Devlin, the others would line up for the chance to take him down.

"Why are you doing this?" She did her best to keep her voice level and calm. Purefoy already showed signs of coming apart, from dilated pupils to beads of sweat on his face. There was no telling what he'd do if she pushed too hard.

"Enough money to make me rich."

The elevator opened in front of them. He gave her a shove and then followed her in. "The Regents give their pet Paladins all the riches and glory. Meanwhile, us Guards make piss-poor money and barely get by."

"But the Paladins fight the Others." And how could he think the Paladins were steeped in glory, when their existence was one of the best-kept secrets in history?

Purefoy snorted. "Oh yeah, they have to fight, what, maybe a few days a month? Even when things go bad, they come back from the dead like some freakin' zombie. We get sent down into the tunnels to back them up, but when we die, we stay that way."

There would be no reasoning with the man. The more they talked, the more he would convince himself that he was on some moral quest to right a wrong on behalf of the Guard everywhere, rather than just being greedy. Meanwhile, the elevator continued its trip downward to the tunnels far below the streets of Seattle.

They reached bottom with a jarring *thump*. When the doors slowly slid open, she got her first view of the dank tunnels where the Others and Paladins fought and died. And where she might die, as well.

Cullen stuck his head in Devlin's doorway. "Hey, Dev, you wanted to know if we picked up any unusual readings."

Devlin looked up from the scan reports that D.J. had printed out for him after hacking into the medical files. He pinched the bridge of his nose, wishing

Laurel was there to interpret the medical jargon for him. He should have made it his business to learn more about how to read the damn things before this.

"What's going on? Is the mountain acting up again?" Lonzo wasn't quite up to speed yet and Trahern was moving slowly; the last thing they needed was another free-for-all right now.

Cullen shook his head. "No, but D.J. picked up a blip on one of the monitors in the tunnels. He's trying to trace it, but it was only that one time."

"Keep me posted."

"Will do. By the way, we're sending out for sandwiches from the deli. Interested?"

He hadn't realized how late it had gotten. "No, I've got plans for dinner." For after dinner, too, but Cullen didn't need to know about that. The only one who knew that Laurel was still staying at his place was Trahern. For her sake, he planned to keep it that way.

"Okay, I'll be gone about half an hour if you need me."

When the door shut, Devlin leaned back in his chair and closed his eyes, hoping to ease the headache that reading and the lack of sleep had given him. He couldn't help but grin, though. Last night with Laurel had been energetic to say the least. The woman must work out, because she sure as hell had stamina. After talking about the current mess, they'd managed to sleep. But then she'd nudged him awake a couple of hours later, and he'd returned the favor just before their alarm had gone off.

They'd also tried out his shower to see how it

compared to hers. Soap-slick skin and pulsating water jets had gotten his morning off to a happy start. They'd run out of hot water; he'd have to order a larger water heater as soon as things calmed down.

The idea had him reaching for the phone. It was almost six o'clock, time to check in with Laurel to see when she wanted him to pick her up. If he shared some of his ideas for the evening, she might decide that some of her work could wait until tomorrow.

He punched in her number and leaned back in his chair. The lab phone rang five times and then kicked over to her voicemail. He considered leaving a message, but there was no telling how secure the system was. The last thing he needed was Dr. Neal or one of the guards listening in.

Maybe she was in the middle of something and couldn't come to the phone. He tried her cellphone anyway. It rang once and then went immediately to voicemail.

They had agreed, when he'd dropped her off at work, that he'd check in sometime during the day. Why would she have her cell turned off? To do so was either careless or stupid, and Laurel Young was neither one of those things.

Son of a bitch, had they underestimated the bastard? It would take balls to snatch her at work, with guards and Dr. Neal likely to walk in at any minute.

He reached for his gun and then picked up his sword. If the bastard had laid a single finger on Laurel, Devlin was going to take great pleasure in carving him up in little pieces.

On the way out, he stopped to tell D.J. where he was going and why, but D.J. wasn't at his desk. Rather than wasting time hunting him down, Devlin got on the intercom and did an all-call for him.

"D.J., get your worthless butt back to your desk!"

In less than ten seconds his friend appeared at a dead run, with Lonzo and Trahern not far behind. One look at Devlin's face and D.J. withheld whatever smart-ass comment he'd been about to make.

"What's up?"

"I'm heading over to the lab to check on Dr. Young."

"Is something wrong?" Trahern pushed past Lonzo. "Do you need me to come with you?"

"I don't know yet. She's not answering either the lab phone or her cell. It could be nothing, but that isn't like her."

"You're right. It isn't." Trahern's own worry showed in the chill of his eyes. "Let me know if you need backup."

"Thanks, I will." He started for the door. "I'll call with an update as soon as I know anything."

He drove straight to the private parking garage provided for the Regents and their staff. The place was virtually empty, the day shift having gone home. No one stuck around much past 6:00 P.M. unless the barrier was acting up and wounded Paladins were expected.

After locking the car, he walked around to the

front door of the building. Once inside, his sense of unease increased geometrically when he saw the guard station was empty. Even when the guard was shorthanded, Colonel Kincade insisted that the front desk be fully manned. The guards stationed there were the first line of defense for the whole building, 24/7. Additionally, they were responsible for monitoring the cameras and microphones in security-sensitive areas like the labs.

He pulled out his cell and hit speed dial; D.J. answered on the first ring.

"The place feels empty and there are no guards at the desk. I'm going back to my car to retrieve my weapons. I'll need you to shut down the sensors long enough for me to get in without sounding the alarm. Can you do that?"

He waited impatiently while D.J. conferred with someone, most likely Cullen. What one of them couldn't do on a computer, the other could. It didn't take long. Just as he expected, D.J. promised him a minimum of sixty seconds of downtime.

"Thanks, D.J. I'll ring your phone twice when I'm ready and then count to thirty before crossing the sensors. Tell Trahern he might want to head this way."

He was relieved to hear that his friend was already on the way and should arrive shortly. More and more, his gut was telling him that something was horribly wrong.

When he returned to the lobby with his weapons, it was still deserted. He punched in D.J.'s number and disconnected after two rings. Staring at the clock on the wall, he impatiently counted down the seconds until he could safely cross. He allowed an extra ten seconds, but even so, he half expected the alarms to start clanging away.

The silence was thick with tension as he crossed to the entrance of Laurel's lab. He walked with a hunter's stealth, gun in hand. His sword hung at his side. It was only when the Paladins fought the Others that they resorted to weapons from ancient times. But here, safely distant from the fragile barrier, he preferred a more modern weapon, one that would make quick work of any son of a bitch who dared threaten his woman.

He approached the door to her lab from the side, working his way to the small windows that would allow him a quick glimpse into the room. It didn't take long to decide that the lab was empty, at least as much of it as he could see. He shoved the door open far enough to step through, holding his gun with both hands. Other than the soft mechanical whir of the lab equipment, the room was silent. And empty.

After settling the gun back in the waistband of his jeans, he started in one corner of the lab and began checking the counters and cabinets and even the empty patient beds for any sign of violence or clues as to what had happened to Laurel. The only thing in the wastebasket was the wadded-up wrapper from the sandwich he'd made for Laurel's lunch. He'd known in his gut that she wouldn't have broken her promise to remain in the building; the crumbs and plastic bag confirmed that.

He slammed his hand down on the counter in frustration. Maybe she'd been called away for a late meeting, but he'd never seen her leave her purse sitting out on the cabinet. And wouldn't she have taken her laptop?

His cellphone rang, shattering the silence. The number on the screen was Laurel's, and he knew even before he answered that something was terribly wrong.

"Bane here."

"Devlin?"

He thought her voice was a bit shaky, but the reception on the call sucked. Either she was almost out of the service area, or somewhere that interfered with electronics.

"Where are you, Laurel? And who are you with?" He kept his voice calm, pacing back and forth across the lab.

"I can't tell you that, but right now I'm fine."

Implying that she wouldn't be for long. He'd kill the bastard three times over.

"He said to tell you that he'll let you know when he wants you to join the party."

The line went dead, then his phone rang again. It was D.J,. telling him that Trahern had arrived and was about to enter the building.

The other Paladin stepped through the lab door just as Devlin stuffed the phone back in his pocket. Trahern lowered his gun and put it back in his shoulder holster, taking in the empty lab with his chilling gaze. "She's gone."

"He's got her," Devlin said.

"Other than he's a dead man, do we know anything about him?" Trahern moved closer, but kept maneuvering room between them in case of any unexpected threats.

"No. He told her to tell me that he'd let me know when I'd be invited 'to join their party.'" Images of what the bastard might have in mind for Laurel flashed through his head, making him want to howl with fury.

"So we find them first." Trahern nodded toward the laptop. "Did you check it to see if she had time to leave us a clue?"

Devlin swore and booted up the laptop. It was a pretty remote possibility, but the fact that he hadn't even thought to check worried him, because it showed how messed up he was. "No recent entries."

He pondered their choices. "Call D.J. and have him send Cullen over to check out the guard station. Maybe one of the cameras caught the bastard on film. If nothing else, he can bring up the logs to see which guards were scheduled to be on duty today."

While Trahern made the call, he forced himself to breathe deeply, searching for the battle calm that came over him just before the barrier came down and the Others came pouring through.

The barrier. There was something about the barrier. He reached over to snatch Trahern's phone out of his hand.

"D.J., did you follow up on that blip you noticed earlier? The one you said was in one of the remote tunnels?"

No, he hadn't had time to check yet, but it had only been that one time.

"Where are the tunnels located? Can you tell me that?"

D.J.'s answer had him running for the door, with Trahern right on his heels.

"Where are we going now?"

"Earlier, something triggered the sensors in a remote tunnel—remote only because it's not near the barrier, but it's right under this building. D.J.'s researching the layout to tell me how to access the tunnel from here. Otherwise we'll have to go down through the Center and backtrack. Until he calls with more information, all we can do is search."

Three hallways converged at the lobby. They picked the one on the left first because it was the shortest. The two of them did a standard search pattern, first one and then the other leading the charge into each room and office they passed. Most rooms were dark, the normal occupants obviously gone for the day.

They started down the second hallway. About halfway down, they struck pay dirt. A woman's shoe was lying near the head of a staircase, and Devlin knew even before he got a good look at it that it was Laurel's. What he didn't know was whether she was leaving him a trail to follow, or if her captor had tossed it there as a red herring.

When Trahern caught up with him, Devlin showed him the shoe. "It's Laurel's."

"Think she's the one who left it there?"

"I'd like to think so, but there's no way of telling." He considered their options. "Any idea where that staircase leads?"

Trahern gave the obvious answer. "Down."

"Thanks." Devlin set the shoe back down. "I figure the stairs are our best choice, but we should do a quick check of the rest of this floor before committing ourselves. I'll finish this end. You take the other. If D.J. calls back, I'll let you know."

It didn't take long to finish their search, which turned up nothing. The kidnapper would have been a fool to take Laurel to one of the upper floors where they could be cornered with no exits. No, they either left the building through a ground level door or found another way out. Dragging an unwilling woman, especially one missing at least one shoe, out onto a public street even for the minute or two it would take to reach a car was too risky.

That left the staircase. Devlin's phone rang just as Trahern returned. When Devlin looked at him, he shook his head. Nothing, which only confirmed what he'd suspected.

"Give me good news, D.J."

His friend's report didn't take long.

"Thanks. No, stay there. I may need you to call in the troops. We'll keep you posted when we can."

He told Trahern, "There's a climate-controlled vault on the lowest floor of the building that houses the Regent's records. According to the schematics that D.J. pulled up, the only access is through a door at the bottom of these steps, and you have to know the security codes to open it."

"I assume D.J. is taking care of that little problem for us."

Devlin shrugged. "He's going to try, but if that fails, I'll blast the fucking thing open."

"Sounds like fun."

chapter 14

*D*evlin checked his gun and the slide of his sword in his scabbard while Trahern did the same thing. When they were both ready, Devlin started down the first flight of steps. At the landing, they stopped and leapfrogged the rest of the way down, offering each other cover in case the kidnapper wasn't working alone.

When they reached the bottom, the first thing Devlin noticed was that the door to the records room was slightly ajar. He dialed D.J.

"Did you open the door? No? That's what I thought." He disconnected before D.J. could ask any questions of his own.

"Devlin, look." Trahern was pointing toward the corner.

Laurel's other shoe was lying in the shadows, almost out of sight under the staircase. That convinced him that Laurel was leaving the clues. If her captor had wanted to lay a false trail, he would have left the shoe out where

Devlin couldn't have missed it. It was definitely Laurel, trying with limited resources to lead her rescuers straight to her. He hoped she drew comfort from her faith that he'd come after her. And once he got her back, he wasn't going to let her go, come hell or high water.

But right now it was time to see what was behind door number three. "Shall we?"

Trahern nodded and followed him through the door and into the darkness.

The cold seeped into Laurel's bones as Sergeant Purefoy dragged her through an endless maze of tunnels. At first she'd tried to keep track of all the twists and turns, but gave up when she realized that his route doubled and tripled back on itself. Even if she managed to break free and escape, she had little hope of finding her way back to the elevator that had brought them down into this hell.

Just when she thought he would never stop, he took a sudden turn to the left. The abrupt change in direction almost sent her stumbling to her knees, and she fought to keep her feet. Purefoy looked down the narrow passage he'd chosen and nodded as if satisfied. Laurel couldn't see anything that distinguished it from any of the others, but didn't care. She was just glad to stop running for a few minutes. Then she saw what was tucked back against the wall and her stomach did a slow roll.

"Welcome to your new temporary home." Purefoy's mouth twisted into a nasty grin as he led her to a narrow cast-iron bed with stained mattress ticking. "I know it's not much on the amenities, but you aren't exactly here on vacation, are you?"

She yanked her hand out of his grasp. "I'd tell you to go to hell, Purefoy, but you'll get there soon enough. About five minutes after Devlin Bane gets his hands on you—if you're lucky. Otherwise, it could take hours." Her show of bravado went a long way toward bolstering her spirits. His eyes immediately flickered back the way they'd come, telling her she'd scored a hit.

"Shut up, bitch."

"Make me." She knew the minute the dare slipped out that she'd made a major tactical error. The man was already running on nerves and adrenaline. She didn't need him to add testosterone to the mix.

His hand lashed out to jerk her toward him. "I figure if you like what Bane dishes out in bed, you probably like it rough."

She could feel the heat pouring off him despite the damp chill in the air. It was a struggle to keep her voice calm. "Don't do this, Sergeant Purefoy. You know you really don't want this."

"That's where you're wrong. I want this a lot."

He ran his free hand up to her shoulder and then back down to knead her breasts hard enough to make her wince in pain. Then he cupped her bottom and squeezed, pulling her against his body. When he tried to kiss her, she jerked away at the last second. He retaliated by fisting his hand in her hair and dragging her face around to plant a wet, sloppy kiss on her mouth. When she tried to resist, he yanked her hair hard enough to make her cry out. She almost gagged when he thrust his tongue into her mouth. To make him stop, she bit down hard.

Purefoy yelped and jumped back, cursing and spitting blood. He slapped her hard enough to make her jaw ache, but at least he made no other move toward her. She'd have another bruise on her cheek, but that little bit of defiance made her feel less helpless.

"Hold out your wrist."

He dangled a pair of handcuffs in front of her face. The manic gleam in his eyes told her that he hoped she'd make him use force. She slowly lifted her hand, the sick feeling in her stomach growing worse. With a quick shove, he sent her flying back onto the bed. He straddled her and snapped a cuff onto her left hand and the other to the rusty metal headboard.

"I'd ask if you were comfortable, but once the Others find you, comfort will be the last of your worries."

He jerked on the handcuffs to make sure they were secure, then leaned down to plant another sloppy kiss. With a cheery wave, he headed back the way they'd come, leaving her alone in the damp chill of the tunnel. At first, she remained motionless, listening to the sound of his footsteps fading. Because the passageways seemed to circle around one another, she couldn't be sure that he'd really gone very far. He could just be lurking nearby to see if she tried to escape.

Why had he picked this particular location to leave her? For its remoteness and its proximity to the barrier? Although she'd seen photographs and film of the barrier, neither had done it justice. In the dim light, the luminescent wall at the far end of the tunnel glowed in a myriad of colors and shimmering textures that she knew no names for.

Her first impulse would have been to reach out and touch it if she hadn't known better. More than one of her Paladins had gotten burns from run-ins with the barrier when they were fighting. It was as deadly as it was beautiful.

She decided she didn't care what Purefoy was doing. Even if he stayed gone, there was always the chance the barrier would flicker, leaving her at the mercy of the Others. She shoved that idea to the back of her mind, refusing to let fear incapacitate her, and concentrated on trying to get free.

Her first few tugs on the handcuffs were tentative, to see if the metal had any give in it at all. The results were discouraging. With just that little bit of effort, the cuff had worn a sore place on her wrist. She struggled to sit up, finding it more difficult than she expected without the use of her hands and arms for balance. Turning to face the headboard, she braced her feet against it and jerked backward, throwing her full weight behind the effort.

Blood dripped down her forearm, but the weld

that attached the pipe to the rest of the frame didn't budge. She breathed deeply, ignoring the pain, and worked herself up to another try. This time she yanked and fell back, allowing herself to yell. Back in college, she'd taken a semester of judo where the teacher had encouraged all of the students to vocalize loudly whenever they practiced. She didn't know if it was the second try or the hollering that helped, but she felt some give in the frame.

Unfortunately, the heavier pipe itself remained intact. She wasn't sure how many more times she could try before she did serious injury to herself. On the other hand, the damp cold of the tunnel was bound to sap her strength if she remained motionless for much longer.

Setting her feet, she inhaled deeply through her nose and released the breath through her mouth. But before she could lunge, a high-pitched buzzing started, growing in intensity until it felt as if someone were stabbing her eardrums with an ice pick.

Sinking down onto the mattress, she watched in horror as the barrier pulsed with ugly splotches of color. Every so often, she thought she caught a glimpse of someone moving on the other side . . . an Other waiting to cross into her world. It had to be. And from what she knew of their general physiology, it was most likely a fully grown male.

Fear, cold and bitter tasting, crept through her. If the barrier were to fail, it wouldn't matter if Purefoy returned. An attack from an Other would play right into his plans: If he made it look as if she'd died at their hands, he might actually get away with kidnapping her. He'd left no obvious clues as to his identity.

Up until this point, she'd managed to remain focused on escaping and waiting for Devlin to find her. With this new and immediate threat, however, what should she do? Think . . . she had to think. She was used to analyzing data and then deciding on a course of action. Doing her best to ignore the buzzing, she looked at her surroundings.

The tunnel walls were uneven, as if carved directly out of stone. Someone had added a layer of concrete at one point, most likely for stability. Electrical conduits ran along the ceiling, interrupted every ten feet or so with motion-sensitive lights. She froze. Purefoy had chained her in a small offshoot of the main tunnel. If she were to quit moving completely, the lights should go inactive, leaving her cloaked in darkness.

Maybe the Other wouldn't see her if she flattened herself against the mattress to become part of the shadows. How long would it take for the lights to go off? She moved again to reactivate their sensors and then stayed still. Counting off the seconds, she waited until the dim lights began shutting down, one after the other, until there was nothing left but the sound of her own breathing and the shimmer of the barrier.

She sat up again. Immediately the lights came up to full intensity, enough so that she had to shield her eyes briefly with her arm to give them time to adjust. Something niggled at the back of her mind about the extreme brightness, something to do with Others and light. After a second or two, it hit her. The lights in the tunnels were set to flare brightly enough to make it harder for the Others to see. Once they had been on for a while, though, the lights would return to normal intensity. It wasn't much of an advantage for the Paladins, but one they made full use of.

The buzzing died away without warning, and the barrier once again returned to normal. While it was under control, she resumed her efforts to break free, knowing the respite might be brief. If the buzzing came back, she would resume her position on the bed and hope for the best.

Damn, he'd thought for sure he had brought the barrier down that time. Stepping back, Purefoy glared at the glowing wall of energy. For a few seconds it had weakened enough for objects on the other side to become visible, but not enough to interrupt the flow of the energy. Where had he gone wrong? He'd tried before to interrupt the flow by stabbing it with Bane's sword, but that hadn't worked. If he hadn't been careful enough to wear insulated gloves, the damn thing would have fried him right there on the spot. As it was, the power had burned through the outer layer of fabric, forcing him to yank his hands out of the gloves before the smoldering heat caused blisters.

This time, he'd come better prepared. After staking out his prisoner where she'd be found by an Other as soon as he brought down the barrier, he'd returned to the stash of weapons he'd secreted over the last week. The small explosion he'd just set off should have put a big enough hole in the barrier. He'd have to try again using more force. Even if it only brought the roof of the tunnel down, that might do enough damage to produce a flicker or two—enough time for the waiting Others to cross over.

Once they caught the scent of a human female, the fun and games would begin. His original plan had been to have her for himself, but with his employer growing impatient and Bane already on his trail, there wasn't time for a bit of rough sex. Once the barrier came down, every Paladin in the region would come pouring into the tunnels.

His plan depended on Bane being the first to arrive. While the Others kept the bastard busy protecting his woman, Purefoy would use a gun to bring Devlin to his knees. Once that happened, he could finish the job with a sword.

And if Laurel Young survived her first encounter with an Other, he still might be able to have some fun with her. It would serve the bitch right; his tongue still hurt where she'd bit it. Maybe after an Other used her a time or two, she'd appreciate a normal human male. Whistling tunelessly, he wiped his hands on his pants and then began the arduous process of wiring his next attempt to blow the barrier to hell and back.

For a second Devlin allowed himself to imagine how good it would feel to get his hands around his quarry's neck and squeeze until the bones snapped. That pleasure would have to wait a while, but still made him feel better. It had taken way too long to hotwire the elevator, minutes that they didn't have to waste.

He and Trahern could have rushed the job, but he didn't want to risk setting off an alarm. The rogue guard had to know that Devlin would be coming after him, and if the son of a bitch felt cornered, he might kill Laurel. So Devlin had been forced to take his time in circumventing the safeguards on the elevator controls. Each extra minute Laurel spent in her captor's clutches filled him with a cold fury.

"There, that should do it." He reattached the keypad and listened with his ear against the door. Somewhere in the depths below, he could hear the *click* and *whir* of machinery starting up. "It's on its way."

"About time." Trahern moved closer. "So what's the plan once we get down there? Should we split up or hunt together?"

"I'm figuring he has a surprise or two in store for us, so we should separate. With luck, he won't have had time to set traps everywhere. Going separate ways gives us a better chance of getting through to Laurel."

Trahern nodded. "If I catch him first, can I kill him or do I have to save that little pleasure for you?"

"I want him to wish he'd never been born, but we've got bigger problems than him. And if he dies, everything he knows dies with him." The elevator *ping*ed softly and the doors slid open. Devlin motioned for Trahern to stand back while he entered the elevator first. When nothing happened, he nodded for his friend to join him. "This guy is at the bottom of the food chain and on somebody's payroll. I want to know who's on top, forking out the money and playing both sides against the middle."

"So we catch him and convince him to talk first." The corner of Trahern's mouth quirked up in a small grin that showed lots of teeth. "Then we kill him."

Devlin smiled back at him. "That's the plan."

"Works for me."

In all the years he'd served in the Northwest, Devlin had never spent much time in this particular end of the maze of tunnels that hugged the length of the barrier through Puget Sound. The area this far north rarely had much seismic activity, although someone was always saying Seattle was due for the big one.

That's all they needed right now. Even the slightest shift in the plates could bring the barrier down long enough to let the Others through. He wouldn't even let himself think about what would happen to Laurel at their hands. It was the main reason that the Regents had a hard-line policy against allowing women down in the tunnels. In fact, as far as he knew, there had never been a female Paladin; he'd always assumed that the Y chromosome had something to do with it.

If he lived through the night, maybe he'd ask Laurel if that was the case. It had never been a particular concern of his because he'd never had unprotected sex; the complication of getting someone pregnant had held no appeal for him. But he and Laurel had skated the edge of carelessness a couple of times. They were both old enough to know better, but the sex between them burned so damn hot that common sense came in a poor second.

The *ping* of the elevator door signaled their arrival at the bottom, just as an image flashed through his mind of Laurel huge with child—his child, their child. The very thought should scare him, but he found himself grinning.

Trahern was staring at him as if he'd grown a second head. "I don't know where your mind is, Devlin, but it better be right here in this elevator with me. When that door opens, who knows what kind of mess we'll be walking into."

"Don't worry. I'm here."

He brought up his pistol, and each of them moved to stand as far out of sight as they could. Only a fool would stand right in front of the door and offer himself up as a target. When there was no immediate attack, Devlin nodded at Trahern that he'd take point. He dropped low and rolled out of the door and back up on to his feet, ready to fire if necessary. Trahern followed close on his heels.

Their motion set off the lights. From years of practice, both of them automatically focused their eyes on the floor, away from the blinding brightness. It wouldn't take long for their eyes to adjust, but for a few seconds they were vulnerable.

"See if they left any trail that way. I'll check in this direction."

Trahern arched an eyebrow. "How many shoes do you think your woman carries around, just in case she needs to leave a trail?"

"Very funny."

Before either of them could move, a wave of energy rolled toward them from the left. Devlin braced his feet wide and stood with his head tilted forward as if leaning into a strong wind, while Trahern did the same. When it had blown past them, he shook his head to clear it.

"What the hell was that?" Trahern stared beyond them, as if expecting a repeat performance.

"My guess is someone is messing with the barrier—most likely our kidnapper."

"Only a damn fool would risk bringing it down. If we're right about this guy being one of the Guard, you'd think he's seen enough of what the Others can do to know better."

"Yeah, but you're assuming this guy is sane. He's the same one who thinks he's going to live long enough to actually spend whatever he's getting to take me out. That alone proves he's three kinds of crazy, but we're going to need help if he does manage to bring it down. There's no telling how far the damage will stretch."

He dug in his pocket for his cellphone, but they

were too far down underground to get reception. "Shit! You'll need to go back and get help. An energy burst like that could have taken down the entire grid of sensors, so they're probably working blind up there."

Trahern obviously didn't like the idea of leaving Devlin alone, but the barrier had to take precedence over the life of one woman or even a Paladin. That was the one truth they lived with.

The tunnel remained quiet. "Go ahead and go. It feels like the barrier held, but he might not be satisfied with one attempt."

"I'll be right behind you as soon as I get back up top and call in."

"I know. Tell Cullen to come from the other end. I want to make sure we catch the bastard between us."

"Will do."

The two of them set off in opposite directions. As he ran, Devlin sent up a prayer to the God he rarely even thought about, asking that He keep Laurel safe. At least until Devlin got there and could take over the job.

The buzzing was back. Already Laurel could see the shadow pacing back and forth on the other side. Fear burned at the back of her throat. Forcing herself to remain calm, she resumed her deliberate attempts to break free of her bonds. The pieces of rusty metal were finally starting to separate. If she could just get it to move a little farther, she might be able to work the joint free.

The humming grew worse, making her ears hurt again. Time was running out. She wrapped her hands around the pipe, closed her eyes to concentrate all of her strength, and tried to turn the pipe. It gave a minute fraction of an inch, but it definitely moved. She tried again and then again. Small flakes of rust rained down on her hands, and it came loose!

Now she just had to bend it down far enough to slide the handcuff chain over the top. And if she could work a piece of the pipe free, it would be a weapon. Several sweaty minutes later, she held a two-foot length of pipe in her hands.

It was time to leave.

The barrier had grown thinner; the clear, vivid colors she'd seen earlier had faded to a muddy tan streaked with sickly green and black. It looked poisoned, as if the beautiful colors had become tainted. And the shadow was no longer a blank silhouette. She could almost make out the features of the Other standing vigil on the other side. As she moved, his head turned, warning her that he could see her just as well—perhaps even better—because she'd triggered the lights in the larger tunnel.

She needed to run, but which direction should she go? Devlin would have found her shoes by now and knew where to start his search. If he used the same elevator, then she wanted to be moving toward him, not away. On the other hand, Purefoy had gone in that same direction.

Going the other way might have its own dangers, ones she couldn't even begin to fathom. Deciding she was better off risking a run-in with Purefoy than an untold number of Others, should the barrier continue to weaken, she sidled past the spot where the Other waited. Once she passed that point, she kept her back to the wall and moved slowly forward. She was already lost; all that mattered now was not being right where Purefoy expected her to be.

As she turned the first corner an explosion shattered the air, the concussion making the world around her heave and roll. She watched in horror as the barrier flickered and then disappeared altogether. A heartbeat later, a pool of blackness, inky and thick, rolled through her mind, and the floor rushed up to meet her.

"Son of a bitch!" Devlin sat next to the wall and waited for the nausea and dizziness to pass. He didn't know what had just happened, but it was bad. He felt as if he'd been flayed alive, because someone had ripped the barrier out by its roots.

He braced himself against the wall and tried to push himself to his feet. It took two tries before he succeeded, and even then he knew the slightest wrong move would land him flat on his face again. Ever so slowly, he stooped to retrieve his sword, aware that he'd be damn lucky if he could even lift it.

Then he felt his way along the tunnel, hoping that his head would clear in time for him to help Laurel.

He didn't let himself think about what the blast might have done to her, closer to the center of the explosion. She was all right. She *had* to be.

The first stirrings of consciousness brought Laurel the unwelcome news that she was no longer alone in the tunnel. She could hear someone moving around, but as far as she could tell she had yet to be spotted. She pushed herself up to her knees and then to her feet. What had caused the explosion?

It had to have been Purefoy, although why he would want to destroy the barrier was beyond her. Did he want their world to become inundated with Others? What good would that do? It appeared that only one Other had crossed in the near vicinity, but that one was headed her way.

The tunnel split ahead. Which way to go? She picked the right hand side because it was dark; something had shut down the power in that particular offshoot. The shadowed entrance was her one hope for refuge from the terror that stalked her.

She reached the darkness just in time. She could hear the steady approach of the Other coming her way. Raising the pipe over her head, she waited until he reached the split in the tunnel. He paused just out of sight, no doubt trying to decide which path to take. What was he doing? It sounded as if he were sniffing the air. With their limited eyesight in the brightness of her world, did they rely on their sense of smell more than humans did?

"Female human, come out." The guttural sound of his voice sent shivers up her spine.

She'd already been the prisoner of one man; she wasn't about to put herself in that position again. Maybe she could catch him off guard.

"I'm coming out. Don't hurt me." She injected as much fear into her voice as she could. Let the fool think she was broken and ready to surrender. Instead she charged out of the tunnel, her pipe swinging around to take her would-be captor by surprise. It worked. Her makeshift club connected with the Other's head with a sickening thud.

A low groan told her that she hadn't killed him. Throwing caution to the wind, she charged down the tunnel, running full tilt. When she turned the corner, she saw the last person she ever wanted to see again. Skidding to a stop, she looked for an escape route, but Purefoy had already seen her. He waved his gun at the pipe in her hand. When she didn't immediately drop it, he pulled the trigger. The bullet ricocheted off the wall by her face, sending rock chips flying and startling her into dropping the pipe at her feet with a loud clang.

"Well, Dr. Young, looks like you've been busy since I last saw you." Purefoy closed the distance between them and grabbed her, his fingers digging into her arm hard enough to leave bruises. He pulled out the key for the handcuffs and quickly snapped the loose end onto her other wrist.

"It also looks like my plan to leave you to the tender mercies of the Others met with failure. And I had such high hopes, too."

"Sorry to disappoint you, Sergeant."

"Well, he can't have been the only one to cross over. And with the barrier still down, there's still hope." He dragged her back to where he'd chained her before.

"You know you won't get away with this. As soon as you damaged the barrier, every Paladin within a hundred miles knew it. If I were you, I'd get the heck out of Dodge while you have a chance."

"And I bet you think I should leave you behind so I can travel faster." He laughed. "The only way I'll leave you behind is if you're dead. Of course, if that's what you want . . ."

A guttural voice said, "Only a coward hides behind an unarmed female, human."

The Other she'd clobbered was waiting for them a short distance down the tunnel. A small trickle of dark blood on his cheek was the only sign that she'd hurt him. He stood leaning against the wall, but his relaxed stance was deceptive. When he moved to block their passage, he brought his sword up in a two-handed grip that seemed second nature to him.

"Human female, step away from him."

Purefoy's grip on her arm tightened. "Get the hell out of my way or die where you stand." At least now he was aiming his gun at the Other rather than at her.

The alien male looked remarkably unconcerned. "Only a coward kills from a distance. I like the feel of my sword slicing into an enemy's gut."

Laurel shuddered. His rough, low pronunciation took all of her concentration to follow. But there was no mistaking the deadly threat he represented. Despite his pallor, he was striking looking, with long hair the color of tarnished silver and eyes only a shade or two lighter. Dressed in unrelenting black from head to toe, he reminded her of a villain straight out of an old black-and-white horror film.

Purefoy risked a quick glance back down the tunnel behind him. If he pulled the trigger, he might very well kill the Other, but any Paladin in the area would come running. She felt his weight shift slightly, warning her that he'd made his decision.

In a surprise move, he turned the gun on her, pressing it against her temple. "Drop the sword or she dies now."

The flat calm of Purefoy's voice sent chills through her. Did the Other understand enough about humans to recognize that Purefoy's words weren't a threat, but a promise? As she counted off what could be the last seconds of her life, it grieved her to know that Devlin would most likely be the one to find her body.

"What's it going to be? Your sword or the woman's life?"

The Other's eyes met Laurel's for a brief second. Had that been regret in the silver of his eyes? The clang of metal hitting stone echoed through the tunnel as his sword hit the ground. The Other held his hands out to the side to show he was now harmless—

not that she believed it. She'd been around too many Paladins not to recognize a trained warrior when she saw one. Unfortunately, that was equally true for Purefoy. He calmly pointed his gun at the Other and pulled the trigger.

She screamed as the Other collapsed on the ground with blood pouring out of his leg. Her captor shoved her toward the wounded man.

"Get him up on his feet. We're bringing him with us."

"I can't lift him with my hands cuffed together." She didn't know if that was true or not, but it was worth trying.

"Fine." Purefoy pulled the small key from his pocket and threw it on the ground next to her. "Get moving. I want to be gone before your lover shows up."

She considered fumbling with the key to delay their departure, but Purefoy was clearly running on the edge. It wouldn't take much to push him over. They both knew he was a dead man if Devlin caught up with him, regardless of whether Laurel was still breathing. She was a bargaining chip and nothing more.

The key worked on the second try. Before she could start on the other cuff, Purefoy demanded the key back.

"Now get him moving."

Ignoring Purefoy, she studied the Other's bleeding leg. "How bad is it?" she asked.

"I will walk."

He avoided her touch by trying to stand on his own. His attempt failed miserably. She wasn't about to let him hurt himself worse out of stubborn pride. They may be from opposing worlds, but at this moment they were bound together by their common enemy.

"I need to bind his leg or he'll bleed out, Sergeant." She glared up at their captor. "I don't know what you have in mind for the two of us, but dead, he won't be any good to anyone. Besides, blood makes for an easy trail to follow."

Without waiting for his approval, she looked around for something she could use as a bandage. Finally, Purefoy pulled a handkerchief from his pocket and tossed it to her.

"Here, but make it fast."

"I'll need your uniform tie, too." She offered her reluctant patient a tentative smile. "I'm a doctor. Let me see the wound."

He tugged up the cuff of his pants far enough to reveal a well-muscled leg with a nasty hole through the meat of the calf. He winced when he tried to straighten his leg. Just that quickly, he ceased to be anything but a wounded patient who needed her care. A quick examination told her that the bullet had gone straight through the muscle. It was still bleeding, but at least that would have cleaned the wound.

"I think it will heal, with care." After she wrapped the cotton handkerchief around his leg, she used the tie to bind it in place and to keep pressure on both sides of the wound. She tried not to think about the possible contamination from touching his Otherworld clothing and skin.

"That should hold for a while. I wish I could do better, but I have no medical supplies with me."

"Your efforts honor me." The Other gave her a grave nod and then accepted her assistance in standing up. He couldn't hide the wince of pain when he put weight on his leg, but then he stood straight and tall.

"All right, move on out." Purefoy prodded her with his gun. He'd also picked up the Other's sword. "We need to be out of here."

Her stomach clenched. "What have you done, Sergeant?"

"I left a little surprise for your lover."

The smug look on his face made her want to smack him. "You're just piling up reasons for him to take you down, Purefoy."

"Not if I kill him first."

She shook her head. "You forget—even if you kill him, he won't stay that way. Eventually he'll be right back on your trail, and Devlin gets testy when someone kills him. But you know that, don't you? You've already killed him once."

"Shut up, bitch."

"Of course, then there are all those other Paladins. I suspect that Trahern's a nasty enemy to have. And the last time Lonzo died, it took six of us to hold him down long enough to restrain him."

She didn't know why she felt compelled to keep

jerking his chain, but she did. Every second he spent reacting to her taunts was one he wasn't concentrating so hard on his plans. Besides, if she was going to die, she wanted her killer to be fully aware that his own hours were ticking away as the Paladins hunted him down like the vermin he was.

The Other stoically marched on beside her. Unless his kind were immune to pain, each step had to be agony, but he gave no sign of it. She never thought to admire anything about an Other, and the unexpected feeling was jarring. Far too many of the Paladins had suffered at their hands for her to see the Others as anything but the enemy. But the man next to her had shown himself to be far from the murdering animal she'd expected.

Surely he wasn't typical of his kind.

"What's your name?" she asked softly. "I'm Laurel Young."

The Other had his eyes trained on the ground ahead of them, as if it took every bit of his concentration to keep moving. After a few steps he glanced toward her, his silver gray eyes bracketed by lines of pain. "Barak."

She surprised them both by smiling. "I am pleased to meet you, Barak. Is that your complete name?"

He immediately turned his attention back to the floor. "It is all that is left of who I was and no longer am."

She wanted to ask what he meant, but Purefoy interrupted them. "You two quit talking. You're here to die, not to become best buddies."

Since Barak showed little inclination to continue the conversation anyway, she fell silent. After a bit, she asked, "Where are we headed? Or is your plan to wander around in this maze until the Paladins find us or you manage to find a door somewhere?"

She was disappointed that he didn't rise to the bait. Instead, he prodded her with Barak's sword. "Veer left."

It was another dead end, almost indistinguishable from the one where he'd chained her earlier. Once they reached the back, she and Barak slowly turned to face Purefoy. With their backs to the wall, she was uncomfortably reminded of pictures of a firing squad. Her thoughts must have shown on her face, because Purefoy laughed.

"Tell you what, Laurel. Show me a little of that same heat you've been generating with Bane, and I might just let you live."

"Not in this lifetime."

"Then chain yourself to your new buddy. I'm sure Bane will love finding his woman in the arms of his worst enemy." Then he tipped his head to one side. "Actually, I guess I'm his worst enemy now."

When she didn't immediately fasten the loose cuff to Barak, Purefoy moved within carving range and raised the sword. "Now, Laurel, or I'll start hacking away. Think Bane will still want you cut up and ugly?"

"Paladins are warriors. He will understand valor even if you do not, human." Barak moved to stand slightly in front of Laurel. "It is easier to fight an un-armed female than to use that on a male. Give me my sword back, and we will see who gets carved up."

Purefoy started to back away and then caught himself. "Chain yourself to the woman, you freak, or I'll shoot your other leg—for starters."

Each minute they kept Purefoy occupied gave Devlin more time to find them, but she wouldn't let Barak get shot just to avoid being chained to her.

She snapped the cuff in place before he could react. "Now what?"

"Turn around and sit down."

For the first time, she noticed there was a line right down the middle of the narrow passage. It looked as if it had been etched there, arrow straight, by a laser, and she realized the barrier itself had cut through the rock. And if they were sitting on that line when the Paladins restored the energy, the two of them would die.

There had already been brief flashes of light along the passage, as if the barrier were flickering back to life. Purefoy started to move away, but in a sudden move he clubbed Barak on the side of the head with the butt of his pistol. The Other slumped against her shoulder and slid back onto the floor.

Laurel braced herself for a similar attack, but Purefoy backed away.

"Dragging an unconscious animal along with you should slow you down. I'd love to stay and watch, but I need to leave." He tipped his head and listened. "I should have just enough time to get in position to watch it all come down."

A few minutes later the lights went out, leaving her in the dark—waiting to see if death or Devlin would be the first one to find her and her silent companion.

chapter 15

$\mathcal{D}$evlin had been cursing for the past fifteen minutes as he figured out how to get around the mess in front of him. The son of a bitch was clever, he had to give him that. Half a dozen or more laser lights were angled across the narrowest point of the tunnel, forming a tangled web. If they hadn't resonated on a frequency close to the barrier's, he wouldn't have even realized they were there. One more step would have triggered whatever little present his enemy had left for him.

The lasers served as a solid wall, trapping him on one side and Laurel on the other. In all those action movies, people always came up with some clever way to avoid the lights—either mirrors or smoke or convoluted body movements that would make a gymnast look clumsy. Unfortunately, he was fresh out of all those things. The best he could hope for was that the lasers weren't hooked up to the current and their batteries would die.

Devlin considered his predicament from all sides.

Within seconds, it hit him: Lasers were energy, and
like all Paladins, he had an affinity for manipulating
the pulsating energy that formed the barrier. Could
he do the same with these narrow beams of light?

He closed his eyes and reached out with his mind
to find them. As his breathing slowed, he felt their
faint but steady flow crisscrossing the passageway.
Bracing himself for the worst, he willed the upper-
most beam to move, bending its path to a point a few
inches higher up the wall.

Success! He rolled his shoulders and ignored the
beads of sweat dripping into his eyes. When the light
beam remained stable, he went back to work, taking
his time with each small adjustment until he'd managed to create enough room to slide under. It would
be a close fit, but he didn't have time to do more. His
fellow Paladins had to be working on restoring the
barrier. If it were to flash back on, the power surge
could be enough to detonate the trap anyway. Worse,
even if *he* managed to avoid triggering the explosion,
Trahern could blunder into it. Using his knife blade,
he scratched the word "laser" in the floor a short distance back and laid the knife down where Trahern
would be sure to see it. It wasn't much of a warning,
but it was the best he could do.

Then he knelt down on the floor and slid his
sword and his gun under the lasers to test the stability of the changes he'd made. When nothing happened, he stretched out on the floor and began
carefully pushing himself along the uneven floor,
knowing that death hovered only a fraction of an inch

over his head. The rasp of his shirt and jeans sliding over the stone echoed in his ears, making him wish even his buttons were thinner. His size had always been an advantage in battle, but right now he'd give anything to have Cullen's slender build. Inch by inch, he crept forward. At the end, he turned his feet out to the sides and dug in hard, shoving himself that last little bit to freedom.

Safely on the other side, he rested against the blessed coolness of the floor, wishing he could stay there longer. Working with energy always drained him, but rest would come later, when he had Laurel safe.

The tunnels in this area seemed to twist and turn more than most, which was both good and bad. He could run for only short distances before pausing to listen when the tunnel veered off sharply enough so that he couldn't see past the turn. It also meant that he wasn't exposed for long distances with no cover.

A flash of light on his right caught his attention. The barrier was struggling back to life. Trahern must have gotten through to Cullen and the others, so that problem was solved. Bit by bit, they'd piece the barrier back together. He could only hope that the unexpected interruption had caught the Others by surprise, too, so that huge numbers hadn't been waiting to cross. But that was someone else's problem, not his.

The barrier flickered again, this time with more substance. Based on the usual pattern, it should come back full strength within the next couple of attempts, which meant he needed to put serious distance between him and the trap in a hurry. Even if the barrier didn't stay up, there was probably enough energy in it now to set it off. He took off at a dead run just as the tunnel lit up with a brilliant surge of light. The resulting explosion wasn't long in coming, but he'd managed to put another couple of turns between him and the worst of the damage.

But his would-be killer didn't know that. As the rumbling died away, Devlin waited, hoping that his enemy wouldn't be able to resist the urge to check. Sure enough, the sound of footsteps whispered through the air so softly that if he hadn't been listening so hard he would have missed them.

He eased forward to peek around the corner and immediately jerked back out of sight. At last he knew the identity of his enemy—Sergeant Purefoy. What had he ever done to him? Hell, he'd gone out of his way to be cooperative with the sneaking little bastard whenever he could. Whatever the man's reasons were for coming after Devlin and his woman, he hoped they were worth dying for.

He listened again, but the footsteps were receding. Damn, he'd hoped the fool would come charging down the tunnel. Instead, he'd disappeared back down the way he'd come, probably to check on his hostage. With his sword in one hand and his gun in the other, Devlin charged forward, determined to reach the other end of the straightaway before Purefoy returned on another scouting mission.

A shot rang out before he'd made it little more

than halfway. He dove for the ground and rolled to the side, dropping his sword to free up one hand to control his landing. Two more bullets ricocheted past him as he scrambled forward, not even considering the possibility of retreat.

"Stay back, Bane, or I'll finish your woman off right now."

"I wouldn't if I were you, Purefoy. She's the only reason you're still breathing." Devlin duck walked another few feet, stopping only a body length away from the final turn in the tunnel. "Turn her loose and I'll give you a head start."

"Not unless I take her with me for insurance, in case your friends are waiting at the other end." His voice sounded farther away this time.

If the bastard had gone to ground, chances were Laurel was close by. Purefoy knew right where Devlin was, so stealth was no longer needed.

He bellowed her name at the top of his lungs, knowing his voice would carry down the tunnel. "Laurel!"

The only response was a muffled sound some distance away.

Cocking his head, he couldn't decide if that had been her answering or not. He tried again.

"Devlin, I'm here!"

This time he was sure it was her voice, but the yelp of pain that followed right on its heels made his blood run cold and his temper hot.

He made sure his gun was fully loaded and retrieved his sword; then he ran full out. He made it to the end of another straight stretch with no sight of his quarry, and he hardly slowed as he rounded the corner. Nothing and no one. The path ahead split in two, one side veering off to the left; the other led closer to the barrier.

Purefoy wouldn't be that stupid, would he? Maybe. Even probably. If he'd stashed Laurel somewhere that would trap her on the wrong side of the barrier, he knew Devlin would sacrifice himself to bring her back. If he couldn't kill Devlin himself, he'd let the Others do it for him.

The barrier continued to flicker and flame.

There was no turning back.

If he were wrong, there'd be plenty of time to check it out. But the seconds were ticking away before the Paladins restored the barrier to full strength. Bracing himself for the worst, he stepped into the right tunnel and marched forward.

"Laurel!"

This time the answer was clear and immediate. "Devlin!"

He could just make her out crouching on the human side of the tunnel. Someone else was on the ground next to her. Purefoy stood beyond her, clearly planning on using her as a shield.

"Stop right there, Bane." Purefoy grabbed Laurel by the hair and pressed his gun to her temple in warning, then he pointed it right at Devlin's chest. "One more step and she's dead."

"What's the point of winning this little game if you're dead, too?" Devlin kept his voice low, as if only mildly curious about the answer. Inside, he was dying.

"If you had stayed dead the first time, Paladin, I wouldn't have had to drag her into this."

"So it's my fault you're a screw up?"

"Shut up, Bane, and back out of this tunnel. Let us out of here, and I'll turn her loose as soon as it's safe."

"Don't do it, Devlin. He's got me chained to an Other who is unconscious. He can't drag us both with him."

Son of a bitch, could it get any worse? If the Other regained consciousness, there was no telling how he'd react. He was already dealing with one crazy; he didn't need another one. He'd settle that problem with a single shot to the Other's head, but he couldn't risk hitting Laurel.

Purefoy shifted from foot to foot, clearly on edge. "What's it going to be, Bane? Her life or my freedom?"

Devlin shrugged and hoped Laurel would find it in her to forgive him. "My job is to protect the barrier, Purefoy, and you managed to bring it down. For that, you die here and now."

"I don't believe you. She means too much to you."

Devlin forced himself to laugh. "Don't be stupid. You've been around Paladins long enough to know that we go through women like water. If you want her, take her, but you have to get past me."

He widened his stance and waited. He didn't have to wait long.

Purefoy shrieked out his frustration and lowered the gun.

"Laurel, drop!" Devlin yelled, to get a clear shot at the desperate Guardsman. She did as he ordered, but even as she flattened down, the dark form next to her surged to his feet and threw himself between Laurel and Purefoy, sending the Guardsman sprawling. Devlin pulled the trigger at the same time Purefoy did, the flashes of gunfire blending in with a powerful flash of light that ran the length of the tunnel.

Purefoy's scream died abruptly as the barrier cut through him, leaving him half in this world, half in the dark world, and dead in both. The echoes of the gunshots died away, leaving only the healthy hum of the barrier to fill the silence.

Devlin surged forward to pull Laurel back into the safety of his arms, but she fought him off with her free hand.

"Laurel, you know I didn't mean any of what I said to him."

She gave him a disgusted look as she struggled to get closer to the Other. "I'm not stupid, Devlin, but right now I've a bigger problem on my hands. Barak's been shot."

"So what? He's an Other. He knew when he crossed the barrier that he was a dead man."

"He saved my life, Devlin. I'm not leaving him here to die in this godforsaken place." Then she lifted her arm. "Besides, I'm chained to him. Where I go, he goes."

"Where's the damn key?"

He wished he could take back the question when Laurel turned toward the half of Purefoy that lay on their side of the barrier. Her complexion took on a decidedly green cast, and she swallowed hard several times.

Her voice quavered when she spoke. "It's in one of his pockets."

Devlin moved to block her view as he patted down the pockets he could still reach, being careful to avoid coming in contact with the barrier. He found the small key in the front pocket of Purefoy's pants. His own stomach was feeling pretty damn queasy when he realized the two halves of Purefoy were no longer connected.

He wiped the blood off the key on Purefoy's leg before handing it over to Laurel.

"If I undo this, will you help me get him out of here?"

He'd promise her the moon and the stars if it would get them both away from the macabre sight behind him. "I'll carry him for you. Let's just get the hell out of here."

Her answering smile went a long way toward melting the core of fear he'd been living with since he'd realized she had been taken. As soon as she stood free, he lifted the Other off the floor, draping the grayish arm around his shoulders and all but dragging him down the passageway. Laurel did her best to help once the path widened enough for them to walk abreast.

The welcome sound of running feet greeted them when they reached the main passage. Devlin stopped and eased his unwanted burden down to the ground. Laurel immediately knelt down and began checking the Other for wounds. The sight made him sick.

"He's not human, Laurel. His kind is bad for our world."

"That may be true. But more than once, he did his best to save me from Purefoy, and he didn't have to do that. I won't let you or anyone else hurt him."

Damn, he was afraid of that. He'd been trying to convince himself that the Other's attack on Purefoy had been a fluke, not a deliberate attempt to save Laurel. He owed the Other a debt he could never repay, especially with a bullet or a sword.

"This is going to cause all kinds of problems with the Regents, not to mention the Paladins. None of them are going to like having their favorite doctor fussing over an Other."

"His name is Barak."

"Damn it, Laurel, he's not a pet who followed you home. You can't keep him." He cupped her face with his hand. "The best you can hope for is getting him stable and then shoving him across to his side the next time the barrier goes down."

The Other groaned and struggled to sit up. "Kill me now, human. I will not go back."

Devlin glared down at his enemy. "I can't. If I kill you, she'll kill me." Either literally or by leaving.

It didn't help his mood any when Barak smiled and shook his head.

Trahern was leading the charge down the tunnel straight toward them. As glad as Devlin was to see them, he raised his sword and prepared to defend the woman he loved and a half-dead Other.

It had been touch and go for a while, but she'd finally gotten Barak stabilized. Since no one had ever treated an injured Other, it had been mostly guesswork and luck that she'd managed to bring the bleeding under control. His blood was too different for her to risk giving him transfusions, so she had pumped him full of saline IVs.

Dr. Neal came in just as she was pulling off her gloves.

"How is your patient?"

"Stable for now." She put her hands on her waist and stretched from side to side, trying to ease some of the stiffness from going too long without rest. "We'll know more by morning."

Dr. Neal picked up Barak's chart. "It would help if we knew what normal was for one of his kind. But as long as the readings don't go haywire, I'm guessing he'll pull through."

He peered over the top of his glasses at her. "And you, young lady, have a lot to answer for."

"I couldn't let Barak die, not when he saved my life." That was true, but she also knew that her patient wasn't what Dr. Neal was referring to.

"When were you going to tell me that you've become . . . shall we say, involved with Devlin Bane?"

He sounded more disappointed than angry. "I can't help you if I don't know the problem exists."

"I know, but—"

"No buts, Laurel. We all get attached to our allotted Paladins, but I suspect you've gone way beyond that. The minute you knew that your feelings for Devlin Bane were no longer what a doctor feels for a favorite patient, you should have come straight to me." There was anger in his voice now.

"And I would have, but there was no time. And then there were his improving test scores. I was afraid someone new might not follow up on them."

He arched an eyebrow and pursed his lips. "Are you saying the rest of us are slipshod when it comes to the long-term care of our patients?"

That was exactly what she'd been thinking, at least on some level. "I'm sorry, sir, but I know the changes are important. Think what it could mean to someone like Trahern if the damage could be reversed. Maybe the changes are unique to Devlin, but maybe not."

"And that is the only reason you aren't being transferred out of here." He glanced past her to Barak. "Not to mention him. You have to know that Colonel Kincade and the Regents will be watching your research very carefully, as will I."

"I know."

"Devlin Bane won't be an easy man to live with, Laurel, but I have an enormous amount of respect for him. I hope he makes you happy."

He threw his arms around her in a surprise hug. "Tell that young man of yours that I owe him a debt of gratitude for bringing you back safely. Now go home and get some rest. Tomorrow will be soon enough to start taking a closer look at the scan results. I'll keep an eye on Barak for you, but once the Regents catch wind of his presence here, there's no telling how they'll react. Just be forewarned."

"Thank you, sir. For everything."

She trudged out the door. Tomorrow she'd be better prepared to do battle again.

It worried her that she hadn't seen Devlin after he and Trahern had lifted Barak onto the lab table. Every time she closed her eyes, she felt the terror she'd experienced watching her lover face down his friends to protect a creature they had been born to hate. He'd done it, though. Trahern and Cullen had finally lifted Barak between them, leaving Devlin free to lead Laurel to the elevator.

When they reached the top, she stepped out into the fresh air, feeling suddenly free of the burden of the entire Earth pressing down on her. It gave her a new appreciation for what Devlin and the other Paladins faced on a daily basis.

With his usual efficiency, Cullen had called ahead for transportation to take her and the wounded Other to her lab. Trahern and Devlin had made the trip with her. She could only hope her insistence on protecting Barak wouldn't permanently damage her rapport with her assigned Paladins. But that was something else she would worry about later.

She tossed her bloodstained lab coat in the laundry bin on her way out. When she reached the lobby, it was divided with nervous-looking guards on one side and one very large Paladin on the other. Just that quickly, her world righted itself. She walked straight into Devlin's arms, no longer caring who saw them.

"Take me home." She snuggled against his chest, needing his warmth and strength.

"My place or yours?" His words rumbled through his chest.

"Yours."

The short distance to Devlin's house seemed to take forever. His silence bothered her. Once they were inside, safe from the rest of the world, she'd find out what was wrong.

He all but carried her into the house, kicking the door shut behind them. He walked straight through to set her down in the bathroom. Still looking decidedly grim, he set about stripping off her clothes. She let him take care of her and then waited patiently for him to get naked, too. After setting the water on full blast and steaming hot, he picked her up again and stepped into the shower. Then there was nothing between them but heat and hot kisses. Devlin took her fast and hard, driving them both over the edge with pounding thrusts that filled her body and her heart.

Devlin feared he'd been rough with her, and for that he was sorry, but they'd both been out of control with need. Afterward they stood under the showerhead for a long time, letting the water wash away the twin stains of death and fear. Finally, he'd turned the shower off and reached for a towel. As he dried Laurel's skin, he quietly checked her from head to toe. The bruises on her face and the abrasions on her wrists made him sick, but he was relieved to see her injuries were minor. She tolerated his first aid attempts without complaint. Then he led her to his bed and tucked her in next to him, not wanting even the thickness of a T-shirt between them. Resting his forehead against hers, he tried to find the right words.

"I almost lost you." Even now, that fear left a mark on him, one that no amount of soap and scrubbing would erase.

"I'm right here." She smiled up at him. "I knew you'd come for me."

"I almost didn't make it. Purefoy was a smart bastard. Smarter than I would have given him credit for."

"Not that smart, Devlin, or he never would have tried to go after you." Her hands slid up his arms to his shoulders. "Someone was paying him."

"That's what I figured. The question is who, but I don't want to think about that now."

She slid her hand down his chest to his belly, and then down some more. With a siren's smile, she curled her fingers around the hard length of him and gently squeezed, the little tease. "Then what do you want to think about?"

He caught her hand and pulled it back up to where he could keep an eye on it. "We need to talk about what I said down in the tunnel . . . about Paladins and women."

Some of the light in her eyes died. "I've heard more than enough about that subject. I don't care about your past, Devlin."

But she did; he could hear it in her voice. "I won't lie to you, Laurel; I've known my fair share of women. But until you, I've never fallen in love, and I've never asked a woman to marry me."

He kissed her long and hard. Both of them were short of breath when he broke it off. "I saved those for you."

He lifted her up to straddle him. "Will you love me back and be my wife?"

She smiled down at him as she rose up to take him deep inside her body. "I will, on both counts."

He decided there was no more need for words. After all, he'd always been a man of action.

epilogue

*T*he phone rang again. He had ignored it the first half dozen times, but avoiding his angry superior wouldn't make the man go away. Bracing himself for the worst, he picked up the receiver. As soon as he identified himself, his boss went on the attack.

"We've got more problems—besides the fact that you obviously picked the wrong man for the task."

"Purefoy was a regrettable mistake, sir, but this time I'll personally make sure Devlin dies and stays that way." Though now that Bane knew he was a target, he'd be harder to corner than ever.

His superior sniffed. "Forget him. He's too busy screwing himself blind with that doctor woman to notice what's going on around him. He's not our biggest problem right now."

"Then what is?"

Silence hung heavily. His superior would start talking when he was ready and not a second before.

"Trahern made some unfortunate phone calls."

That unwelcome news made him want to cuss loud and long. "What do you want me to do?"

"Handle it, damn it. I don't care how, but handle it."

"It could get messy. Trahern's friend has connections in high places. Besides, the judge is squeaky clean and always has been."

"Then make him look dirty, and take the bastard out before he causes us any trouble."

"Yes, sir. Consider it done."

The phone line remained open but silent again. Finally, his superior spoke again. "You've failed me once. Don't do so again."

The finality of the *click* on the other end of the line sent a chill up his spine, but he ignored it. There was no time for fear in his life—not when he had plans to make and people to kill.

He reached for a pad of paper and began making notes.

**Pocket Books
proudly presents**

Dark Defender

The next thrilling novel
by Alexis Morgan

Turn the page for a preview of
Dark Defender. . . .

"Come on, honey, let's go on up to the room," Trahern told Brenna. "I can bring in our luggage later. Right now I've got other plans for us."

She was appalled when he actually winked at the cute little blonde behind the counter. Lord save her from women who giggled. Then he had the nerve to wrap his long arm around her shoulder and all but drag her toward the elevator, as if he couldn't wait to get her alone.

Once the elevator doors closed, Brenna jerked free from his embrace. Some of the makeup she'd slathered on to disguise her bruises had left a streak on his shirt, which pleased her.

"What was *that* all about?" she asked angrily.

"Hotels find it odd when customers have no luggage. I don't have anything but the bare essentials with me and you have nothing. If she thinks we're in a hurry to get to our room, she won't wonder so much why I've only got this one small bag."

That was logical, but that didn't mean she had to like it, or like him leering at some sweet young thing right in front of her. A flash of what felt suspiciously like jealousy burned through her. Though she had no right or reason to feel that way, Blake's reappearance in her life was too new for her to want to share.

When the elevator doors *ping*ed, Blake pulled his

gun from his waistband and checked the hallway before he'd let her come out. She didn't like the unspoken reminder that she needed his protection until she could figure out who were the good guys and who were the bad.

A few seconds later, he opened the door to their room and tugged her inside. She was dying to shower and then crawl between clean sheets and sleep for hours. But Trahern stopped abruptly, blocking her view of the room. She tried to shove him out of the way.

"Brenna, I swear I didn't know."

"Know what?" She leaned over to look past him.

At the bed. One. As in a single place to sleep. If he didn't look so genuinely shocked, she might have suspected he was lying.

"So request another room."

"I can't."

Her temper flared. "You mean you won't."

He sighed. "She said it was the last room available. I suppose we could go someplace else, but . . ."

"Never mind. I'll sleep on the floor." If she didn't get horizontal soon, she would fall asleep standing up.

"Like hell."

"Fine, I'll sleep in the chair then. Right now I don't care."

She headed for the shower, only to realize that she had nothing to sleep in except that hideous hospital gown. She couldn't sleep in just her underwear with Blake Trahern in the room. No matter how bruised and battered she was, he still managed to stir up thoughts and ideas she had no business even thinking about.

"Here. Thought you might want something clean to sleep in." Blake tossed her a white T-shirt.

"Thank you." She blushed at the thought of wearing his clothing, but the alternative was unthinkable. Besides, it was a clean shirt, so it shouldn't be all that different from wearing one of her own fresh from the laundry.

As much as she would have enjoyed a long soak in the tub to soothe her aches and pains, there wasn't time. She wasn't the only one dead on her feet. At least she'd had a decent night's sleep at the hospital; Blake had spent it in a chair that was too small for his long frame. Skewing the water to the hot side of comfortable, she stepped into the shower and let the stinging spray wash away some of the day's problems. It took some work to lather up the small bar of hotel soap, but at least she was clean again.

The bandages on her arm got soaked, but that was unavoidable. Once she had dried off, she carefully pulled the bandages away and checked the stitches underneath. The wounds looked as if they were healing just fine, with no hint of redness.

All in all, she'd been lucky. She'd gotten off pretty lightly, considering how close she'd been to the explosion. Her poor father . . . No, she was *not* going to think about him. If she allowed one tear to fall, she wouldnt be able to stop.

She toweled her hair dry before pulling on Blake's

T-shirt, glad that it came to mid-thigh. Thank goodness he was so tall. Feeling a bit shy, she hesitated before opening the door. When he'd lived in their home, she'd thought nothing of running around in not much more than what she had on.

But that was when he was a teenager and she was still a little girl. He had always been older in some way than most of the other boys his age, probably because of the hard times he'd experienced before her father had rescued him.

He definitely wasn't a boy anymore, not with those broad shoulders and powerful muscles. He didn't have the beefy build of a weight lifter, but more the kind of strength that one often saw in well-trained firemen or the military. Somehow, she didn't think either of those were what he did for a living. He'd hated rules and regulations as a youth, and judging by his actions over the past two days, he still did.

And he hadn't wanted to be with her when the police came to interview her in the hospital. Why was that? Was he afraid of them for some reason? She poked at that idea for a second or two before rejecting it. The idea of Blake being afraid of anyone was absurd. He had good reason not to care for the law in general, and she'd already seen him bend more than one rule; but he'd never walk on the wrong side of the law. Her father had meant too much to Blake.

A niggling little voice reminded her that Blake had also chosen to leave fourteen years ago and hadn't returned until after her father's death. How much could she really know about the man he'd become?

Enough to know that he'd keep her safe for the night, and for now that was enough.

Stepping out of the bathroom, she saw Trahern sprawled in the chair, sound asleep. If she tried to move him, it would only start another fight that she'd probably end up losing. So for now, she'd take the bed.

The cool sheets felt like heaven as she snuggled in between them, and she turned to face Blake. The small light she'd left on in the bathroom cast his face in faint light, softening his features as he slept.

Now it was easier to see the Blake she'd known fourteen years ago in the face of the hard-edged man he'd become. Clinging to that small bit of familiarity, she let her eyes drift close and slept.

Blake frowned. Normally he didn't mind a raccoon or possum invading his yard, but right now all he wanted to do was sleep. If the creature didn't quiet down soon, he'd have to scare the damn thing off.

The whimper came again, this time loud enough for him to recognize the sounds of pain and fear. Crap, it was probably an abandoned baby animal, looking for its mother. That was all he needed—another night spent trapping a scared animal and getting it to a wildlife rescue shelter.

After a bit, the noise stopped. Satisfied that mother and baby had been reunited, he tried to turn over and sink back into deep sleep. Something was wrong, though. Either his bed had shrunk or he was sleeping in a chair. His eyes reluctantly opened, first one and then the other. Son of a bitch—he *was* in a chair, not his decadently comfortable king-sized bed. And the whimpers he'd been hearing weren't from some lost animal, but Brenna crying in her sleep.

He stood up, every joint in his cramped body protesting. After stretching a couple of times, he pulled his chair close to the head of the bed and sat down.

"Brenna, it's all right. I'm right here." He rubbed her shoulder and back slowly, hoping his touch wouldn't startle her awake. From the way she was crying, it appeared that she was trapped in a dream, most likely a replay of the explosion. He hoped like hell that she wasn't one of those people who dreamed in color. She didn't need to see her father blown to bits in vivid clarity.

"Hush, Brenna. It's all right. Don't cry."

Please don't cry, he added silently. He could face down a dozen Others armed with razor sharp swords and not blink an eye. But a woman with a tear-streaked face was enough to unman him completely. He bet his friend Devlin Bane, back in Seattle, would be rolling on the floor right now, watching Blake try to comfort her. But then, maybe he wouldn't be. Devlin was just about the biggest, baddest Paladin of all time, yet he was in love now. And with his Handler, of all people.

But the two of them seemed to be happy together, making all the other Paladins more than a little jealous. What Devlin and Laurel shared was more than just good sex. In all the years that he'd known him, Blake had never seen Devlin more content.

He suddenly realized that Brenna's crying had tapered off. He slowly pulled back his hand, but she began thrashing around again until he put it back again. He left it on her shoulder, figuring it was little enough to do for her when she was in such obvious pain. But after a few minutes, his back was protesting loudly over the awkward position.

A glance at the alarm clock on the bedside table told him that it was hours until dawn. He wouldn't be able to move in the morning if he sat this way for the rest of the night. Reluctantly, he joined her on the bed. As long as he stayed on top of the covers and she stayed tucked in nice and safe under them, there should be no problem.

Would she have found comfort in his touch if she knew the truth about him? he wondered. No rational woman would. Even if she could accept knowing that he was hardwired to fight and kill Others, there was the problem of his rapidly shrinking hold on his humanity. The last time he'd been badly wounded, his Handler had bought extra strong chains just for him. That hadn't kept him from trying to break free from that cold steel slab, screaming for hours and shredding the skin around his wrists and ankles until they bled.

He remembered the pain in Devlin Bane's voice as he offered to end Trahern's life permanently to stop his misery. He'd been so tempted to accept, but that would have been the coward's way out. When his time came to be put down, he wanted it to count for something—not happen because he was afraid to face another day as a Paladin.

He had no right to touch someone as innocent and beautiful as Brenna Nichols—but that didn't stop him. When he tried to gather her into his side, she came willingly, snuggling in to rest her face on his chest with his arm wrapped around her. It felt like heaven, even if the predictable effect on his body was a living hell. How many times over the years had he dreamed of this exact moment, holding Brenna Nichols in his arms with her warmth and scent filling his senses? Of course, in his dreams they were both naked and sated after a night of wild monkey sex. But even this version wasn't too bad.

Blake had gotten up first and left to get breakfast for them. As Brenna got dressed, it dawned on her that sometime during the night, the makeshift bandage on his shoulder had come off—and his raw bullet wound was now only a new-looking scar. Her own gashes, although days older, looked much worse than his. How could that be? She sat down hard on the bed as her world rocked with her newfound knowledge.

Blake Trahern was everything he claimed to be— a Paladin, who lived and died and then healed from wounds that would prove fatal to anyone else. And if that were true, then so was his wild claim that his kind fought a secret war to fight off invaders from other worlds. Not only that, but her father had been part of Blake's world, living a double life that she hadn't known about.

She didn't know whether to weep for the hard life Blake lived, or to rage because neither of the men in her life had trusted her enough to share that until it was too late. Her father had died because of the Regents, and Blake lived a solitary life because his calling would eventually pull him down into madness.

The urge to move, to run, to deny everything, had her up and moving. She swiftly stuffed her personal belongings back into her suitcase, then set it on the floor by the door. With nothing left to do, she sat on the bed to await Blake's return, grateful for the time to come to terms with what had happened.

Last night, she'd taken a lover who wasn't completely human.

Blake knew the minute he stepped back into the room that something had changed. Brenna accepted the food he'd handed her with a quiet thank you, but she had yet to look at him directly. Granted, he doubted she was an old hand at sharing breakfast with a man after a night and morning of hot sex. But he'd thought they'd gotten past that awkwardness in the shower.

Something was definitely wrong. It was in the tense set of her shoulders and her sideways looks when she thought he wasn't watching. And her bag was sitting right by the door as if she were ready to bolt.

Her silence bothered him. She'd been so vocal in

her approval of their lovemaking, but now she'd withdrawn to someplace inside that didn't include him. Part of him knew it was for the best—they'd agreed that last night had been unique, something to revel in and then walk away from. Perhaps this was her way of doing just that, but he didn't have to like it. Not one damn bit.

"What's got into you?" Besides him, last night, but he wisely kept that snide little remark to himself.

She jumped, as if she thought he was going to attack her. He'd never shown any violence toward her. Where did this sudden fear come from? Had she finally accepted what he'd been telling her all along?

"What happened to convince you that I'm a Paladin?" Blake stood with his legs apart, a warrior's stance. He couldn't change what he was and wouldn't apologize for it either.

She looked at his shoulder. "Your wound isn't only healed, but it's already just a scar."

"That's part of the Paladin package, honey."

She glared at him, not appreciating his attitude. Too damn bad. He was what he was.

"And just how does one become a Paladin?"

Now she was resorting to sounding like the college professor she was—rather snooty. He didn't like it.

"One doesn't *become* a Paladin, Brenna. You are born that way. The doctors in Research could tell you more, but I doubt that you'd find it very interesting."

Her chin came up. "Is Dr. Young one of those doctors?"

"Yeah, she is. How do you know about her?" What was that odd note in her voice?

Brenna concentrated on cutting her bacon into very small bites. "She called earlier. Since I didn't know if she could be trusted, I asked her to have your friend Devlin call."

Though no expert on women's emotions, he was pretty sure that was jealousy in her voice. While that pleased him on some selfish level, now wasn't the time to put more strain on their relationship.

"Devlin is the top dog in the Seattle Paladins. Dr. Young is our Handler—that means she puts us back together and decides if we've got enough humanity left to live. She and Devlin are lovers." He shook his head. "None of us saw that coming."

"What's wrong with them being lovers? It happens all the time."

Yeah, and look how well *that* was turning out. "It's never happened before in all the history of the Paladins. Handlers and Paladins have no emotional involvement—that makes it easier when the Handler has to decide to put down a Paladin for crossing the line."

Her eyes were wide with shock. "What line?"

"Damn it, Brenna, haven't you been listening? Paladins live and die and then live again, right up until they awaken stark raving mad and have to be put down like a vicious animal. We all travel that path at different rates, but we all get to the same destination eventually."

One emotion after another flitted across

Brenna's face—shock, horror, then the worst of all, pity.

"Why, Blake? Why does it have to be that way?"

He shrugged. "Genetics. Dr. Young thinks she can change that, but I'm not holding my breath."

"She's your Handler, too?"

"Yeah, she is." And one of these days he was going to cause Laurel Young a whole lot of pain, when she had to grab that needle full of toxins and shove it in his arm. They'd all seen how devastated she was the first time she'd ended a Paladin's life, even though he'd been a complete stranger to her.

Devlin's move toward becoming more like the Others had evidently slowed down. No one knew why, but all of Research was interested in finding out. Devlin didn't think much of being considered a lab rat. But if it meant saving some of his friends from certain death, he'd put up with a few extra needle pokes and tests. Besides, it gave him an excuse to hang out with his woman right under the nose of the higher-ups. Devlin was perverse enough to enjoy that.

Brenna had shoved her unfinished breakfast plate aside. She seemed to have run out of questions for the moment, so Blake concentrated on finishing his bacon and eggs. They had a long drive ahead, so it might be awhile before they had a chance to eat again. And he'd need another couple of days to recoup the energy he'd lost to the healing process.

When he was finished, he made quick work of packing his few belongings. He'd left Seattle in such a hurry that he'd only thrown the bare minimum into his duffel. One T-shirt had been lost to yesterday's gunshot, and Brenna hadn't returned the one he'd loaned her. Not that he'd ask for it back. He liked the idea of her sleeping in his shirt—unless he had another chance to keep her naked in his bed.

Yeah, like that was going to happen again anytime soon.